GUNPLAY & LeTavia

Shawty Want A Thug

2

A NOVEL BY

LEO SULLIVAN
PORSCHA STERLING

PREVIOUSLY

Le Tavia

Taking a deep breath, I tried to calm the butterflies in my stomach as I watched Gunplay get out of his side of the car and walk over to mine, while holding a single rose in his hand. He was trying extra hard to get me back, and I had to at least give him that. He wasn't the romantic type, but he was trying his hardest and it was working.

His 'great idea' for a date had been to drive for damn near an hour all the way to Times Square so we could walk down the sidewalk and act like tourists. I was born and raised in Brooklyn, but not once had I been to Times Square. In my mind, that was what white people and tourists did. But when Gunplay took me there, I was 'oohing' and 'ahhing' just like a white ass tourist.

The lights, the food, the smells…everything was so different from where I grew up. As I looked at everything around me, I imagined that one day I would get an apartment somewhere around there as soon as I could save up my coins. As soon as I pulled up the internet to see how much a small one-bedroom apartment near there cost, I realized that I would be saving up until my bones turned to dust.

"You stick it out with me and I swear that I'll give you everything you can ever dream of... even if what you want is to live in that closet that cost damn near $1,000,000 dollars," he'd told me with a straight face that immediately made me laugh.

Grabbing his hand, I kissed him lightly on the cheek and relaxed my body into his as we walked down the street, passing by swarms of people. But the only person I could see was him.

Gazing up, I looked into his eyes when he opened my door and placed my hand in his to allow him to help me out. My heart was fluttering, and the space between my legs was throbbing. More than anything, I wanted to invite him inside my place, into my bed and then into my body, so he could do all the things to me that he'd done to me before. But I wasn't quite sure I was ready for that. I was afraid that once we got into the moment, the only thing I would be able to think about would be how I'd been tarnished by Cutta.

"You sure you don't want me to come in?" Gunplay asked, sensing the desire I felt for him. Staring into his eyes, I could see that he was feeling the same way I was.

Sighing, I shook my head softly. "No... not yet. I just want to take it slow for now."

He gave me a hard look as if he was wondering whether or not to push me on the issue, and then his shoulders slumped as he nodded his head.

"Okay, as you wish," he agreed.

Then a smirk crossed his face as he reached up to push a strand of hair out of my face.

"I know you ain't gon' hold out for too long anyways, witcho lil' freaky ass," he joked.

Laughing, I pushed him away, but he grabbed me around my waist and held me close to where our lips were almost touching.

"I said we gotta take it sl—" I started, but he stopped me by pressing his lips to mine, instantly silencing my words and my will to resist.

Reaching behind me, he grabbed my ass cheeks and pressed me even closer to his body, until my mound was situated right on top of the bulge in his pants. Somewhere in between feeling like I was falling in love brought on by my lust for him, I began to panic. My body tensed and became rigid and my heartbeat went from a subtle thump to a speeding locomotive in my chest.

"Not yet! I can't," I yelled much louder than I initially intended, and pushed Gunplay away, with my hands firmly planted on his chest.

I watched him as he stepped away with his hands up and a frown on his face. An emotion passed through his eyes, but it was so intense that I couldn't look away. He didn't understand why I was acting this way all of a sudden, but I could see that he was hurt by it.

"I'm sorry," he apologized. "I know I did some fucked up shit in the past with Quisha, but I just wanna move past that."

"No, it's not that...I—"

Clamping my mouth shut, I stopped before I told him more than I wanted to tell him. If he felt that my reaction was because I was still feeling some kind of way about him and Quisha, I would let him think that.

3

Gunplay nodded his head before walking up to me and kissing me on the forehead.

"I'll give you a call tomorrow. Have a good night, Tavi," he told me.

Still not at ease, I pressed my lips in a straight line, giving him my best version of a smile before opening my door, muttering 'bye', and closing it right behind me. From how dark and quiet it was inside, I assumed Sonya wasn't home and I was happy for that. I felt awkward enough without having to deal with someone standing right in front of my face.

As soon as I walked into the bedroom, I began to feel lonely and regretted not inviting Gunplay in just to chill with me until Sonya returned home. Grabbing my phone, I ran my thumb over it as I played with the thought in my mind.

Should I call and ask him to come back?

Before I could even decide, I heard a knock at the door. A tingly sensation traveled down my spine as my chest twanged with hope that it was Gunplay coming back. I dropped my phone on my bed and walked to the front door. When I checked the peephole, I saw it was covered. A signature Gunplay move.

Smiling, I unlocked the door and opened it wide. But when I saw Quisha standing in front of me with a twisted grin on her face, my jaw clenched with anger.

"What are you doing here?" I snapped. "On second thought..."

Stepping back, I went to slam the door in her face, but she stuck her hand out to stop it, barged in, and shot right past me with the quickness. My hands folded into fists as I watched her casually glide into my apartment as if she owned the place, flipping her hair in the process. Something falling out of her hair caught my eyes and I squinted at it when it landed on the floor.

"Are those leaves? Bitch, don't tell me your ass was hiding in the damn bushes!"

Leaning down, I took a closer look, and sure enough, this bitch had little pieces of leaves and twigs falling out her hair. When my eyes went back to her, I watched as she grabbed the bottom of her hair and began pulling a few other pieces of debris out before shrugging and tossing it back over her shoulder.

"Yeah, I was in the bushes, and what?" she snapped as if she didn't sound utterly ridiculous. "I've been waiting for your ugly ass to get back so I could show you something."

I was fuming, on the verge of going the fuck off, and although I wanted to beat her ass all the way out the front door, curiosity got the best of me and I paused.

"What could you possibly show me? I already know that you and Gunplay was fuckin' around! He told me, and he also told me that he had his daughter and was done with your ass," I informed her. "I can't stand bitches like you! How many times a man have to tell you that he don't want your ass before you decide to move on? A baby don't give you the right to keep a nigga who don't want your ass!"

The more I spoke, I could see I was hitting a nerve because Quisha's face became more twisted by her fury with each second. By the time I was done talking, it was a wonder that she didn't have steam coming out of her head. She was heated, but I was just getting started. If she wanted to keep standing there looking stuck on stupid, I could come up with a lot more to say.

Suddenly, Quisha's expression changed and a gloating grin replaced the snarl that had been there. Crossing her arms in front of her chest, she jutted her chin in the air and looked at me like I was beneath her, and not even worthy of being in her presence.

"Well, have you told Gunplay that you fucked the nigga who is tryin' to kill him?" she asked calmly as if she was solidifying her stake in a battle she'd already won.

"What?" I replied with a frown. "I didn't—"

Before I could say another word, she pulled out her cell phone, scrolled for a second, and then pressed play. I heard the sounds of my moaning before my eyes even fell on the screen. My heart came to a halt in my chest and my blood went cold. Closing my eyes, I tried to blink away the image of Quisha standing in front of me playing the video of me and Cutta, but it wouldn't go away.

"That's right, bitch! This is you and Cutta. If you didn't know it, let me fill you in on a few things," she began with an icy tone. "Cutta is the one who has a hit out on Gunplay. That shoot-out that he was involved in? When he got locked up and had to call *me* to pick his ass up? Cutta was the one who ordered it. And you fucked him! Of all the niggas in the world you could have gave the pussy to, you picked him."

Tears came to my eyes, which were transfixed on the screen, as she continued to allow the most horrific night of my life to play before me. Before I knew it, they were rolling down my cheeks. My knees felt weak. Reaching out, I placed my hand on top of the table next to me so that it could steady me.

"But I—I didn't want to do that!" I cried, wiping my tears away. "He *raped* me. He had a gun...he told me to make it seem like I liked it or he'd shoot."

Although I tried to appeal to a side of Quisha that I wasn't sure she had, the empathetic side that would allow her to see me as another woman who had been taken advantage of and used, it didn't seem to work. Instead of her sympathizing with me and understanding the terrible predicament that Cutta had placed me in, she seemed to be elated by my revelation and tossed back her head in laughter, a sinister dry cackle that sent chills down my body.

"The fact that you think I care trips me *the fuck* out!" she squealed. "Bitch, I don't give a shit about you being raped! Who the fuck you think recorded this shit?! Matter of fact...who do you think got the bartender to slip a pill in your drink?"

Fresh tears came to my eyes as she continued to cackle like she'd just heard the funniest joke in the world. I couldn't believe what she was saying.

She did this? She helped Cutta rape me...

"Matter of fact, I couldn't have planned that shit better!" she continued, as her laughter died down. "Let me tell you how the fuck this shit is gonna go. You are gonna leave Gunplay the fuck alone. You're not the one for him anyways; you're just an undercover hoe and a temporary distraction. Plenty of bitches been in your position and have come and gone, but I'm still here. And I'll always be here."

And with that, she smiled wide as she turned the phone to face her and watched the video of my assault for a few more seconds before cutting it off. Suddenly, something clicked inside of me and my hurt and devastation turned to rage. Yeah, she might have had a video of what had happened saved somewhere else, but she wasn't about to make it out of my shit with the one on her phone, or without getting her ass beat.

"...and furthermore, bitch—"

Before she could even finish her statement, I completely lost it. Like a bat out of hell, I lunged at her with my fist flailing, swinging wildly. I felt my fist connect with her teeth, then the side of her face, then I came back with an overhand right hook to her nose. I heard the bone snap as blood squirted, her eyes spread wide with fear, or maybe it was the terror of the moment that was consuming us.

Then, somehow, she managed to get off a kick that stung my inner thigh momentarily as she swung and missed badly. I could feel the wind from the blow pass by my face. Suddenly, she ran at me and we locked on each other with our arms out like rams. I felt the wind leave my lungs from the impact.

We were caught up in the throes of a female catfight when her fingers reached out to gouge and scratch my eyes. I pulled my head back but her fingers scratched my neck and she pushed me back further, making us slam against the wall. The impact knocked a picture down, and glass shattered. Her face was only inches from mine, and I could smell alcohol on her fetid breath as she bared her teeth, flashing her gold canines at me as she sneered. I fought to get her off me, and then the bitch bit me hard in my face! Locked on my cheek like a fucking pit-bull. It was the most excruciating pain I'd ever felt in my life, like a million volts of electricity surging through my body. As her eyes held mine, I noticed she was actually growling.

My face fuckin' hurts! my mind screamed, panicked.

Then we both heard it at the same time. A blood-curdling wail, like a bestial howl, inhumane and unreal. It was me, screaming at the top of my lungs. This crazy bitch was trying to bite a chunk out of my face. I needed to get her crazy ass off of me.

With both hands, I grabbed her hair, lassoing it around my arm and waved, yanking it with all my might. Her tooth released from my damaged skin as bits of her hair broke free from her scalp. With windmill motion, I used my fist and pounded her face with a four piece of clean upper cuts, then a flurry of rabbit punches to her already bleeding nose before yanking her hair even harder with my other hand. Spinning around, I tossed her around about the room by her hair like a rag doll. She was completely off balance and at my mercy.

"Naw, bitch!" I taunted, as I dragged her ass by the hair with her still trying to fight back.

"You better let my fuckin' hair go—" she started, but she was in no position to be issuing out demands.

I uppercut her several more times as her legs wobbled, but she would not fall. She cried out and tried to ward off the blows. Swinging again, her strength waning, I seized the opportunity and kicked her in the stomach, satisfied when I heard the sound of air being knocked out of her. She bent over, blood from her nose staining the linoleum floor, as I slammed my knee into her face. The sound was maddening, like wood being smacked into concrete.

Instantly, her legs wobbled but she still wouldn't fall. This bitch had some fight in her ass but so did I. I was sick of her shit and I was determined to show her just how much. As her legs nearly buckled, I yanked hard on her hair again and shot her a quick three-piece uppercut, extra crispy, straight to her jaw, and finally her hood rat ass fell to the floor like a sack of potatoes. There was a loud thump as her head hit the corner of my heavy oak wood coffee table. She landed on her back with her hair covering her face. I had knocked her ass the fuck out. Her hair was splayed over her face as sanguine-red blood oozed from her nose.

Walking over to her, I reached down and tore the phone from where it lay near her fingers.

"Checkmate, bitch," I mumbled to myself as I went to the video and deleted it, smearing her blood from my fingers all over the screen in the process.

A sense of relief passed over me when I confirmed that the video was gone, and I finally turned my attention back to Quisha who was still lying, completely knocked out on the floor.

"Wake the fuck up, you evil bitch," I muttered as I kicked at her feet.

But something about the way that her neck was crooked to the side made an uneasy feeling settled upon me. Something wasn't right.

"Oh my God!" I gasped as I released the phone straight out of my hands, and it hit the floor.

Dropping to my knees, I leaned over Quisha's limp body and pushed her hair out of her face. Her face was covered with blood and there was a large gash on her head where she'd hit the edge of my coffee table. But what had me in a state of panic were her eyes, which were wide open, glassy and staring at a distant place that only she could see.

She was dead.

"Shit!" My stomach churned so badly it felt like I was going to vomit, as my mind raced 1,000 miles an hour.

Gripped with terror, I fearfully scurried away from her and nearly slipped in a puddle of blood, as the horror of what I'd done set in on me. Quisha was dead... and I'd killed her. A million thoughts invaded my mind as I tried to figure out what the hell I could do and who I could call. I couldn't go to prison for this. Could I plead self-defense? No... I couldn't. The bottom line was that I'd attacked her and she'd died at my hands.

I was a murderer.

KNOCK! KNOCK! KNOCK!

Suddenly, there was a loud knock at the door. My heart nearly jumped out my chest.

RING! RING!

Whoever it was rang the damn doorbell with urgency!

My eyes darted from the door to Quisha's body as she lay there with her eyes open as if staring at me accusingly, with the daunting trail of blood like a signature of her demise. And once my thoughts merged in my mind, my ass stood paralyzed with fright, completely devoid of what the hell I needed to do. Panicked, I crawled quickly over to her body and grabbed at her shoulders.

I have to hide her! I thought as I tried to lift her up.

But as lightweight as she seemed to be in life, she seemed to weigh 1,000 pounds in death. I couldn't even get her to budge. The worst part of it all was the more I tried to shift her, the more blood oozed from her face, and she continued to stare at me with morbid eyes that mirrored the terror that engulfed me completely. Tears stung my eyes before cascading down my face.

Releasing her, Quisha's body fell to the floor with a *smack* as her face splashed into her own sea of blood. I used my forearm to wipe away the tears that were blinding my eyes, and smeared some of the blood on my face. Gasping, I looked at my hands, which were covered in blood. There was no way for me to get rid of it. There was way too much.

KNOCK! KNOCK!

"Tavi! Open the damn door! I know you hear a nigga...don't make me start singing and shit again!"

It was Gunplay. What the fuck was I going to do?

"Go away!" I cried out through my tears. As soon as I heard my own wavering tone, I regretted it.

"Tavi...what the fuck? Are you crying?! Open up this fuckin' door!" Gunplay yelled as he continued to knock.

The more I hesitated, the harder his knocks got until he was banging on the door. Covering my ears, I squeezed my eyes closed and cried silently, praying that he would give up and just go away. Then finally, the sound stopped. Slowly, I uncovered my ears and opened my eyes. Was he gone?

Standing up, I padded over to the door to see if he was gone. Just as I got to the door, I heard the shrill sound of glass shattering from my room and I gasped, whipping around in terror with my eyes stretched wide, as the thumping sound of heavy footsteps followed. Feeling my knees getting weak, I almost fainted when, right before my eyes, Gunplay's long and lean form emerged from the hall, his eyes stricken wide and focused right on Quisha's dead and bloodied body.

Grasping the edge of the counter next to me, I felt myself began to go weak as I watched his eyes travel slowly from her body to mine. His brow knotted up when his eyes traveled from my bloody hands and soiled red clothes, and then finally to my battered, bruised and bleeding face.

"Fuck... Fuck..." he cursed, slapping his forehead like he was trying to wake up from a bad dream.

Staggering slightly, he gazed at Quisha's body with a stare filled with absolute devastation, like what he was seeing wasn't real. In his eyes was the look someone gave after coming to the terrifying conclusion that the person they loved had done something so incredibly horrific and left themselves with no way out.

"Tavi," Gunplay began quietly in a calm tone, with a hint of grit in his voice like he was fighting a battle of emotions. "What the *fuck* did you do?!"

CHAPTER ONE

Gunplay

Months Later

The one thing I couldn't stand was to be involved in somebody's bullshit. Shit like that irked me to no end because it stopped me from being able to make moves. That was one reason I kept the women in my life to a minimum.

Just like any other nigga, I liked to fuck. Getting my dick wet off sexing bad bitches was my favorite pastime. But with women came problems, and I didn't have time for nothing that would distract me from my #1 goal: to take over the fuckin' city.

All that said, that's why I was mad as hell, sitting inside of the fuckin' police department talking to the head pigs in charge on Quisha's case. According to them, they had received information concerning her disappearance that made me a person of interest. I wasn't feeling this shit, and to make matters worse, they had kidnapped my ass right off the street like I lived in a third world country. I stepped outside my crib to go pick up some money from one of my workers, and the next thing I knew, an unmarked cop car swooped down on me with two pigs inside, one black and one white. The black cop, Jefferson, asked my name, and I figured 'what the fuck?' I didn't have no warrants out on me, hadn't recently bodied a nigga, so I gave it to him.

Big mistake!

As soon as I told the cops my name, all hell broke loose. It seemed like every parked car, including a garbage truck on my street, was an unmarked cop vehicle just waiting to pounce. They took me down to the station after threatening to whoop my ass; however, in street lingo, when a cop threatens to whoop your ass, that's just them being humble. What they were really saying was that they were going to *shoot* my ass. In light of the recent current events, I got my ass in the car without a word, even though I had about $20,000 in cash in my pocket and a quarter ounce of loud.

"Can you tell us again where you were on—"

"I'm not tellin' you shit," I replied back, cutting Jefferson off as he crossed his thick ass arms in front of his chest and scooted his chair closer, fully intent on intimidating me with that whack ass 'cops and robbers' ploy.

Leaning back in my seat, I shook my head, making my long dreadlocks fall away from my face so that I could glare at each of the detectives in front of me. One thing was for certain: I knew my rights. I wasn't new to the game; my street cred was impeccable. Best believe these pigs had already looked a nigga up thoroughly, so they should have already known this.

"Unless y'all gon' charge me with some shit, you need to let me the fuck go. I got shit to do. Plus, I done told both of y'all, I ain't got shit to do with my baby moms or whatever happened with her. Ya wastin' ya time… and mine," I continued, my eyes narrowing in on Jefferson, who seemed to be the leader of the two.

To me, it was obvious that Jefferson was the type of cop who felt like he had something to prove to his white counterpart when it came to questioning other niggas. He took it upon himself to go especially hard with the 'bad cop' role, to show he could rough up another black man just like he was one of the good ole boys. I knew his type and I couldn't stand his ass.

"Listen here, jackass," Jefferson said through his yellow teeth, the edges of his mouth turning upwards into a hideous sneer like he had just taken a bite out of something sour. "You won't be leaving out of here until I tell you that you can. And you won't be doin' shit until you tell me what the hell I want to hear… got it?"

"Fuck outta here," I muttered loud enough for both of them to hear.

I simply focused my eyes in on Jefferson's mustard-colored face, noticing the twinge of red that had started to appear at the top of his hound dog eyes, like either he had been going days without sleep or he was mad as shit at me. Probably both. He was getting frustrated by my lack of cooperation, and it was funny as hell watching him get all worked up over a case he wouldn't win with his dumb ass fear tactics.

Listen, muthafucka, I'm a career criminal and them white boys ain't tag me with that shit for no reason. I know my fucking rights.

Finally, Jefferson sighed audibly as he interlocked his stubby fingers and leaned back in his seat. He looked like he was five months pregnant with twins. His fat ass probably had a donut back at his desk with his name on it. It was going stale, but he was ignoring it to sit here and question me about this stupid shit. And I was just about to inform him that it was time for his fat ass to go stuff his face, when he suddenly said something that made me lose my train of thought.

"Well, we also did get a lead on another person of interest… a woman by the name of LeTavia Miller. You know her?"

The edges of his mouth curled up into a sinister smirk, and for the first time and, on cue, his partner's face lit up like a Christmas tree. He strode over and tossed a chair, causing it to slide across the freshly waxed linoleum floor, making a loud, screeching sound. The chair landed less than a foot away from me, but I didn't even flinch. He straddled it backwards and spoke with hubris and a mysterious twinkle in his eyes.

"We know about your bitch, LeTavia Miller, and she can either be an accessory after the fact, or we can stack up a first-degree homicide case against her," he said in singsong voice that would have been comical had it not reeked of deadly intent.

Jefferson couldn't help but chuckle at his partner's antics as he watched on. The other cop, Mike Taylor, sounded whack, like one of them white boys trying too hard to talk and act black. But something was wrong and I couldn't place my finger on it.

I glanced up at the camera that I was sure was hidden behind the large two-way mirror across the table from us. Taylor must have read my thoughts. He inched closer and lowered his voice, leaning in like he was personally speaking to me.

"Ain't no cameras, no witnesses, no hidden people behind the glass. Just us." He snickered derisively.

"I don't give a fuck. I know y'all muthafuckas ain't got shit, so you gotta let me go," I said angrily. "I know my damn rights."

"Well, you need to give a fuck! And you must have been watching too many episodes of First 48, talkin' 'bout some fucking rights!"

"Tell 'em, Mike." His partner chimed in, instigating with a gleeful grin. Gay ass nigga.

I reared back in my chair to get a good look at them both as suspicion crept deep in my gut like a plague threatening to erupt. They were up to something, and I had a feeling that shit was going to quickly go from bad to worse.

"Yeah," Mike continued. "'Cause we don't believe in that bullshit 'all black lives matter' mumbo jumbo. We believe in all black ass whoopings matter! Now, you need to start talking or we gon' start beating your ass in here. As it is, we have probable cause."

Silence.

I held my tongue, conscious that crooked cops were worse than any gang. Fuck, to be real, they were the real gangs in America, dressed in blue, with a track record for gettin' niggas' names written on tombstones.

"Cat got your tongue, nigga?" black ass Jefferson boasted.

That was it.

I couldn't help it. Them muthafuckas was toying with me because they knew I was gonna flip, and they got exactly what they were asking for. There was something about niggas showing off to impress their white friends that always struck a nerve with me. I fuckin' lost it!

"Naw, y'all on some fuck shit! I ain't stupid and you, with yo' boot-licking ass, gon' let this cracka turn you into a fuckin' Uncle Tom! You can miss wit' this bullshit, ole gay ass muthafuc—"

Before I could finish the statement, Jefferson smashed his fist into my mid-section, knocking the air out my lungs. Fuck! His ass sucker-punched the shit out of me. Had me thinking back to the first time I got my ass beat by this clown after I picked a fight with his brother for peeing in my mama's yard. Dude's name was Maurice Blevins, and I swear I'd never forget that name until the day I died. Nothing stood out in your mind like your very first ass whooping.

Grunting, I would have keeled over on the floor had it not been for my arm being shackled to a steel rod that was protruding from the wall.

"Fuck is wrong with you? Don't you know we will *kill* you in this muthafucka?! Handcuff your punk ass and push you down a flight of concrete stairs, break your *fucking* neck, nigga, and say you fell while you was trying to escape!" Jefferson raged as spit flew from his mouth. He stood over me with his fist balled tight, like he wanted to strike me again.

All I could do was keep my head down, forehead near my leg as my lungs, deflated, searched for the oxygen that had been depleted by the massive blow.

"Fuck you want with me, mannn?" I groaned painfully. It was hard as hell to keep the thug shit going when a nigga couldn't breathe.

WHAM!

I was struck again. This time with more force in the back of my head, causing my face to come down hard on my leg, nearly bussin' my lip. Seeing stars, I nearly blacked the hell out. I heard white ass Taylor chide me, mockingly.

"See, told ya. Black ass whoopings matter." He laughed like it was the funniest joke on Earth.

"This is what we want. We want you to tell us where Quisha is. We know you killed her. Just tell us where her body can be found and we might take it light on ya for not makin' us work," Jefferson said as if I'd really fall for the oldest trick in the damn book.

For some reason, he was breathing hard, nearly panting. He had an evil, sinister look in his eyes. Maybe it was from the adrenaline rush he'd got from knocking the shit out of my ass. Or maybe he was excited because he was giving serious consideration to pushing me down a flight of concrete stairs while my hands were handcuffed behind my back.

"Mannnn, I told you—"

He snatched me up by my hair so hard that one of my dreads came out and sailed across the floor, as he reared back to punch me in my face. For some reason, he paused, but his fist was poised, ready to strike me, when he yelled in my face.

"Okay, enough of this cat and mouse shit! The reason why we want to question your girl, LeTavia, is because we found evidence that your old bitch paid a visit to your new bitch on the last day her mama had seen her," the cop Taylor spat, playing a weak gambit in hopes that I would go for that shit and start talking.

Not!

"Man, I told you, I dunno shit! Either y'all gon' beat a nigga to death, take me to a cell, or let me the fuck go!" I raised my head and spit blood onto the floor next to the white cop.

Suddenly, the mood in the small interrogation room shifted. Things began to feel awkward, like we were all trapped in an uncomfortable elevator. I watched the two cops exchange uncertain glances, finally realizing that I really wasn't gonna say shit.

This was another day for them at the New York City Police Department – 47th Precinct and, like me, they also had shit to do. They had many more victims to harass, more innocent people to abuse... oh, I mean, more people to serve and protect while struttin' around talking 'bout "black ass whoopings matter."

Of course, they roughed me up some more and threatened to toss my ass out the window. Eventually, I was taken to a cell, battered and bruised, but the very next day, I was released. Fuck a probable cause, they had to let me go!

And as soon as my feet hit the ground on the other side of the door, I turned around and shot them niggas a bird.

It was on!

Le Tavia

"Do you have anyone to take you home?"

I jumped slightly, not even noticing that the nurse had returned to the room. Tilting my head, I focused my attention on the petite, blonde woman ahead of me, and muttered out the word 'no' while ignoring the sting of shame in my cheeks. I shouldn't have been embarrassed, because the only reason I didn't have anyone was because I didn't tell anyone what was going on.

"I—It would be a lot better if you had someone to help you home. We gave you a lot of medication."

Under the hood of my eyelids, I watched as the woman's bright blue eyes dimmed a little and the edges of her lips tugged downward at the ends. She felt sorry for me and that made me feel even more like shit.

"I'm fine… I have no issues gettin' home on my own," I blurted, disconcerted. I tried to tell my lie with a straight face, even though I was emotionally distraught and felt physically battered and bruised, not to mention embarrassed.

I can't speak for no other woman, but for me, there was a feeling of inhumane humiliation and degradation after I had my abortion. Especially since I didn't have money to go to no fancy place. Everybody in this place looked at me like I was just another hoe trying to clean up my mistakes. I hated it. I'll never forget the grotesque feeling of a tube being shoved up my vagina with a vacuum suction that sent an ungodly shiver throughout my body. I had thought I would get a pill and be done, but I was too far along.

WHOOSH, was the sound that was made. And, just like that, a baby was sucked out of my precious womb and placed into some type of plastic bag like discarded trash. But it was a human life. My child.

"Well, you might have some cramping… and you should stop bleeding in a week or so," the nurse began saying as she handed me a hideous looking box of pads. They were huge and looked like large pampers. She intensely watched me as I moved about, in a daze, lethargically stumbling around the room while grabbing my things and looking everywhere but into her eyes.

"We'll prescribe you some medication to take in case you experience any discomfort, and make sure to give us a call if—"

Before she could complete her sentence, I tucked the box of Maxi pads in my bag and was out of the room. By the time I was able to make it out of the front door, I was already in pain and could feel something resembling a mini flood between my legs. I felt myself began to break down. I remember faces, gothic-looking people with gaunt eyes, watching me as I stopped at a nearby water fountain. Before I could take a sip, my emotions took over me. I broke down and cried.

I cried because of the rape.

I cried for my child.

I cried because I was humiliated.

My God… *what* have I done?

Then a soft hand came to rest on my shoulder as people walked by, gawking at me. Slowly, I looked up and saw that it was the nurse. The same damn nurse that had helped the doctor conduct the abortion. I blurted out an uncontrollable sob, and shoved her hand off of me as I tasted the salty tears in the back of my throat.

She had been only trying to help, but her face was a constant reminder of all that I had done. I couldn't take seeing her anymore.

I walked briskly, my mind in a stupor. With each step, the pad between my legs shifted. It was uncomfortable and bulky, like I had a damn boxing glove hidden down there. At some point, I could have sworn it was making some sort of squeaky, wet sounds. I just needed to get home.

The last couple months had been the most trying of my life. After Gunplay helped me dispose of Quisha's body, I went into a deep depression over what I'd done, shutting everyone out completely. Gunplay had decided that we shouldn't be seen together for a while until things blew over, so he had no idea what I was going through, and I'd preferred it that way. But I couldn't lie and say that I didn't miss him. My birthday had come and gone months before, leaving me devastated when he didn't even show. I longed for him.

One day, the cops came knocking at my door asking about Quisha, saying that they heard she'd planned on visiting me the last day anyone had seen her. After that, I tried to get as ghost as possible and moved into another place. Sonya stayed for a short while after that, but ended up moving to a more luxurious apartment on the other side of town. About a week after, I found out I was pregnant with Cutta's baby.

I played with the idea of keeping it for a while, but I knew I couldn't, so I made the choice to have an abortion… which brings us here.

The bus pulled up as I stood in line waiting to walk up the few short steps; my body was cramping so bad that, by then, I was walking nearly bent over in a slump. All I could think about during the long ride was a long, hot bath, and some pills to soothe my pain, as I tried my best to erase the memory of what just happened to me.

It was times like these that I missed Gunplay. He was more than a boyfriend, he'd become my best friend, my lover, and I told him everything. Almost everything… No matter what, I just couldn't bring myself to tell him about Cutta, the abuse, the humiliation. Once again, I choked back a sob, fighting a gall of emotions that threatened to consume me.

With my forearm, I mopped at the tears that were streaming down my cheeks as we approached my stop. My phone began to ring, but I was too busy struggling to get up and couldn't grab it before the caller hung up.

"You okay?" the driver asked, his thick brows bunched up into a frown on his weather-beaten mahogany face. Pressing my lips together, I nodded 'yes' and stumbled slowly down the steps.

I turned the corner only a few buildings away from my place. A dog barked from across the street. I looked up, locking eyes with my neighbor, Bruce. He was walking his big ass ferocious pit-bull. Him and his dog actually looked alike. He had the nerve to wave and call my name like a damn lame. I ignored him and kept it moving.

He was a muscle-bound guy, and kind of nerdy and ugly, with

hound dog eyes. I had made the mistake of telling him my name to be cordial when I first moved in my place. He saw me struggling with some bags and I let him help me. Big mistake. Second day after I moved in, he showed up at my door, drunk, at eleven o'clock at night, asking if I wanted to smoke with him. But his eyes were asking for pussy. He's been creepy to me ever since.

I hobbled along, searching in my purse for my house keys with my head down, and that's when I heard a voice I knew all too well. It sent a slight shiver down my spine.

"Damn, shawty. What tha fuck goin' on wit' ya and why ya walking like that? Ya gotta take a shit or somethin'?"

In spite of my current condition, the sound of his voice made my heart leap in my chest as his rugged tone echoed in my ears. Lifting my eyes, I saw that Gunplay was right ahead of me, sitting on the hood of a shiny new dark red Benz, which was parked right in front of my door.

My baby had come back to me.

CHAPTER TWO

Le Tavia

"What are you doing here?" I asked him, ignoring his question as I straightened my back and felt another sharp pain. The last thing I needed was for him to ask any questions regarding what was wrong with me or where I'd come from.

"I came to see you," he told me, while slyly caressing his private area and cocking his head to the side. Then he gave me a sexy smile, the kind that could melt panties in three seconds flat.

His eyes swooped over my frame and I turned away to the side to avoid his intense stare. He got off his whip, and I felt his presence moving closer to me. Suddenly, I felt conscious about my condition, my cardinal sin making me feel like I had betrayed him. With a stutter step and an involuntarily shiver, I wrapped my arms around my body, enclosing myself with my arms and creating a barrier between the two of us. Time seemed to stall.

As I gave him a shy glance, trying to read his thoughts while taking in his demeanor, I couldn't help but notice that he was peering directly into my face. We were doing that mental telepathy thing that lovers often do on an unconscious level. Lust was pollinating between us as we stared at each other for the first time in what felt like forever.

"You been good, ma?" he asked in a husky voice as the murmur of street life stewed around us. His brow raised, his hand was still on his crotch as he gazed at me. My legs wobbled, making me gravitate closer to him as I tried my best to appear normal.

"Yeah, I'm okay." My voice cracked and I winced, willing myself not to break down in front of him.

Don't lose it, Tavi, I admonished to myself.

"Then why ya walking 'round lookin' like your dog died or some shit?" he asked and reached out to me as he held an open envelope. "And why you ain't been goin' to school, nigga?"

Gasping, I snatched the envelope from his fingers and pulled out the letter inside, reading it quickly.

"You read my mail?! What the hell is wrong with you?" I snapped, gawking at him.

Instead of seeming apologetic for his illegal invasion of my privacy, Gunplay simply shrugged in a way that was so sexy it made my cheeks hot. He shifted and my eyes fell to his body. Damn, I missed him.

"You ain't been talkin' to a nigga so I had to see what you was up to! It's been a minute, na'mean?" was the only excuse he lent, and he said it as if it was a valid reason for going through my shit like it was his. He was still the same Gunplay with his crazy ass!

"No, I don't know what you mean! And don't be going in my

mail!" I snapped, pretending like I had an attitude.

But who could be mad at a nigga who was so damn fine? He was dressed in a simple black silk Polo sleeveless shirt, showing off his tats, and his nice arms and chest. He had on some loose-fitting jeans and black, shiny Gucci sneakers that perfected and completed his style.

"And not seeing me for the past few months was a decision you made on your own," I continued, still feeling a little hurt by him pushing me out of his life. "That was your call."

As expected, Gunplay completely ignored me. He just reached around behind me and grabbed a handful of my ass, palming it in plain daylight, like he was sampling food or something.

And I let him. At least for a moment.

"Really, DeShaun?" I said as I brushed his hand away.

"Well, I'm makin' a new call," he told me with a chuckle as he stood in front of me, so close that I could smell the scent of his cologne. It was hypnotic, and I sucked it up through my nostrils like it was the oxygen that I so desperately needed in order to live. It was crazy to me how one person could pop up in my life and completely change the way I'd been feeling for the past couple months.

Gunplay stood in front of me, straightening his back and making it painstakingly obvious to the both of us how much he towered over me. But he made me feel safe, secure. It took everything in my power not to melt into his arms. Lord, I missed that man so much. Looking down, he allowed his brownish-blond dreadlocks to fall forward, nearly brushing against my cheeks.

I closed my eyes, took a breath and tried to calm the beating of my heart. Any louder and Gunplay would be able to pick up on the sound and know that I was still crazy in love with him, something that his cocky ass did not need to know right now.

"I had to take a break to get my shit together, and also to make sure that there was no heat on you after that shit happened…"

He paused when he saw me flinch at him mentioning the incident with Quisha. Pulling back slightly, he ran his finger over the top of his upper lip and looked me over once more. I felt on edge, wondering if he was going to speak what was on his mind. Slowly, his eyes rose to my face and held me, twinkling, his gaze sending a fluttering sensation through me that traveled all the way down to the space between my thighs. Feeling my anxiety creeping in, I began to rub the back of my neck, a nervous habit I'd picked up recently.

"Either way, I'm here now and I'm ready for us to get back to how things were again," he told me, his eyes focusing on my hand that was still rubbing at the back of my neck. I stopped suddenly and forced my hand down to my side. Then Gunplay flicked his thick tongue slowly over his gold grill, and I almost lost my damn mind.

"Let's go inside," he said seductively, nudging me towards my apartment as he licked them sexy ass lips of his while letting his eyes drop below my waist, fully revealing his lustful intentions.

He was ready to sex me. And it was twisted as hell, considering what I'd just been through, but I was ready to sex his ass too! But I was leaking like a broke facet and my vagina felt violated like a truck had just drove out of me.

Opening my mouth to respond, I was instantly thrown off by

Bruce's creepy ass.

Bruce's pit started growling, and I saw when Gunplay flinched and moved for his strap. My mouth dropped, hoping he wasn't about to bring out the thug and cause even more bullshit between me and my creepy ass neighbor.

"Yo, Tavi, what you ain't speaking to a nigga now? And that's fucked up what you did the other night. I been meanin' to tell you that shit," Bruce said and walked up on us with that damn dog barking madly like it was crazy with some type of white foam dripping from its mouth.

I was hurt but I wasn't stupid. I moved my ass right on the top step of my resident landing. I already had enough shit going on and didn't want to get bit by some rabid looking ass dog.

"Tavi, who the fuck this clown ass nigga is and what he talkin' 'bout 'the other night'?!" Gunplay asked with his face twisted, jaw askew like he had just got his teeth pulled without using any Novocain for the pain.

"I...I..." My tongue searched for the words in my mouth that were as evasive as smoke in a bottle because I knew what was coming next. And it did... like a train wreck about to happen, and my ass was standing directly in its path.

"Nigga, what you just said?" the big nerd asked boldly, to my surprise. He walked even closer, inches away from Gunplay's leg with that vicious dog snapping its large teeth threatening to bite a chunk out of him.

Hell to the naw! I hopped my ass up three more steps with one leap as if I was trying out for the Olympics or some shit. My eye on the dog that was still growling and walking steadily closer, I began seriously thinking about taking off running.

Gunplay moved in one quick motion and pulled out a big ass gun, a .44 Desert Eagle, cocked it and aimed! The dog yipped and began to cower with what almost sounded like a human whimper. Then it ran behind its master with its tail between its legs like it didn't want to get shot.

"Man, it ain't all that serious. I was only playing with you and Ms. Tavi. I didn't mean no harm, I swear," Bruce said, devoid of any bass in his voice like he was about to start pleading for his life.

CRACK!

Gunplay whacked him so hard upside the head with that big ass gun, he nearly stumbled and fell. Thankfully, he didn't draw blood, but Bruce was in a daze.

"GUNPLAY!!" I shrieked and felt a sharp pain in my stomach that nearly bent me over.

"Nigga, you fuckin' 'round wit' my bitch?!" Gunplay yelled with deadly intent in his voice. I could see an angry vein pulsating in his forehead.

"M—m—man, please, don't shoot!" the guy pleaded and I felt so sorry for him. There was sweat dripping down his wrinkled forehead as he held the place where Gunplay had whacked him.

"Gunplay, stop! Leave him alone!!" I shouted so loud to the top of my lungs. I was conscious that a few street people stopped what they were doing to watch.

"That nigga better start talkin'!" Then Gunplay's crazy ass stopped and ran his eyes over at me and said, "In fact, both of y'all muthafuckas better start talkin'. I'ma have both y'all sharing an ambulance if somebody don't tell me what the fuck is going on!"

He turned, focusing his attention on me. I don't know if it was intentional or not, I'm not exactly certain, but at that moment, I almost fainted. Dating a thug was like petting a poisonous snake; you just never know when they were going to turn around and bite you. But Gunplay was way worse because his ass was crazy. I know that most people think I mean crazy in the non-threatening kinda way, but fuck that. I meant it in all seriousness; his ass was straightjacket, padded walls *crazy.*

"Boy, I don't know what you're talkin' about! I don't fucking know him!"

Again, I screamed to the top of my lungs, hoping it would work some sense into him. I was motivated by my fear. Standing across from me, staring at Gunplay with his eyes in a tight frown, Bruce continued to plead his case.

"Man, it was nothing. I stopped by and tried to holla at her one night and she turned me down. I ain't know she was ya bitch!"

"What the fuck you just call her, fuck nigga?!" Gunplay yelled, and Bruce began to look confused, his lips wiggling although no sound came out. Hell, I was confused too. Didn't Gunplay's ass just call me a bitch like two seconds ago?

"Fuck all this. I feel like both y'all tried me," Gunplay said with a fiendish look in his eyes.

Then to my utter shock, Gunplay raised the gun in his hand and fired, point-blank range.

BOOM! The shot roared like a cannon!

Bruce screamed in anguish, grabbed his ear, and began to walk in place like he was climbing a steep mountain, legs moving high. The sound of his wail echoed throughout the hood and in my ears like we were standing in the Grand Canyon.

But he wasn't hit. Gunplay had intentionally shot past his head to put the fear of God in him. And it worked. Bruce had peed on himself, and I was holding onto the stair railing so tightly, my knuckles paled.

"Haul ass, fuck nigga! And if I see you round my bitch—" Apparently, I was a bitch once more. "—again, I'ma slump ya fuck ass. Get somewhere!!" Gunplay threatened through his teeth.

Bruce took off running right past his apartment. I don't know where the hell he thought he was heading, but he was trying to get away, and I didn't blame him.

Just then, somebody hollered, "Five-O!"

Sirens blared. The police were coming. People started to scatter like roaches with the lights on. I felt another sharp pain ricochet through my stomach. It hurt so badly that I bent over and gasped out a harsh breath, as my legs got wobbly.

"Let's go, Tavi," Gunplay said and stashed the banger in his pants, but I was stuck.

My legs wouldn't move, the pain was excruciating.

"Fuck wrong wit' ya?!" Gunplay raised his voice and, before I knew it, he'd reached down and scooped my ass up in his arms before taking off up the stairs. "Damn, Tavi, yo' ass is sexy slim, but you solid like a damn linebacker!"

Holding onto him, I groaned and winced through another sharp pain, ignoring his blunt mouth and crazy antics. This was just a normal day with Gunplay.

LaTavia

Gunplay really had some fuckin' nerve.

After being gone for months, not only did he pop up unexpected, pistol-whip the shit out of my neighbor, shoot a gun in my pretty peaceful neighborhood, but now he was sitting his ass in my living room, peering out the window for the cops, while simultaneously rolling a blunt. He was a typical thug but, for some reason, I couldn't help but be happy he was here, even though he irked the hell out of me.

"Country ass nigga better be glad I didn't light his ass up with that .44." He licked the blunt, eyeing me in a threatening manner like I should have been happy too. Then he got up, a goofy grin on his face before walking over and grabbing my arm, affectionately beckoning me to come to him.

"Let me get up in them guts. You know you want it. Look like you been missin' a nigga for real."

"Ugh! Nigga, is you buggin'?" I snapped, pushing his hand away from my arm, which he was using to forcefully direct me towards my bedroom. "You think you can just pop up, act a damn fool, and we'll continue from where we left off. Hell naw!"

"Man, I didn't tell that nigga to do that stupid shit, and for real, for real, I was thinking about smoking both y'all ass for a minute," he said and tried to grab me by the waist with one hand as he held the partially rolled blunt in the other.

Frowning, I batted his hand away.

"Really?!" I shrieked, shocked that he could say something like that so calmly.

"Shit, it won't be the first time a nigga shot a bitch and her side nigga in a jealous rage."

"Who you calling a bitch?" I asked him, finally sick of hearing him say that shit. I was nobody's bitch and that included his ass, too.

He gave me a shrug. "I'm just saying, shawty."

"Well, what you saying, 'cause you called me a bitch while we was outside. Then you wanted to act all mad and shit 'cause Bruce—"

"You mean 'Fuck nigga, Bruce,'" he butted in with his correction.

"—because he called me it too, but you said the same damn thing!"

"It's just a figure of speech, love," he muttered under his breath. "You know you worth more to me than a bitch. You ain't never been that to me."

I didn't say anything, and that was all he needed to be convinced I was done fussing. Satisfied all was good, he turned, fired up the blunt, and blew smoke at me like a dragon. I rolled my eyes, watching him act like he was a pro at it. He was acting hard, trying to play all cool and shit, but then began to choke and gag on the smoke. I couldn't resist clowning his ass.

"That's what your crazy ass get, nigga! Coming here, popping up all of a sudden, like you think you're going to get you some!"

He suddenly stopped coughing, but his eyes were rimmed red and glassy as he stared at me, taking a step back, his face twisted with confusion and shock.

"Think? I *think* I'm about to get me some?" he asked, genuinely looking perplexed at the idea.

Of course he's shocked, I thought, fighting the urge to roll my eyes. *What woman has ever refused Gunplay?*

"Tavi, why yo' ass trippin'? You been fuckin' that Bama lookin' ass nigga?" he asked, delivering an accusatory glare.

The edges of his mouth curled up into a sneer and my breath caught in my throat as I felt his rage multiply in an instant. I hadn't even confirmed his statement, but from the murderous stare in his eyes, he'd already confirmed it for me. If he was acting like this over the thought of me possibly messing around with some ugly nigga, how would he act if he knew that I had gotten pregnant from Cutta, his #1 enemy? My heart lurched in my throat, beating fast, as I thought about a threat he had made earlier.

Y'all two finna be sharing an ambulance.

Just the thought of what he might do made my blood turn cold, and I knew that I needed to stop this thing with Gunplay before it became the death of me. Even if I did tell him that Cutta had forced himself on me, would he believe it after all this time? I should have told him right when it happened, but it was much too late for that now. And I knew from experience that a secret that big is never left untold, so I had to leave him alone.

"No!" I yelled out once I'd finally found my voice. "I haven't been with anyone else, especially that ugly ass, backwoods ass dude," I snapped.

"Then why you was beggin' and pleading and shit for me to stop beating his ass?"

"First off, he was innocent. He ain't do shit but try to holla at me, like all niggas do. Second, who pistol-whips people in broad daylight?" I retorted.

"Shit, ain't no timeline for a beat down. A nigga get out of line and I'ma check his ass viciously, na'mean? I don't give a fuck 'bout it being day or night. And I'll bust yo' ass too, if I find out you fuckin' with a nigga behind my back."

"You know what? You need to go!" I yelled, tears stinging my eyes. I was sick of his threats, and what he was saying was hitting too close to home. In the past, it was normal for us to go back and forth like this, so I know I had to be confusing him, but I couldn't help it. With the reality of my situation staring me in the face, they no longer felt like jokes to me.

But instead of reacting like any normal nigga, Gunplay just turned and grinned at me with them damn eyes dancing back and forth all over my face. He grabbed me and all the playfulness fell from his face as he cupped his hands around the back of my waist and looked at me with sincerity and heavy emotions. I felt flutters erupt inside of my stomach.

"Ma, you taking things too serious. A nigga just missed you and that fat ass. The love you give me fucks my mind up... I can't get enough of it and I can't get enough of you. You can't blame me for gettin' mad that another nigga got to taste somethin' I been wantin' for so long and couldn't have."

I cut my eyes at him. But I was only playing hard. Something about that line and his smile had tugged me right back on his side. Fuck. Love made people stupid.

He passed me the blunt. At first I hesitated, but then I took it and tried to take a small puff. When I started coughing about as bad as he had, Gunplay looked at me with an impish grin.

"It's Purple Kush straight from Afghanistan," he explained and stole another glance out the window. I twisted up my lips, wondering how in the world he'd gotten weed from Afghanistan and wondered if he was playing with me. Finally, his eyes settled on me just as I started feeling good. He looked me over, his eyes lingering shamelessly on my hips and thighs.

"Aye," he started, still eyeing me with crinkled brows. "You ready to go to the room?"

Scoffing, I rolled my eyes and ignored him. Our silence stewed like the halo of Kush smoke engulfing both of us in its gray haze. I took a couple more tokes as I watched him watch me. It instantly mellowed me with its potency. Then Gunplay said something that nearly blew my high.

"Maybe since you don't wanna be wit' a nigga, we can just chill and smoke weed all day and let that be it. I got this new chick I been chillin' wit' and she wifey material, so I'm 'bout to go see what's up. Might put a baby in her sexy ass since you don't wanna do shit," he told me with a straight face, and I fell into a fit of coughs.

"Nigga, whet?!" I snapped, ready to get all up in his ass. I placed the blunt down and narrowed my eyes at him, waiting to see if he had the courage to repeat what he'd just said.

"April Fools!" he yelled and started laughing as I glared at him.

"What the hell are you talking about, DeShaun? It's August!"

Despite his crass humor, he chuckled, grabbed the blunt and inhaled deeply, staring sexily at me as smoke rose from his mouth and nose. Then he stood up, walked to me, and wrapped his arms around me, holding me tight as he kissed all over my neck. God, he smelled good. Did he always smell like this? And I could feel the rock hard bulge in his pants, pressing against my leg.

Did he always *feel* like this?

"Fuck them details. I'm just saying, I was playing. I wasn't ever really jealous of dude and, as for you... I think you know what kind of caliber nigga I am. I play for keeps, na'mean? Once mine, always mine. Ya got it?" he said with a cocky arrogance that was part of his demeanor.

There was something about his ego that worked me like an aphrodisiac; I hated it, but it was irresistible at the same time. He made my head spin. He was so dangerous, so unpredictable, but so alluring in the most uncanny of ways... a wild child turned savage who I couldn't help but to love. Before I could respond, he moved forward and scooped me up into his muscular arms.

"Stop actin' like you ain't still feelin' a nigga because I know you are. Walkin' around here all booted over, like your back hurt or somethin'. You just need some dick in yo' life to set that ass and back straight."

He began to pepper my face, neck, and breasts with kisses. He seemed to grow an extra set of hands like an octopus. One hand was on my ass, another was on my breast, and it felt like he had another hand trying to go between my legs.

"Stop... Nigga!" I yelled, attempting to wrestle him off.

But the instant his lips touched my skin, nearly every bit of resistance I had left in my body chucked me the deuces and walked the fuck off, leaving me at the mercy of the throbbing muscle between my legs. He felt so good and it was a long time since I had anyone really make me feel that way. Like a real woman with lustful needs that only he could tend to.

"GUN... PLAY! STOP... IT... NO!" I moaned weakly. But to him, it must have sounded like an impetus for him to move on, because he pulled out my breast and squeezed it once before licking it like it was sweet nectar.

It felt so good my toes curled up. This has always been another hazard to dating him, a roughneck thug. He had a tendency to take what he wanted instead of asking, but this was not the right time and I couldn't fold.

I started to twist, trying to free myself from out of his tight hold. But I could barely move as he held me even more tightly the more I protested.

"Stop all that buckin' when we could be fuckin', gul," he told me in a playful tone, as he walked towards my bedroom with his legs wide to keep his unbuttoned jeans from falling lower.

I felt his penis, throbbing hard against my leg, about a foot long. All I could think about was the freaky things he liked to do, like that one time when he bent me over the bed pouring liquor all over my body and licking it off. And the shit that he did with his pistols, rubbing them tenderly against my clit while he pushed his fingers up inside of me. Damn.

He tried to carry me to the room. I resisted some more right before he tossed me down on the bed.

"Yo, check this, ma," he started, a serious expression on his face. "Don't try to fight a nigga that you know you want. You know you would be fucked up inside if I was with another bitch, just like I would be if you were with another nigga. So this that bullshit you don't need to be on. Now stop playing with a real nigga, my dick hard as Japanese arithmetic," he said like he was nearly out of breath from wrestling with me.

"Uhh, huh, nigga, I told you I'm not doing anything with you. You must think this some shop and go pussy," I spat sassily.

Lying down beside me, he couldn't help but snicker at that, and wrapped me up in his arms. I nestled in and released a content sigh of relief as he held me close, his head on my chest as if he were trying to doze off to the beating of my heart.

My baby really was back.

In minutes, he fell asleep and began to snore lightly. I couldn't help but watch his handsome face, his rigid features. His calm, serene presence in my bed as the blunt smoldered, still burning between his fingers. He was about to set my bed on fire and possibly himself too. I grabbed the blunt, causing him to stir softly in his sleep as I watched him, unbridled masculinity captured on the screen of my mind like a painting. Gently, I reached over and caressed his face, light as a feather.

"Damn, I missed your crazy ass," I muttered and took a toke off the blunt.

To my surprise, his eyes opened and he pulled me tighter in his arms like he never wanted to let me go, flipping me so that I was lying back against his chest. I swallowed hard, realizing that was exactly how I felt. This was what I had been wanting for so long.

To feel his touch.

To feel loved.

I snuggled back against him and ignored it when his massive hands palmed my ass and spread my cheeks, positioning me right on top of the rise in his pants. He kneaded my ass like he was trying to create a permanent memory of how it felt to him; it kind of hurt but I realized at that moment I never wanted to let him go.

We cuddled like spoons in a tight space with my butt pressed against his manhood, hard and throbbing. I started to pull it out and play with it, but I didn't want to get him started when I couldn't do shit about it.

"Man, this feels good... love you, shawty," he said breathlessly into the back of my neck and then fell right back to sleep. My eyes jolted open at the sound of his declaration of love and I looked at him, realizing that he'd said it while nearly asleep. He probably didn't even know what he'd said.

Exhaling slowly, I laid back, cuddled in his arms and listening to the silence while in the solitude of my thoughts.

Love you, shawty.

His words, heavy with his northern accent, resonated in the dark crevices of my emotion-filled, feminine mind again and again. But still, I couldn't help but wonder.

What if... what if Gunplay found out about Cutta? Would he still love me then?"

Nope, he would kill your ass, the voice that I believed the most rang so loudly in my mind.

I couldn't tell him about this. The baby was gone, Cutta was locked up, and Quisha was dead. The secret was hidden for now, and I was going to try to keep it that way.

CHAPTER THREE

Gunplay

One thing about a street nigga… we always had major shit on our mind. For that very reason, I didn't sleep much. And even when I fell the fuck out, like I did at LeTavia's spot, I couldn't stay asleep for long. I had to admit I was knocked out for a minute, only to wake up to her staring at me. Normally, I would have been unnerved or even spooked, but the look I saw in her eyes was nothing but love and admiration for a nigga. I dozed back off, feeling more comfortable than I'd felt in some time. Probably since the last time I was with her. She kept my mind at peace.

I woke up in the middle of the night, reaching for my banger out of habit, and then relaxed when I felt LeTavia snuggled up at my side. Rolling over, I got out the bed to take a piss and then found myself thinking about how long it had been since I'd seen her ass. For some reason, I couldn't shake the idea of her being with another nigga while I was gone, and it was fuckin' my head up. I know I sounded silly as hell being worried about it after I'd been gone so long. And, to be honest, I ran through chicks left and right the whole time we weren't together, but I couldn't deal with thinking she was up to the same shit. It made my dick hard thinking about how many ways I would gut a nigga up if I found out he'd been kicking it with LeTavia. Crazy, I know. But I'm a lot of damn things and sane ain't ever been one.

After making sure that she was asleep, I started to walk around the apartment, inspecting every little thing to make sure I didn't see evidence of a man anywhere. If LeTavia had tried to move on from me and was fuckin' some other nigga in her spot, there would be evidence of him somewhere. That was the type of shit men did.

Or at least, that was the type of shit I did. I'd already left one of my guns in the bathroom in a spot that could only be seen if you were standing up taking a piss. And just in case any muthafucka she called herself dealing with had any questions on who the gun belonged to, I left my gold chain with the double pistols lying right on top of it to let him know.

After walking around the apartment and not finding a damn thing, I grabbed my phone out my pocket, satisfied that LeTavia was still the same woman I was diggin', ready to get back to business. Once I looked at the screen, I saw that E-Class had been hitting me up back-to-back while I was sleeping, but his messages didn't say much beyond that I needed to give him a call ASAP.

Glancing behind me towards the hall, I walked into the kitchen to grab something to drink. As soon as I opened the fridge, I saw that LeTavia was on some bullshit. Wasn't no Kool-Aid, soda or a single Heineken in sight. Her ass had the fridge stocked with bottled waters and some vegetable juice shit. I'd only been gone for a couple months and already she was forgetting that she needed to have stuff prepped for a nigga in case I decided to swing by. This was some bullshit.

Barefoot on the cold barren floor, I walked over and glanced out the window as I dialed a number. It rang several times before he picked up.

"Nigga, what's good?" I greeted E-Class as soon as he answered the phone.

"Aye, good to hear from yo' ass, nigga. Where you been at?"

His tone was somber. He took a long pause before he continued speaking so I knew it was bad news. I continued to stare out the window. There wasn't a soul on the streets. A stray alley cat was walking on top of my car like he owned it. It took everything in my power not to bang on the window.

"Here and there. Now I'm chillin' with Tavi."

"Tavi? She back in the picture?"

I chuckled a little, shaking my head as I answered the question. "She always been in it. She is the picture," I added, more to myself than to him. "But I know you got news. I'm listening."

"Man, I just heard some niggas in my club talkin'… they was sayin' some shit about Cutta. I knew they wouldn't say shit if I was around so I sent one of the girls over to give them some special attention and listen out for me."

He paused and I frowned. Cutta was in prison, pressing his bunk, and I was on the streets running the fuckin' city. What the hell could he be up to that I'd give a shit about?

"And, nigga? Why the hell should I be worried 'bout the shi—"

"It's Rayshaun, bruh. Somethin' ain't right 'bout him. The niggas that came by was plotting some shit. They said that Cutta was giving orders from the inside and he'd rallied up some niggas on the street to handle shit for him. They ain't mention nothin' concrete 'bout what they were plannin', but the chick I sent over there said that one of the men took a call during the conversation. He said it was Rayshaun callin' before he walked off," E-Class finished, and I felt my blood begin to boil.

Deep down, I knew something about Rayshaun was foul ever since he had brought that whack ass wannabe Colombian to meet up with me. Shit hadn't been kosher between the two of us since then, and the only reason I hadn't already hemmed his ass up with a pistol to the gut was because of the fact that he was one of my oldest homeboys. We ran the streets as kids and I wanted to believe that nothing could come between that bond.

"But that's not it," E-Class continued. "You need to watch your back too. Word is that Cutta paid some niggas to kill your ass. From what I hear, these niggas be on they shit. I'm worried bout'cha, man."

"Ain't no need to be worried 'bout me, E," I told him with a solemn tone as I twirled one of my pistols around on my pointer finger. "Any nigga gunnin' for me gon' end up resting in peace in a body bag. A nigga would rather walk through hell with gasoline drawers on than to be fucked up with me, homie."

E-Class laughed on the other end but the frown deepened on my face. I wasn't the least bit worried at all about Cutta's plans but I didn't like this shit to be popping up right when I'd decided to bring LeTavia back into my life. That would fuck me up to have to break away from her again just so I don't pull her into some street bullshit.

"Yo' ass still play by goon rules. You ever thought about a new lifestyle?" E-Class asked but I didn't bother answering. Wasn't any need; E-Class already knew I feared no man. I appreciated that he was giving me info, but I stayed ready to have a reason to pull out on somebody.

"Let me know if you need anything, bruh. But, for real for real, I think you need to think about havin' an entourage when you out and about. That's on some g-shit."

Sucking my teeth, I frowned and tossed a crazy look at the phone like E-Class could see me.

"Nigga, I ain't worried 'bout no nigga who in the pen tryin' to keep Big Bertha's dick from runnin' up his ass! Besides, I keep an entourage with me, about twenty-five deep. I got this shit handled."

"You rollin' twenty-five deep? Word?"

"Muthafuckin' right, nigga! Sixteen in my nine milli and nine in that muthafuckin' .44 makes twenty-five! And I'm generous with them hot balls. I don't discriminate, any bitch can get it, na'mean?"

"True, true. A nigga know you 'bout ya business, son," E-Class said, enthused.

"You just let me know if you hear anything else, a'ight?"

I heard the floorboard squeak along with the patter of feet coming from down the hall. When I looked up, it was LeTavia. From the look on her face, I couldn't tell how much of my conversation she'd heard, but I knew I didn't want her to hear anything else.

"A'ight, playa. I'll holla at'cha later, my nigga."

"One."

Hanging up the phone, I turned to LeTavia who was lookin' sexy as hell in them lil' ass pink, satin pajama shorts she loved to wear that had her booty cheeks hanging out the bottom.

"You leaving or you coming back to bed?" she asked me, her voice soft, but I still heard a hint of something else there, like she was worried I was about to leave her. I didn't want her to be worried about no shit like that ever again.

"You want me to stay or go? I mean, I know it can't be easy putting up with a nigga like me."

While speaking, I studied her. She just stood there stoic and nibbled on her bottom lip like she was actually considering what I had said. She was weighing her thoughts and looking beautiful while doing it. How I'd managed to stay away so long, I didn't know. Obviously, the need for me to know she was safe had won the battle in the end, which is why I kept my distance. But I didn't want to miss out on another day.

"Yea… I want you to stay." Her words came out shy but melodic, like one of them old school Anita Baker songs my mama used to listen to when she wasn't trying to act all religious.

"You're sure about that?" I said in a husky tone, bubbling with excitement and something else I couldn't describe. Just her nearness turned me on, the silhouette of her body carved out in the limpid light being cast from the window. She smiled and wiped at a ringlet of hair on her delicate forehead then looked away. I stole a glance at her breasts, next, her curvaceous thighs, and felt my nature rise.

I walked closer, fragile steps, hearing the floorboards crack underneath my foot. Then we both heard it at the same time; from somewhere in the distance, a police siren shrilled and we both flinched then looked at each other deeply, both of us having a nostalgic moment about the first time we'd laid eyes on each other.

"Alright... but I might not be able to control my hands from rubbing up in that fat ass."

She just grinned at me sheepishly, and I thought I saw a glimpse of one of her sex faces, tempting me, inviting me. Or did I imagine it because I wanted her so bad? She placed a hand on her round hips and rolled her eyes. Then, suddenly, her expression changed and she pulled her chin up, declaring capriciously, like a declaration of femininity.

"We can't do anything. I'm on my period." For some reason, she watched me intently, maybe she was secretly waiting for my usual ignorant reaction. I did my best to keep all the playfulness at bay... at first.

"Okay, I understand. It's cool."

"Really?" she mused, adjusting her stance to one side and cocked her head to the side. Smirking at her shock, I made a rookie mistake. I glanced down at the phat ass pussy print in her tiny ass shorts and then failed miserably.

"Yeah, but this some fuckin' bullshit," I hissed under my breath and inadvertently kicked the coffee table, knocking over a picture. LeTavia flinched and squinted her eyes at me.

I was pissed and now so was she.

"Boy! My grandmother gave me that coffee table and you knocked over her picture!"

I ignored her anger. Absentmindedly, I grabbed my manhood. I was already hard and ready to bury myself in the confines of her hot sex, but she wasn't having it.

"Man, shit. Maybe we can think of something else? Be creative."

I reached out and squeezed her nipple. She swatted my hand with a furtive dose of fingernail, enough to let me know she could claw my ass, if need be.

"Creative, Gunplay? Like how?" She frowned at me dramatically, and then bunched her lips up, twisting them to the side doubtfully.

"I'on know. But them sexy ass lips looking awful luscious right about now," I hinted. She countered with a dry laugh and rolled her eyes once again, but I didn't crack a smile. I was dead ass serious. I looked at her, totally hypnotized by her sensuous hips and mouthwatering breasts with her nipples erect, pointing upwards as if in defiance with gravity.

My dick got harder and I groaned.

Then it suddenly dawned on me why I couldn't leave—why I made up an excuse to come back to her. The reality was I didn't have a choice. My body craved her. My mind needed her and, on some real nigga shit, I couldn't even fathom being without her. She kind of had a hold on a nigga. I needed to rebut that and redeem myself. She really had me in a fucked up situation and didn't even know it.

Maybe she did?

I shifted my manhood around in my pants as to not look so pathetic—mind over temptation. It wasn't so much that I wanted to fuck her. I wanted to make love to her. Go deep within the walls of her tight sex. Lose myself in the wails of her crying. Listen to her calling my name as fingernails raked my back. Fill us both with ecstasy. Bring out the carnal beast in me with each deep stroke.

"So you leaving now?" she asked in a loud clipped tone that seem to resonate throughout her small apartment.

"Naw, but still, this ain't fair. My dick hard as a muthafucka and I ain't seen you in a minute—"

"Whose fault is that?" she shot back with an attitude.

"Yours."

"Mine?"

"Yep. If you hadn't done that shit to Quisha, I wouldn't have had to get ghost for so long."

"Humph! And if your crazy ass baby mama hadn't come to my place with that bullshit, if only you would have *checked* her ass instead of having sex with her, this wouldn't be happening."

I tensed, not liking where this conversation was going. I'd disrespected LeTavia in the past in ways I would never do now. I didn't like that she was still hurt about that.

"What wouldn't be happening? Your period?" I responded, feigning stupidity, just to change the line of conversation. It worked.

"Nigga, you know what the fuck I'm talking about!"

She raised her voice and took a step closer. I enjoyed the swells of her breasts with her sudden movement, and it was as if my hands had a mind of their own, which was always the case with LeTavia. I reached out and grabbed her. To my surprise, she didn't resist.

"How long your period been on?" I inquired in my most gentle voice, the pussy plea bargain voice niggas used when they were determined to bust a nut by any means necessary. I began to palm her ass, digging so deep I nearly touched her anus. I heard her purr like a kitten in my hands as she responded to my question.

"Why?"

"Well, uh, if it's just a little drip-drip, that ain't so bad. It's like pushing through the red light at a traffic stop when it's just about to turn green, get it?" I persuaded and continued to squeeze her ass like my life depended on it.

Gasping, LeTavia's body went rigid, stiff as a board in my arms, as she frowned and gave me a look like I'd lost my damn mind. I didn't know what the fuck was wrong with her. Shit, I was serious. In my book, it had been a *long* damn time since I'd ran up in somethin' and I wasn't in prison no more. I ain't wanna wait any longer.

She pulled away from me and I tugged her back as she looked up at me, straight in my eyes like her vanity was wounded. Like I had overstepped my boundaries.

"DeShaun, really? Niggas will say anything for a piece of ass. Let me go!"

She resisted.

So did I.

I resisted in not letting her go. Opening my mouth, I tried a different angle. I had to redeem myself. I looked into her face and paused. Damn she was beautiful.

"No, it really wasn't so much about the sex, shawty. It's the intimacy, it's being inside of you, hearing you call my name, us bonding like some 'Heaven on Earth' shit. I missed you. I just really wanted to make love to you and hold you in arms. Word is bond."

By the time I finished talking, I was winded. Silence lulled over the backdrop of nocturnal noises coming from outside the open window. LeTavia just stared up at me with starry eyes glistening. Then her facial expression changed, like a chameleon, and she relaxed some more in my arms. For that infinite moment in time, I could feel her heart racing right next to mine. She exhaled a deep breath and moved her fingers, like tiny feet walking down my thigh before caressing my zipper.

"You should have been an actor," she breathed out, barely above a whisper.

"Why you say that?" I palmed her ass harder and was rewarded with a subtle moan.

"Because… hmmm… those were some of the sweetest words. Like you're acting, playing a role just to get some pussy."

She smiled and I felt my chest get tight. I couldn't keep my eyes from off her.

"Naw, that was just my heart talkin'. A nigga missed the fuck out of you."

"Ouch! DeShaun, that hurt! That's my ass you're squeezing between your fists!"

I pulled back and smirked at her, unable to hide my true motives any longer. I was too turned on for the games.

"Man, a nigga tryin' to enjoy your body. And what the hell is that strapped to your ass, a fucking pamper?"

"It's a pad. I told you I was on my period, with your crazy ass." She rolled her eyes and pushed away from me. I frowned. A pad? Since when she started wearing all that artillery?

"Man, if you got a pad on that big—shit, you need to be in the emergency room!"

"DeShaun, you're about to ruin the mood!" she snapped with grit in her voice.

"I was just playing."

"No you wasn't, nigga."

We both laughed. Leaning over, I kissed her softly on the lips. She opened for me immediately and I pushed my tongue inside, growing rock hard when she sucked on it. She giggled, feeling my hardness pressed up against her torso, and then unzipped my pants. After wrestling to free my pulsing dick, she finally got it out and gasped, licking her lips.

"Damn, I forgot how big you were." She started stroking it, slow at first, and then with so much vigor my toes curled.

"You gon' kiss it?" I muttered in a strained voice, wanting nothing more than to feel her soft, sweet lips wrapped around me. Plenty of women gave head, but none of them did it for me like she did it. I needed it.

"Maybe," she whispered coyly and stroked me faster. I was about to lose it and bust a nut off in her hand. A wasted seed? Never that. I grabbed her head softly and tried to nudge her down.

"DeShaun, STOP!"

"What?" I asked, looking down. She was holding my dick so tightly, the mushroom head looked like it was going to explode.

"Stop pushing my head down. I don't like that."

"Sorry, I apologize. But damn! You killing me softly with that hand job. I—I—I thought you was going to kiss it," I stammered, gurgling my words. For some damn reason, she giggled.

"I will, but tell me how much you missed me again." She used her other hand and stroked me like I was a plunger in a stopped-up toilet. Her soft hands were giving me the business. I was at the mercy of her soft manipulation.

"Are you s-s-serious?"

I was past the point of no return as her hands worked their magic. Like I was having some out-of-body experience, I watched. I will never forget the devilish look in her eyes, mystic and mysterious. It was as if she was enjoying having control over me... control over my body.

"How much you missed me?"

She got down on one knee and looked up at me with sparking eyes filled with mischief. Teasing me into thinking of all the pleasure she could bring. By then, my dick was throbbing, rock hard, only a few inches from her face. Already, her fingers were saturated, wet and sticky with pre-cum. She stroked even faster, then blew on the head of my dick.

"Damn, I missed you so much—missed you like a muthafucka. Please, bae, you're dick teasing the shit out of me," I pleaded. Again, she smiled up at me and began to lick around the rim of my dick.

More torture.

Her breath was a torrid of wanton ecstasy. Then she took me all the way in her mouth, to the back of her throat, and held me there in place as her lips lubriciously worked feverishly like a vacuum. It was as if she was inhaling me, devouring me as I stood captive on my toes, the balls of my feet in the air like I was stuck in quicksand.

"Goddamn—muthafuckin—son—of—a—bitch!" I exclaimed.

She worked me with her mouth lovingly, enduringly taking me past the brink of no return just when I was about to cum deep in her mouth, the back of her throat.

"You gon' swallow it?" I winced, placing both hands on her head to keep up with the fevered tempo of her rhythm. She continued to guide my pole further down her throat. Then it felt like my legs were about to give way, like a drunken sailor, inebriated by her lips.

She just stared up at me with a quizzical expression. Then I came like a broken faucet. She pulled her mouth away and aimed my dick at her succulent breasts, causing a jet stream of silky white cum to spray her titties. She removed her hands causing my dick to dangle as she pulled her bra strap down and let her pendulous breasts swing free. She began to massage my cum onto her breasts and soft brown erect nipples.

"Damn, you almost swallowed that." Just thinking about it made my legs go wobbly.

"If you were my husband I would have," she flippantly replied and stroked my dick with admiration.

"Be careful what you ask for."

Afterwards, we lay in bed smoking blunts and pillow-talked. Being with her was better than anything I could have asked for. But I still had things on my mind and a score to settle. A young gangsta's biggest opponent is always the streets and I needed to claim it and start my empire with LeTavia by my side. I wanted to give her the world, but first I had to take it.

Gunplay

I showed up on the block, my old stomping grounds, and things were still the same. Niggas was hustling cocaine rocks, molly, pills, heroin, and just about anything you wanted. Including sex. The hoodrats in my neighborhood were always on the prowl, walking around, scantily clad, wearing too much cheap makeup and not enough clothes; always in search of their next victim, a nigga with some chips to sponsor their frivolous lifestyle of weed, pampers, and Section 8 bills.

I spotted Polo posted up on the corner. He was dressed in thoroughbred blue jeans and an Obama t-shirt with the words plastered across it, "Yes We Can". He donned a wave cap and some old Nike sneakers.

"Aye, nigga, I ain't seen you a few days. What you been up to?" Polo asked me as I approached.

In the distance, either a shot was fired or a car backfired. Either way, it caused me to reach for my strap. Polo ducked and turned around just as an old pickup truck passed, fumigating both of us in thick gray smoke coming from the tailpipes. I glanced inside and spotted two white crackheads. They called out to Polo and he scurried across the street, nearly avoiding getting hit by a car. I watched him serve the white boys dope that he had stashed in a brown pill bottle, and then walk back across the street, counting some crumpled up bills.

At the time, I was walking towards my mama's crib so that I could check in on her and Imani. With me being in the streets trying to provide for the two women who meant the most to me outside of LeTavia, I couldn't handle raising Imani on my own, but my mama stepped in without a second thought. Every day I thanked God for my mama, and I was determined to get my mama and baby girl out the ghetto.

"Yeah, I was chillin' with my lady for a minute but I'm back on the map now grinding, about to pick it up a notch," I told him, bumping his fist. "So what's good, nigga?"

A blue Chevy with candy-paint rode by with its music blasting, and niggas inside grilling us like they were considering trying to make a move on us. I caressed my strap, a gesture to let them know shit wasn't going to be easy. They kept it movin'.

Polo continued. "Oh, I know how that shit be, nigga. Gotta stop by and make sure the home base is right, huh? Rock lil' mama to sleep and then get back in these streets, huh?" he joked, but he had spotted the hoodlums in the whip too. As they rode by, I peeped that Polo had his hand on his strap too.

For some reason, I had a bad vibe and started darting my eyes across the street. I felt like I was being watched but there was no one there. Shaking it off, I figured it was just E-Class's warning fuckin' with me.

"Yeah, my nigga. Shit's gravy. Like I said, I'm about to boom this bitch, shake up the block with a new product, cop a new connect and get it poppin'. And if a nigga ain't with me, he's against me, feel me?" That was my caveat to a silent threat, to which Polo nodded his head. "For now, I'm just over here checkin' on my moms and handlin' business."

"That's cool," he told me. "I gotta get back to this hustle anyways. You know me, I gotta slang this shit to feed my fams because ain't no other muthafucka gon' do this shit."

Smirking, I looked at him and nodded my head. "You keep stackin' up them big faces, nigga. I might have to see you when it's time. Yo, I'm finna shake up the Earth and a lot of niggas finna fall off."

"Bet," Polo said with his eyes focused on the street. He planned for his next verbal exchange to be with a customer or potential victim.

But then, just as I was about to walk away, he turned and called my name.

"What's up, yo?"

"My bad... Fuck, I forgot to tell you something. My mind been on this street shit plus my ole girl back in the hospital—she had another heart attack and it got me slippin'. But I need to holla at you 'bout some emergency shit."

"What?" There was something about how he asked me that piqued my curiosity.

Polo was a self-proclaimed street nigga about my age, and I had mad respect for him although he was crazy as a muthafucka. His mama was a crackhead and, word was, she'd been smokin' dope the day she had him and that was what caused her to go into labor. Polo came out his mama addicted to crack and it was like a bad omen, something he couldn't shake. Even though he didn't smoke on a pipe, he liked to smoke dirties—crack and weed rolled in a blunt, that had him doing dumb shit. Once, he even shot at his mother for stealing his dope, only to find out she had never stole it, he had misplaced it. Another time, he kept his pregnant baby mama chained to a pipe in the basement for months because he was paranoid about her seeing the doctor too much. The dope was telling him that she was an undercover informant working for the police. She ended up delivering their baby two months early because of the stress he put on her, only for him to then toss her out on her ass, convinced the child wasn't his because her delivery date was off.

However, what couldn't be denied was Polo was what the streets called 'a functioning addict'. He got high as fuck and still managed to get money. Polo drove a brand-new BMW and would shoot a nigga in a heartbeat. You got some dope fiends like that in every hood, a real product of their environment.

"It was some niggas in a blue Crown Vic riding around showing your picture to everybody on the block. They was asking where you or your mama lived at."

"Whaaat?! Fuck you talkin' 'bout?" I nearly jumped two feet in the air. "Who asking where me or my mama live? What the fuck you tell them? What they look like? Why in the fuck you ain't been told me this?" I snapped! I was livid, talking a mile a minute and my heart was beating even faster.

Polo was responding too slowly for my taste, still looking back and forth on the block for potential clients before talking.

"Nigga, I ain't got you on speed dial! And, like I said, my mama in the hospital and I got other issues too."

"Fuck you mean you ain't got me on speed dial, nigga?! You know where to find me. You could have said something!" I yelled so loud the pigeons on the street scattered and a group of hood-rats stopped and stared at us. I was making a scene and didn't give a fuck.

"How? Nigga, I ain't seen your ass in a minute!" He stood his ground and reached behind his ear to retrieve a partially smoked blunt, crack mixed with weed. He fired it up.

"Who else might know somethin'?"

He blew a palm of that stanky ass smoke at me. I watched his eyes roll around in his head as he spoke, now more focused but paranoid than before. As crazy as it may sound, paranoia in the dope game can be good. It's hard as hell to sneak up on a junky.

"Them crazy niggas, Pookie and Jabari. They was the ones who told me. I ain't see shit, that's why I forgot. But Pookie and Jabari in jail now. Got busted in the trap on 49th Street. The Feds raided that bitch. They found cocaine, AK-47's and some mo' shit."

"Is that who was looking for me? The Feds?"

My pulse began to thrum. Every nigga in the hood knew when the Feds come looking for you, it's end of the ball game. And they was giving niggas basketball numbers for sentences.

"I'on know. Like I said, they didn't ask me and I didn't see them," Polo replied curtly. He knew like I did, whoever was in that Crown Vic looking for me or my mama was nothing but trouble.

"And what the fuck they want with my mama?" I pondered to

myself and ran my fingers through my dreads in frustration. Then it suddenly occurred to me I needed to get home ASAP. I took off in a trot with my pistol in my pocket. The only thing I could think about was my mother and my baby girl. Homicides in the form of home invasions were all too common in my hood. An old woman with a child was an easy target.

Fuck. I ran faster.

****

Unlocking the front door with my key, I walked in my mama's house and was immediately hit with the smell of whatever good shit she was whipping up in the kitchen. She was sitting in the living room in her favorite La-Z-Boy chair. Imani was curled up in her lap, knocked out sleep. All I could do was let out a big sigh of relief. And, like a true to the bone mom, she could sense my distress.

"Boy, is you okay? It looks like you've seen a ghost or something!" She raised a brow in concern.

"I'm good." I tried to play it off.

I was winded but, even more than that, I was tense. Still, there was no way in hell I was going to tell her that she and my baby girl could possibly be in danger. I didn't want them worried about something I would take care of. My daughter was my heart, and I hustled hard as hell to give her the world, hoping it made up for the loss of her mother.

"You sure?" she pressed further. But in a mother's lingo that really meant she knew I was lying and I needed to tell the truth.

"It's just been a long day." I leaned over and kissed her cheek. "You need to wake that big ass girl up!" Reaching out, I tried to poke

Imani in her side, but my mama slapped my hand out of the way.

"Shush, boy! She sleepin'!" she scolded me with a frown. "She had a long day."

Blowing out hot air, I walked to the kitchen to check inside of her pots.

"A long day doing what? It ain't like she workin' a 9 to 5. Spoiled ass."

B-muthafuckin'-I-N-G-O! I thought as I grabbed a piece of golden fried chicken from off the stove and placed the entire wing into my mouth.

Chomping loudly on it, I licked my fingers as I stomped into the living room and sat down in the chair next to my mama. That's when I felt the hot chicken, fresh out the frying pan, burning the roof of my mouth. It took everything in my power not to spit it out and, judging from my facial expression, my mama got a good kick out of seeing my anguish.

"See, that's what you get, putting your hands on my food without washing them. No telling where your hands been." She chuckled with a sparkle in her eyes, and then quickly changed the subject, giving me a pained expression as she looked at my daughter.

"Well, you might not have realized it, but we are coming up to the holiday season and it got Imani thinkin' about how long it's been since she seen her mama. I pray every day for Quisha that she is okay. I just can't imagine her up and leaving Imani like this. Something had to happen to her. She had her problems but the girl did right by my granddaughter."

Still chewing on the chicken wing in my hand, I didn't say a word as my mama spoke about Quisha. One thing I hated to do was lie to my mama. She had never asked me directly about Quisha and, even though I was grateful she didn't, I felt like her reasoning was that she knew I had something to do with it.

"And when you gon' bring that girl you been with around for me to really meet her?" she asked all of a sudden.

Sitting up, I looked directly into her face, a slight frown forming between my brows.

"Who you talkin' about? Tavi? How you know I'm back messin' with her?"

She winked at me but didn't say a thing as she picked up the remote and went back to the show she was watching. I don't even know why I asked. My mama always had a way of knowing all kinds of shit about me. Thank God she wasn't the Feds because my ass would always be locked up.

Checking my watch, I began to get restless. I had come over to look out for my mama and play with Imani, but with the threat of them possibly being in harm's way, I couldn't focus on anything but how to keep them safe. I needed to think of a way to protect them, fast.

"You got someplace to be? Boy, what is wrong with you? The last time you was looking like that was when you got in trouble by shooting that boy," she said just as I stood up to throw the bones in my hand away. A mother's intuition is about as close as you can come to God's blessing. Moms always be knowing.

"I told you I was good. I'm just a little stressed out. I'ma hit up a

"Yeah, workin' on some shit for Queen. Just doin' some research and shit before I do what it is I do. She got me dealin' with some Atlanta niggas. I might need you to come through at some point, fam," he told me and I smiled on the phone, shaking my head.

"You know whenever you call, I'm there, and some shit is 'bout to go down!"

Trigga was my nigga for real. We met as young kids, wrecking the damn city. Remember when I said the first and only nigga to beat my ass was some nigga named Maurice? Well, that was Trigga. His dumb ass twin brother, Mase, had peed in my mama's front yard and I beat his ass bloody… only for his brother to come and whoop my ass like I stole something. After I got my ass beat, Trigga helped me to my mama's front door, rang the doorbell, waited until she answered and told her why I got my ass beat, and even convinced her to make my ass apologize. He was a savage from the moment he took his first breath.

Ever since then, Trigga has been like my big bro who I loved to death but on the low, I couldn't help feeling some type of way about the fact that he was the only nigga who always had one up on me. He was on a genius level with this street shit, a skilled killer who worked for Queen, a bad ass chick who had a drug empire worthy enough for me to envy, but she was too deadly for me to even think of touching her territory. He was her prized possession and the sole reason for her success. If I had Trigga on my team, I would have it all. Him and I together was unstoppable, but I wanted to do things on my own. We were both leaders, we'd clash… it could never work.

"Aye, I need to talk to you right quick, bruh," I told him as I walked into the closet connected to the master bathroom and grabbed a shirt to pull over my head.

"Fa sho. Meet me at E's spot. I'll see you when you get there."

Hanging up the phone, I pulled my locs up into a ponytail and placed a cap over my head, pulling it down low. Polo was still on the block serving. I waved at him before jumping in the whip and driving off. It only took me about fifteen minutes to get to the club, and Trigga was already there waiting for me.

"Yo, what up, nigga?" Trigga asked as I walked over to where he was sitting.

"Nothing, man," I replied before reaching out to dap him up. He bumped my fist and I waved a stripper over to get me a drink. It was early in the day so E-Class wasn't around. He normally didn't come to the club until late.

"If anybody told me you was gon' walk up in here with some custom-made gold and black Jordans with double pistols on the side, I would've told them they was a damn lie. But I be damned if you don't come in here with that sparkly, leprechaun shit on."

"It ain't sparkles, these *diamonds*, nigga," I corrected him, holding my foot up. "Get'cho mind right. I can save lives with these shits right here." He was playing but I was dead ass.

My shoe game stayed on point, just like everything else about me. If I ever let this street shit go, I could get into making a clothing line *easily*. If niggas like Kanye West could make millions off of convincing people to wear dingy cleaning cloths and rags that looked like he'd wiped his ass with them, then I knew I could create an easy come up just off my personal wardrobe.

"You buggin', yo," Trigga laughed, shaking his head. I frowned at being clowned about my gear and then I heard Trigga click his teeth.

"And don't be gettin' in yo' fuckin' feelings about my opinions either, wit'cho emotional ass," he continued. "You always finding some shit to get mad about, but you know you can't pull the heat out first on a nigga so don't even get yo'self worked up."

I clenched my jaw but I didn't say shit. I lived up to my name, but Trigga was ill with his shit. There had been many times that we'd pulled out pieces out on each other after shit got tense between us, but Trigga always got the draw on me. That shit kept me in my fuckin' feelings. And his ass was always calling me emotional but for real, my sensitivity is what made me so damn deadly.

"You know I don't normally come to you 'bout no advice but I got a question." I paused and Trigga just looked at me with them funny colored eyes, waiting for me to talk. I couldn't even believe what I was about to say.

"Yo... I'm thinkin' about making shit real with Tavi. You know, at my age, I'm an old man in the streets. It might be time for me to make her wifey."

"Damn," was all Trigga said. He reached in his pocket and pulled out a blunt. I watched as he lit it before handing it over to me. Just from the smell of it, I could tell it was some good shit.

"Nigga, who you got this shit from?" I asked as I eyed the blunt suspiciously. I knew it ain't come from me or my team just from the scent of it.

"That is coming to you, courtesy of The Queen's Cartel, nigga. Only shit I smoke," he told me with a smirk as he teased me. He knew I was sensitive about my product and the fact that Queen's shit was better than mine always fucked with me. I had some good shit, premium shit. But still, hers was better.

"Fuck outta here wit' dat bullshit," I told him with attitude, but I still grabbed the blunt anyways.

"On the real though… I don't know what to tell you because I ain't even thinking about no bitches right now. It's the furthest thing from my mind. Damn sure ain't tryin' to wife no chick up, B," Trigga said as he scratched at his jaw with a wide-eyed expression on his face.

I shook my head and blew out smoke, knowing exactly what he was saying.

"Yeah, I ain't think my ass would be even saying this no time soon."

Trigga nodded his head quietly and then he looked up at me, a frown caught in between his eyes.

"Nigga, is *that* what you met me here to ask 'bout? You know I'm not the one to ask 'bout no chick." He laughed and I joined in.

"Naw, I heard some niggas been askin' 'bout where me and where my moms stay. I know you always got your ear to the streets so I just need you to let me know if you hear anything."

Trigga's brows shot up in the air. "Word? Some muthafuckas tryin' to find your mom's spot?" I nodded my head. "I ain't heard shit, but I'm definitely about to check on that shit. I just was over there yesterday though, checking to see if she was good."

"At my moms?" I quipped, and he nodded his head, frowning slightly as if I should've known.

"Nigga, I was checkin' on yo' moms every damn week since you got locked up. Now that you're out, I don't. But she calls me every now and then to come over and get me a plate. Can't nobody cook better than she can."

"Say that shit, nigga. That's my baby though," I said, thinking back on my mama. "But if you hear somethin', hit me up. E-Class been helpin' me out, but Rayshaun been ghost since he almost got my ass locked up trying to find me a plug."

With a stone face, Trigga nodded his head. "I heard about that shit. It's fucked up, but I don't think he meant to get you cased up, nigga. That's our homie… since we was little."

"I know it."

Sighing, I stood up and knocked fists with Trigga. I didn't have time to waste.

"You leavin' so soon? You usually don't leave out this bitch until they cut off the damn lights. I guess not since you got wifey at home." He was teasing me for being a love-struck ass nigga, but I couldn't help but laugh.

"True, but more importantly I need that info, a new plug, and to get my stacks up."

"You know, if you ever need assistance with that shit, just call me, nigga," Trigga offered, standing up. Smirking, I nodded my head even though I knew I wouldn't be calling him to help me with shit unless I really couldn't handle this on my own.

"You just do what you need to in Atlanta. I got this, bruh. Who Queen got you trackin' anyways?"

He clicked his tongue and shook his head dismissively. "Nobody big. Some whack ass country boy in Atlanta named Lloyd. She said his weak spot is his side bitch. Some chick named Keisha who got a love for that nose candy, na'mean?"

"Hell naw... how the hell a kingpin got a junky as a side bitch. That's some warped shit. I definitely wanna know how that shit ends."

We bumped fists again. He promised to hit me up as soon as he heard anything and I thanked him right before leaving out. Once my feet hit the asphalt, my entire mood changed. I had shit to do and people to see.

This was my city and New York would house my empire. I was going to take it one block at a time.

CHAPTER FOUR

Le Tavia

Classical music piped through the store speakers as shoppers meandered about the department store I was in. I found myself, once again, thinking about Gunplay, when I should have been focused on the task at hand. But the truth of the matter was, after what felt like forever, my body was finally back to normal again, and I was ready be that sexy chick that I used to feel like whenever Gunplay was around. As soon as I saw him later on, I was going to jump right up on his lap and show him exactly what he'd given up the moment he decided to run off and leave me hanging all those months ago.

I probably should have felt embarrassed by the fact that I'd just had an abortion and already was thinking about sexing him in all the nasty positions he liked, but I wasn't... not at all. After spending the last few nights playing touchy feely, being groped and physically molested—so to speak, with all them damn hands Gunplay seemed to have—and not being able to have real sex in bed with his fine ass, I was ready. There was nothing like the feeling I got when his hard penis penetrated my warmth. It was an addicting feeling, even suspenseful because of his tendency to use his pistols for foreplay. Shit, I even missed being sore the next day from him twisting me up in all them different positions, and I definitely craved his deep stroke game. Some days, I swore he was trying to literally blow my back out. He hungered me and the pain hurt so good.

But for now, I was in the mall shopping with my little sister, Nori. My grandmother was getting too old to handle Nori and Peanut on her own, so they were going to be living in Miami with our mom's sister. I hated it, but my grandmother had enough health problems as it was. Nori hated it too but she was now 17-years-old, she wouldn't be there long and could come back once she finished her senior year.

I'd offered to help her with my brother and sister but she was dead-set on refusing my offer, saying that she wanted me to live my life so I could make something of myself. So I decided to at least take Nori shopping so that she could start at her new school with new clothes.

Just as we passed the Gucci section, my mind wrapped up in a sexual fantasy, I heard a squeaky voice calling my name. Something was also tugging at my sleeve.

"LeTavia? LeTavia! You act like you're not listening to a word I'm saying," Nori interrupted, pulling me out my reverie. I just happened to look up and a dark-skinned chick was putting on some expensive Gucci designer sunglasses, her eyes roaming the area as if checking for security. She looked suspicious to me.

"I heard you, girl! And stop pulling on my blouse."

"Why do we have to go live with Aunt Nessa?" Nori whined. I happened to look up again and see the dark-skinned woman take off the expensive designer shades and stuff them in her pocket. Then she casually strolled over and stood next to us. That was when I spotted the store security, a fat guy dressed in a light blue uniform and sunglasses, and a female store clerk. They were both watching the lady like a hawk.

"Doesn't she stay in the country?" Nori asked with her nose turned up like it was a conviction.

"No, she stays in Miami," I corrected her, shaking my head and casting an evil eye at the chick who had come and stood next to us like we were all together.

What the fuck? I thought, glancing at her once more. That's why I didn't like going to this ghetto ass mall. There was always some weird shit going on.

"Not everything 'bout the south is country, little girl. And you'll like it there."

Focusing on the lady, I tried to keep a straight face but it was hard with her ducking around behind me. The security guard was looking in our direction, watching her hard with his walkie-talkie to his mouth. I moved around, increasing the distance between us to show that we weren't together.

"Will you come visit?" Nori asked and I stopped, looking her right in the eyes so she would know that I was telling her the absolute truth.

"I will be down there every chance I get and even more if you call me and say you need me."

Just then, the store security guard walked up along with the female clerk, an older white woman with gray hair in one of them old fashion pompadour styles. She wore thick bifocal glasses, the kind that had the string attached, making her look sort of like the 'Cat Lady'.

"Ma'am, can you come with me?" the security guard asked casually as the female clerk hoovered in the back drop.

The woman got loud and belligerent.

"Hell naw! Come with you for what? Fucking rent-a-cop. Hell naw I ain't coming with you, and if I wasn't black, you wouldn't be harassing me and shit." She turned and looked at me to co-sign her statement.

I took several steps with Nori in tow to distance my ass. I told her not to pay any attention and glanced over my shoulder. By then, the lady and the security guard were in a boxing match, with the guard getting the bad end of the deal. The woman was throwing blows like a dude while walking towards the front door to make her escape.

"They fighting!" Nori exclaimed excitedly while I nudged her out the door. My phone began to ring and I grabbed it, answering it on the first ring as soon as I saw it was Gunplay. As soon as I was distracted, Nori dived back in the store to watch the drama.

"Hey, baby," I cooed through the phone, smiling shamelessly as several store employees ran by us in a hurry.

"Oh, I'm baby now, huh? You must be missing a nigga. Your situation changed?"

"Situation?" I scrunched my nose up.

"You know... yo' aunt Florida or whatever y'all chicks be callin' that shit."

"You mean, Aunt Flo?" All I could do was crack up laughing, causing Nori to look up at me with a poker face.

"Yeah, her. She got her ass the hell on yet?"

"Yes, she did, and I was more than ready for her ass to go."

"Good, 'cause I been wantin' you so bad, I might suck the fuckin' fallopian tubes out your pussy."

Damn!

I almost choked as I took the phone away from my ear, looked at it, and then smirked at his mannish ass. Gunplay was born without a filter and didn't know how to be any other way than blunt as hell. It was something that I wasn't sure I'd ever get used to but he made me laugh so, in some twisted way, I guess it worked.

"I'm ready to see you," I said seductively as I walked back inside after Nori. The commotion was over and now she was looking through the clothes once again. "I got some new stuff I wanna try."

"Ewww," Nori chimed in and I rolled my eyes at her.

"That's wassup," Gunplay replied and I could hear the smile in his voice. "What you gettin' into?"

"I'm shopping with Nori right now and then—"

My voice cut off suddenly when I saw a man leaning up against a wall staring at me. He was dressed in all black, sweatpants and t-shirt, with black Timb boots, showing off a sleeve of tats on each arm. Something about the way he was looking at me made me feel like he wanted me to see him there. Then, just as he noticed me looking at him, he pushed off the wall and walked away, leaving out the mall through a side door like he was in a hurry.

"Hi!" a little voice tore my attention away and I looked down, right into the eyes of a little girl. She had to be no older than maybe one-year-old. She had a beautiful brown face with the prettiest little dark brown eyes.

"Hi," I mumbled back, smiling at her as she stared up at me.

"Quisha!" a woman snapped and I froze in place, feeling a chill rising up on my spine.

I watched as a young black woman, around my age, ran up and grabbed the little girl by her hand, pulling her away.

"I'm sorry." She muttered an apology to me before turning to her child. "Quisha, I told you about talkin' to strangers. Damn!"

What in the hell? Now I felt creeped out to the fifth. What was the probability of me running into a child whose name was Quisha?

"Tavi? Man, nigga, what the hell you doin'? Just holdin' the damn phone?" Gunplay's words interrupted my train of thought, but the eerie feeling at the nape of my neck remained.

"Naw, I'm here," I told him. "I'll be back home in about an hour. See you then."

"A'ight," he said before hanging up the phone. Gunplay had this thing about saying bye. He never said it, just hung up in your face. Usually, I would call his ass back and cuss him out about it but this time, my mind was on something else.

Turning around, I searched for the woman and her daughter,

eager to put my mind at ease and shake off the feeling that something wasn't quite right. But after walking around the other stores, checking everywhere they could have gone, I didn't see either of them.

***

"Aye… why you lookin' all sour? I came and I got what you want." Gunplay walked in my bedroom donning a sheepish grin that made me roll my eyes. "We doing somethin' tonight?"

"We can," I sighed. I tossed the book I was reading by Walter Mosley on the table next to the bed. I looked at Gunplay and saw the frown, noting the confusion in his eyes.

"Okay, well damn, shawty. I know ya ass heard me walk in through the door. Why you still wearin' clothes? I thought you said you were ready." He shot me a sexy smile as he grabbed his crotch. "Didn't you say you wanted to try some new shit?"

"Yeah, like maybe I can hang upside down from the chandelier or something," I joked. He gave me a quizzical expression like maybe that wasn't a bad idea.

Biting back a laugh, I started to pull off my clothes slowly but I was so not in the mood. After the incident at the mall earlier in the day, I couldn't shake the weird way I was feeling. Sex was not on my mind. Gunplay must have sensed something was wrong. Before I could get my jeans off, he stopped me.

"This not how you was sounding earlier. You need to talk to me. Something's on ya mind and I wanna know what it is," he said and sat down on the bed, looking at me with a vexed expression that told me he wasn't moving until I explained what was going on.

After taking a deep breath, I told him everything that had happened at the mall, starting with the man who had been looking at me and ending with the little girl named Quisha. Gunplay was quiet for a while as he thought on my words, but then he sighed and pulled something from behind his back. It was one of his pistols. The gold-plated Desert Eagle, his favorite.

"Let me show you how to use this shit and tomorrow, I'll get you one of ya own."

I tensed up when he placed the weight of the gun in my hand. I turned it around and looked at it, feeling a surge of energy come upon me. Clutching it in my hands gave me a sense of power I couldn't explain.

Gunplay showed me how to refill it with bullets, cock it, put the safety on, and clean it. By the time he was done, I knew how to do everything, and the only thing I hadn't tried was to shoot it, but he promised to take me to the range the next day to do that too. Something about the way that he took care with showing me how to protect myself when he wasn't around got my kitty purring, and as soon as he was finished and set the pistol on the dresser, I was ready to go.

I stood seductively and wiggled out my designer jeans. Never once did I take my eyes off him and he kept his on me. It was as if both of us were in a sexual trance, ravishing the moment. It's a beautiful thing when your man can turn you on without even touching you. There was nothing like that telepathic connection; he didn't just have my body, he had my mind.

"Damn, you got a beautiful fuckin' body," he whispered as he ran his hands along both sides of my hips. Then he stuck his large finger between my legs, rubbing my kitty like it was on fire. He placed his finger full of my juices in his mouth and sucked on it like it was sweet molasses. My clit twitched and I creamed even more.

"Fuck. Mmmm," I groaned, already drunk on the emotions he was creating within me.

Leaning down, he picked me up like I weighed nothing more than a feather. Doing some type of balancing act, using pure strength, he nibbled gently on the bottom of my thigh, teasing me just the way that only he could, and I let out a low moan. The more he teased me, the more I moaned, and the harder his erection became until it was like he couldn't hold back anymore.

Suddenly, Gunplay eased me back on the bed gently. His hands were hungrily groping my titties, then my ass, as he tried to pull down my panties all at the same damn time. He moved swiftly, with desperate urgency, like he was trying to satisfy a need. Finally, he lost patience and pushed my panties to the side, seeking to quickly satisfy his desire.

He stroked his finger deep inside of my warmth and I swear to God it felt like he was caressing and rubbing right on my g-spot. I squirmed and began to thrash around on the bed when he covered one of my raisin nipples with his mouth, sucking gingerly. I couldn't help it. I let out a mini-orgasm on his finger. Again, he placed his finger in his mouth and sucked, noisily licking the juices.

"Fuck, Gunplay, what are you doing to me?"

Using his street name ignited a fire in his eyes, and I could see the wheels in his head turning. He was about to do some off the wall shit and I couldn't wait. I could see cum cascading down my leg and my clitoris was throbbing. It had been a minute since I had some dick, and I was ready for him to bust me open with every bit of them twelve inches, as painful as that always was. He came up high, kissing me on the lips and slipping his tongue inside of my mouth as he grinded his hard and erect bulge against my mound, making me soak up my panties even more.

God, he was a roughneck, but I liked it in that carnal, kinky, rough kind of way. His hands ravenously moved for my kitty and I sucked in a breath, anticipating the touch of his skin against mine after all this time. A shiver ignited deep inside of my stomach and then quickly pushed downwards, settling between my legs in the place that yearned for him.

Caught up in the feeling of his muscular, hard body against my soft skin, I allowed a small moan to escape my lips. In response, Gunplay grunted his content as he ran his tongue in figure eights down the back of my neck, continuing all the way down my body like he wanted to take a trek down south.

"Shiiiit, ooooohh dayuuuum," I moaned as I bit down hard on my bottom lip to stop from screaming out loud.

He pulled away from me and I instantly felt cold. Opening my eyes, I looked at him and saw that he'd released himself from his jeans. He fell back over me and let his rock-hard erection overlap on my thigh, enormous and long, elongated like a black serpent. I could feel its heat, a fiery warmth of lust. It was pulsating, and ramrod hard as he pressed it against me, rubbing it up and down my leg, as if measuring the depths of my womanhood. My entire body was on fire.

Never in life would I have described a man's dick in this way but Gunplay had a gorgeous one. It was the kind that made your mouth water when you looked at it. I had never liked the idea of giving head but with Gunplay it was almost something I craved. The feel of his mushroom head pushing down my throat and the sexy moan that followed when I rolled it around in my mouth and attempted to swallow him whole... Shit! I couldn't take any more of a delay.

I needed him badly.

I couldn't help it.

And Gunplay must have felt the same way.

He ripped open my thighs, his eyes wild with his need to feel me as he grabbed his manhood in his hand and aimed it right at my opening. Hesitating for only a second, he bit his lips before pushing in slowly, giving me only the head. Then he pulled out and did it again. Only the head. I pushed my hips up, begging for more but he only smiled and shook his head no. This is why I couldn't stand his ass.

"Damn... fuck, DeShaun!"

He was driving me crazy.

Finally, just when I was about to start cussing his ass out, he lunged forward, pushing the entirety of his manhood into me. I gasped loudly, curling my toes when he filled me completely. We fit together just the way we should... like our bodies were made for each other.

"Goddammit, Tavi!" he groaned, pulling up partially. I looked up at his face, noting his eyes were squeezed tightly shut. He was biting on his bottom lip as if he was battling something in his mind.

"Shit!" he said as he finally opened his eyes. "You feel so fuckin' good. Almost made a nigga bust quick as hell."

He started to laugh and I joined in. But the giggles were replaced with moans and screams of pleasure once he began winding his hips into my pelvis, wrapping me up into his spell and pushing closer and closer to the ultimate pleasure.

"Fuck!" I winced, when I felt the exhilarating feeling rise in my body, starting from the tips of my toes. Gunplay sped up his pace and I fell right in rhythm, fucking him as he fucked me. The lovemaking had to wait until later because that was nothing like what this was. Pulling himself up, he began slamming down into my body, damn near breaking my bed. The frame began to squeak and I just knew we were going to end up on the damn floor.

"Don't fuckin' give my shit to nobody else, Tavi! You hear me?" he growled as he beat up in me even harder. It hurt so bad but felt so good at the same damn time. I gritted my teeth as he kept thrusting, wondering if it was possible for him to actually shake some shit loose inside of me.

"I won't!" I told him, meaning every bit of what I was saying. I would never, ever, ever give to another man what was his. Every part of me belonged to him and that's how it would always be.

"Promise me. Fuckin' promise me that shit!" he yelled, clenching his jaw as he began to wind his hips, throwing his dick in a circle.

"Shit! I promise!" I screamed and arched my back, feeling like I was just about to cum. Before I could, he pulled out and flipped me over, pushing my back down to arch my ass up. I purred and raised it high in the air, giving him a good look at my pretty pussy that I knew was glistening with my juices. Then I felt him reach over for something and the next thing I knew, he'd cocked his gun.

"One in the chamber."

I shivered even though it wasn't cold.

Gunplay was exactly that in every bit of the word. He was passionate and dangerous, even in love. Call me crazy, but the shit turned me on.

Using the barrel of his pistol, he parted my ass cheeks and swiped it slowly down the crack of my ass, pausing only when he was pointing the barrel right at my puckered hole.

"When you gon' let me hit you in the ass, shawty?" His voice deep and robust, almost ragged with lust. My already rock hard nipples got even tighter and I felt a little of my honey drip down my clit.

"Whenever you want, baby." I arched my back even more, grinding my ass on the barrel of his gun and I heard him take in a sharp breath.

"Damn, you so fuckin' sexy, Tavi."

He pushed the cold steel down even further, running it across my hard clit and I moaned in pure ecstasy. The feel of it against my skin turned my mind to mush and I began to grind against it, my only thought was to satisfy my craving for more pleasure.

"Cum on it, baby," he coaxed me and I grinded against it even more. Gunplay stuck his finger in his mouth and pulled it out, making a soft popping noise. The next thing I knew, he was sliding it up into my ass. There was pain… then pleasure… pain, then… shit, it felt so fuckin' good. He raised the barrel up and stuck it in my pussy, jabbing the metal dick right into my cave. This nigga was crazy as hell but so was I. We were a match made in hell.

"You like that?"

He began to dive the barrel further up into me and I replied by crying out, gushing all over it when he sped up the pace. My pussy started contracting and I came hard, pushing out my thick cream all over his piece. Gunplay removed it quickly and then bent over, pushing face-first into my ass, and lapped up my juices from behind. His thick tongue curled all up through my folds as he drank from me until there was nothing left. I groaned, I fought, I tried to push him off me but he wrapped his lips around my hardened clit, sucking until I screamed. Another orgasm began to build up within me.

"I need this pussy," he whispered in a guttural tone. Then he flipped me around on my back and dived right back into me, quick and hard with no mercy.

Gunplay wrapped his arms around me, pulling me closer into him, totally caging my body inside of his, before delivering short, fast jabs straight through me. In no time, I was at the precipice of another orgasm, this one even stronger than the last. I came at the same time that he did, both of us moaning so loud that I knew every damn body in the building, Bruce's lame ass included, knew exactly what the hell we were doing.

"Damn, we fucked up the sheets," Gunplay noted as he pulled

out of me and kissed me with emotions, sort of in a way I couldn't remember him doing before, like he meant it. Then, rolled over to his side of the bed as if sedated, satiated, and slightly winded.

"Baby, you got some good ass pussy. The kind that'll make a pussy-whipped nigga wanna make you wifey," he teased with a smile while staring at my body. He concentrated his gaze between my legs with lust brimming in his eyes like he wanted to go another round.

"You know it's only so long you can get the kitty for free, so maybe it would be a good idea to place a ring on it. Sort of like coochie insurance, your dick and mouth will always have a permanent home to come to," I teased him back with a mischievous smile.

"Permanent? Fuck you mean a 'permanent home'? You sayin' it ain't like that now? You talkin' like I'ma pop up and a nigga gon' be here beatin' in your guts just cause we ain't married!" He raised his voice as he balanced himself on his elbow atop the pillow, boring down into my face.

I gave him a dead serious expression and said with gaiety, attempting to imitate the way he spoke, "Naw, I'm just sayin', shawty. You never know... you just might need to get yaself some of this coochie insurance so that don't happen." I tried to keep a straight face and not burst out laughing.

WHAM!

Before I could dodge it, his ass hit me upside the head with a pillow, twice, the first blow a little too hard. But the last blow had me seeing little red spots in front of my eyes. Then he reached back to strike me with the pillow again.

"STOP!!" I screamed at him, slapping at his arms.

Frowning at me, he paused suddenly, holding the pillow above his head. Leave it to Gunplay to get all in his feelings just from me playing around.

"If I come up in this bitch and you got another nigga in this shit, I'ma wet both y'all up. Y'all muthafuckas gon' be sharing a coffin," he threatened with grit in his voice. "Now play wit' it if you wanna!"

Shaking my head, I couldn't resist chiding him more. He made it too easy to get up under his skin.

"Damn the last time you had me and another nigga sharing an ambulance. Now we done graduated to a coffin?!"

WHAM!

Rearing back, he came forward hard and smacked my ass with the pillow again, then pushed me out the bed, making me fall onto the floor, right on my ass. The entire time, I couldn't help but laugh so hard that my sides hurt.

"And I ain't playin' wit' ya ass. Yeah, I got love for you, but that shit don't mean nothin' if I find you fuckin' around. G shit."

Tilting my head to the side, I sat up and peered at him from beside the bed.

"Oh, you love me?" I asked him, a smile tickling the corners of my lips. I could see the thoughts merging in his mind as he ran back through what he'd said.

"I said 'I got love for you,'" he informed me, carefully repeating his words.

"So, that mean you don't love me?"

Gunplay looked back at me and I could see the inward battle raging through his mind as he pondered whether or not he should fess up to his feelings. Then the corner of his upper lip rose slowly and I knew then that I'd won.

See, niggas be acting so hard like they don't care, but every nigga got a heart and with it comes the ability to fall in love; it just takes the right female to bring it out of them. And, from the looks of it, I was bringing it out of Gunplay.

"Yeah, I guess you can say I do," he said, and then fell back on the bed, staring at the ceiling with a nonchalant expression on his face. He tried it. I was not about to let that fly.

Jumping up on the bed, I straddled him, pinning him down by placing my arms down on either side of his head as I leaned over into his face.

"Say you do what?" I queried with a sly grin.

"That I love you." He said it just above a whisper with his eyes closed. Then he opened them and looked at me, the gentle expression on his face sending a chill straight to my core.

"I love you, Tavi," he repeated and my heart skipped a beat and a half.

"I love you too, DeShaun," I told him as I kissed him lightly on the lips. "I always have and I always will."

LeTavia

"Wake up."

I blinked a few times in fast sequence, as I tried to straighten out my blurry vision. Sitting up in the bed, I looked up right into Gunplay's eyes. He was fully dressed, standing over me with a peculiar expression hidden between his eyes.

"What's wrong?" I asked, rubbing the sleep away. I glanced at the clock. It was only a little after six in the evening.

"Nothing. Just get dressed. I need to take you somewhere."

And with that, he turned away and walked out of the room without another word. Rolling my eyes, I got up and rushed to the bathroom to take a shower and clean up so I could get dressed. Dealing with Gunplay was always exciting because he was so unpredictable. He brought color to my otherwise dull life.

When I stepped out the shower, I noticed that he'd already pulled out something for me to wear: a nice black dress that was somewhat form-fitting, but casual and cute. I paired it with a diamond necklace, earring and bracelet set that he'd bought me, did my makeup and hair, then slid my feet into some nice black heels. A half hour later, we were pulling up to a group of apartments I knew too well. The last time I'd been over this way was to help Sonya move after her father died. When Gunplay pulled in front of the one next to Sonya's old place, I turned and looked right into his face with my eyes wide.

"We're going to see your mother?"

He nodded and smirked, cutting off the engine.

"She wanted to meet you," was all he said, giving me a slight shrug.

"She did?" He nodded again and I swallowed hard.

Although we'd been dating for a while, Gunplay kept a lot of stuff regarding his family secret. It wasn't that I felt like he was hiding them from me, I just felt like it never really came up. When we were together, we were so consumed with each other that we almost forgot a world and people existed outside of us.

"Let's go. She cooked."

He stepped out of the car and then ran over on my side to open my door. I frowned up into his face and shook my head as I stepped out.

"Don't be tryin' to act all like a gentleman just because yo' moms is lookin', nigga," I teased him with a smile before leaning over and giving him a light kiss on the lips. "But I appreciate it anyways."

He smiled deeply and I was almost taken aback. He was so sexy to me. I was so caught up in him that it scared me. I'd always heard that passion too intense died off fast but I just couldn't see that happening with us. Gunplay was dressed in a pair of nice blue jeans, stark white sneakers, and a white Polo with icy diamond jewelry in his ears, around his neck, and his wrists. He looked good and smelled even better. I was just as caught up in him today as I had been the first time I saw him. My passion for him hadn't decreased one bit. In fact, it had grown tremendously.

With his hand right above my ass, he ushered me to the door which opened wide as soon as we got to the top step.

"Daddddyyyyyyy!"

Out came Imani who I hadn't seen in forever. She ran and jumped straight into Gunplay's arms.

"Hey, big ass girl!" he greeted her, and I rolled my eyes, laughing as they embraced in a tight hug.

"Well, hello, Ms. LeTavia."

With my smile still plastered to my face, I turned and focused right in on Gunplay's mother's face. She was a beautiful woman, and looking at her made me miss my grandmother who I hadn't seen in a while. I made a mental note to check in with her.

"It's so nice to meet you, ma'am," I said with sincerity, walking over to give her a hug. She held me tight and I melted in her arms. I'd always thought Gunplay gave the best hugs but I had been wrong. I inhaled her scent and felt so relaxed. She smelled of honey and peppermint, a seemingly odd combination but it blended perfectly with her natural fragrance.

"You are such a beautiful woman!" she gushed, looking me over. Then she shot her eyes to Gunplay and smirked. Her sly smirk was identical to his.

"You did good, son."

"I know," he replied, grinning hard with Imani in his arms. I ducked my head and blushed.

"C'mon in! I cooked and I don't want the food gettin' cold!"

As if hearing her words, I felt my stomach churn and I realized how hungry I was. I'd eaten earlier with Nori but all that had been used to fuel my sexual encounter earlier with Gunplay. It was hard work satisfying a beast and now I was starving.

As soon as I walked in her home, my nose was filled with the alluring aroma of whatever delicacies she had prepared for us. I was ready to dig in.

"It smells good as hell in here, Mama!" Gunplay said, stomping to the kitchen. He immediately began lifting pots and peering in them to see what was inside.

"DeShaun! Don't you think you need to wash your hands?" I chastised Gunplay who only turned around and gave me a smile. He shrugged and I frowned at him. His mama looked back and forth between us with a smile on her face.

"Get out of those pots. Let me wash up and I'll make your plate," I said."

"Yes, ma'am." He fixed back the pots and stepped away from the stove, giving his mother a sheepish expression.

"So, she gets on your case for the same thing I do, I see!" she told him, laughing heartily.

"Tavi always gettin' on my case 'bout somethin'," he replied, acting like he was annoyed about it. "She bad as you, Ma."

"Well, that's good because she should. I approve of you already, Ms. Tavi."

I beamed, smiling hard as I quickly rinsed off my hands and dried them.

After dinner, Imani and Gunplay went to her room to play and I sat down in the living room to chat with Gunplay's mother. My stomach was in knots because this was the first time I'd ever met anyone's mother. I had no idea what to expect. I felt like she liked me but how could I be sure?

"You're good for him," she said as soon as Gunplay was down the hall. I relaxed instantly, happy that I seemed to have her approval. Nothing was more important to a woman than her children but there was a special place in a mother's heart for her son. Most times mothers never felt any woman was good enough for their sons, so I counted my blessings that this wasn't the case for me.

She cleared her throat and I turned to look at her, waiting for her to continue.

"My son… he needs a strong woman in his life. He is a very strong man; he's always been that way. Even when DeShaun was younger, he's always been so headstrong, focused, and fearless. That last one has caused me the most worry," she chuckled but I knew it wasn't because anything was funny. Gunplay's fearlessness kept me awake at night sometimes too. I understood exactly what she meant.

"When I was younger, I was an alcoholic. DeShaun is my youngest… the other ones have nothing to do with me, even though I've changed. My other family have little to do with me so it's always just been me and him. He's very protective of me but he's also very dependent on me. I'm not going to live forever and I've been asking

God to give him the right woman to take my place once I'm gone."

I'd only just met this woman but already tears were in my eyes just at her mentioning needing me to take over once she was gone. I could see how Gunplay was so protective and dependent on her. With her dark brown eyes filled with so much wisdom and compassion, she instantly made me fall in love with her presence. Then she said something that rattled my spirit. She frowned deeply before speaking, as if it pained her to say it.

"My son is a hard one to love. He has a darkness in him that I could never get to. I've tried to encourage him to go with me to church... to see my pastor, but he always refuses. I'm sure you've seen it sometimes." She looked expectantly at me, but I only averted my eyes from hers. I knew what she meant but I didn't want to say anything bad to her about Gunplay. It would feel like I was betraying him.

"You've seen it but you don't want to talk against him. That's okay. That's why I like you." She nodded, giving me a weak smile before going on. "His anger is uncontrollable. When he was younger, he'd do things in his anger and later wouldn't remember it. It was almost like he blacked out. I would punish him, thinking he was lying but he wasn't. He truly had no recollection of the things he'd done. I got him help but it only allowed him to be cognitive of the things he was doing but he still isn't able to fully control it. They tried to tell me my baby was crazy... that he needed medication. There is nothing crazy about my son... he was just a young black boy who was forced to become a man far beyond his time because of his environment. He was forced to figure out how to survive. He learned early that only the strongest survive and that's who he's become."

She stopped speaking and I could see the pride showing in her face. She was proud of everything Gunplay had become, proud of the way that he was able to make the best out of his hard upbringing. She may not agree with how he did it but she loved him anyway.

"Have you told him your secret?"

I froze in place. I swear my heart had skipped a beat or maybe stopped beating altogether.

"M—my secret?" She nodded her head.

"Yes, your secret. You love him but I can tell you also fear him. You're too cautious… like you're trying not to anger the beast. I can tell it and I know he can too."

She looked at me, staring deeply into my eyes and I felt cold and naked. I licked my lips and tried to relax in my seat to seem at ease. She gave me a knowing look and I knew I couldn't fool her.

"Whatever it is you're keeping from him, continue to keep it. Don't ever tell him unless you absolutely must. People always say honesty is the best policy and full-disclosure is preferred but it's not true. Sometimes, things are better left unsaid when saying them could hurt a lot of people. My son loves you… I've never met a woman he's been in a relationship with. Even with Quisha, I met her after she had Imani and they were no longer together. And it wasn't because he never brought a woman by, it was because they never lasted long enough to even get to that stage. DeShaun is a great man to be with, but you have to learn how to live with him."

They were the truest words I'd ever heard. Speaking to Gunplay's mother put a lot of things in perspective for me. I'd been feeling like I was alone in the world when it came to Gunplay... I had no one to speak to because no one could understand how it was possible to be so in love with someone but so scared at the same time. Speaking with his mother cleared things up for me and allowed me to better understand the type of man he was and how I could make it work with him.

For both of us.

That night, we went back home and made love so long that my whole body was sore by the time we finished. Something about getting his mother's approval changed something in Gunplay. For the first time since we'd met, he wasn't an animal in bed. There were no pistols, no biting, no slamming into me, or knocking the bed against the wall. There was only sweet lovemaking, tender kisses, and sensual rubbing all over my body. I fell asleep in his arms, listening to the sound of his breathing and knew right then that there was no other place I'd rather be. Ever.

Gunplay

LeTavia had some shit between her legs that would have a nigga losing his damn mind. She wondered why I was so fuckin' crazy about her ass and that was a big part of it. The sex was like none other, plus she had a bangin' ass body, and was smart as hell. I wouldn't admit it to her but I liked the fact that she was one of the only women, other than my moms, that wasn't afraid to go toe-to-toe with me.

Okay… I'll admit it: she had a nigga sprung. I've known for quite some time that I loved her; I just didn't want to really say it. In a strange kind of way, I felt it was a violation of my thug code but it felt good, she felt good and that was all that mattered.

God created the ultimate delicacy in the form of a wet, juicy vagina. But when he combined it with a beautiful sexy body, along with a pretty face and a smile, it was a wrap. He created something that wars would be fought over, something men would die and betray each other for. Fools fell victim to the wiles of feminine enchantment and I was trying not to be that fool.

Not at first, anyway.

After feeling her for the first time in some months, it took me three days to get myself together enough to leave her ass alone and get back to work. But I eventually found a way from in between her legs and, now, I was lighting up and sitting in the middle of my favorite place to be: E-Class's club, and wrestling with the uncanny voice in my head that kept telling me the same thing over and over vehemently, almost to the point of badgering me.

She is the one. She is wifey material.

Of course, I kicked the thoughts out my head like a bad habit, only for them to return later. Love was a muthafucka but I had other plans. It was time for me to spring into action. I had long thought about rubbing off my old connect and getting a new one. The last time I copped some coke from Freddy, he had shorted me thirteen grams and blamed it on a bad shipment. He promised to reimburse me but he never did. And to make matters worse, the dope was weak like it had been stepped on too many times.

Rumor on the streets was, Freddy had begun to get high on his own supply and was tricking off some chick named Shaquita who was beating him out of his money and dope. Freddy failed to heed the codes of the streets: don't get high on your own supply, and it ain't trickin' if you got it. It was obvious that Freddy didn't have it. Freddy was sinking like the Titanic and the streets were talking. I knew for a fact if I didn't get him, another nigga would. This was the ghetto food chain; the strong prosper and the weak die.

The first thing I did was contact Shaquita, which was easy thanks to E-Class, who had her number and address. According to him, she had worked for him in the club for a little while a few years back, until he found out she was underage. Now she was only nineteen-years-old. She lived in the projects in the Bronx with her mama and two-year-old daughter. Ironically, me and her brother, J-Rock, went to high school together back in the day and she had a crush on me.

At the time, I didn't know it. In fact, I didn't even remember her, but I acted like I did and it helped when I rolled up on her in my Charger sitting on 22s. She smelled money on me like a starved Ethiopian at a chicken buffet and agreed to help me with the lick, hook, line and sinker, under one agreement: we get together afterwards and I pay her $500. She even took it a step further and showed me where Freddy Black lived, and agreed to be there when I ran up on him so that everything went smoothly.

We agreed to meet up on Tuesday and that was because she knew firsthand from ear hustling, that Tuesday was the day Freddy got in a large shipment of cocaine.

It was on!

"So, I hear everything is a go with Shaquita," E-Class said as he sat down across from me, holding two identical glasses of brown liquid. He pushed one over to me and I nodded my head.

"Yeah, good lookin' out too, fam. We movin' on this nigga's shit on Tuesday. Once it's all said and done, I'll give you a cut for the hook up. I owe you big for lettin' me use your spot to get my shit together. How much you want anyways?"

E-Class shrugged. "Just ten percent works for me."

I lifted one brow. "Ten? You sure?"

He nodded his head again. "From what I hear, Freddy gon' have millions up in there. Ten percent is way more than enough, fam. I ain't tryin' to break ya."

"Listen, nigga. You don't know how much I appreciate you helpin' me with this shit. I know I ain't been able to drop bread on you for all this info you giving me like I used to, but it's only because I'm in the building phase. When I get my chips together, I'm takin' over this fuckin' city and I'm bringing you with me."

I meant that shit, too. Trigga, E-Class, and Rayshaun were like brothers to me. Part of me felt like less than a man because I couldn't make moves as fast as I wanted to, but I wasn't really worrying about that shit because I knew in only a little time, I would be on top. It was always safe to gamble on a nigga like me because I made shit happen. At the same time, I didn't like that E-Class was letting me use his club for meet ups and shit with my growing team and I hadn't been able to drop bands on him to show him I appreciated using his resources. But I would be changing that soon. And I still needed to catch up with Rayshaun.

"You heard anything from Rayshaun?" I asked E-Class and he shook his head.

"Not really. He came up here asking for a job but I don't trust that cat, ya know?"

I didn't respond. I was feeling some kind of way about what I was hearing about Rayshaun, but I hadn't spoken to him yet for myself.

"He asked you for a job? Why the hell he ain't come to me? I ain't even seen that nigga in weeks. He can't still be feelin' crazy about that shit with that Colombian."

"He probably just knows that was some foul shit he did and trying to keep his head low."

"Yeah, plus, I been hangin' with LeTavia a lot lately."

As soon as I mentioned LeTavia, something passed through E-Class's eyes. Something I didn't like.

"Aye, you trust her?" he asked me and I frowned deeply.

"Hell yeah, I trust her. Why wouldn't I?" He paused, giving me an uneasy look and I didn't like it one bit. "E, you know some shit 'bout her that I don't know?"

"I heard some stuff but it's not important. Bitches always talking about another bitch… probably just jealous shit."

Immediately, I was on edge. What the hell could he have heard about LeTavia? It wasn't like she was a ghetto broad who always had her business all in the streets. There was no way he could have heard something about her that I didn't know.

"Naw, nigga. Tell me what the fuck you heard. I'm not with these secrets and shit."

Sitting back in my chair, I grabbed a blunt out of my pocket and lit it. A stripper came to our table asking if we wanted her to refill our drinks and I waved her away. The DJ started playing some trap music and the bass bumped heavily in my chest, the perfect soundtrack for my brewing anger.

"C'mon with it, nigga!" I pushed angrily, blowing out smoke and E-Class finally opened his mouth and started speaking after expelling a heavy sigh.

"I heard that while y'all was together the first time, she was seen fuckin' around with a nigga in Harlem. One of Cutta's men."

"WHAT?!"

Before I knew it, I was blinded by my rage. I jumped up so fast that I knocked a chair over in the process and almost knocked over the table that sat between us as I lunged for E-Class. With the blazing blunt still between my lips, I jacked him up hard by the collar, pushing steadily backwards until his body was pressed against the wall behind him with only the small table between us. The music still blared around us but nearly every eye had turned to us, everyone was wondering what in the world was going on between the boss and Gunplay. I was out of line but I didn't give a single fuck.

"If I ever hear about Tavi fuckin' around with a nigga from Cutta's crew, I'ma fuckin' kill her ass and I put that on God. So, unless you fuckin' know for a fact that this shit 'bout Tavi is true, you need to fuckin' dead that shit, nigga! You get what da fuck I'm sayin'?!"

E-Class narrowed his eyes on me, matching my intense glare with one of his own.

"Yes," he replied in a clipped tone. "Can you release me now?"

By this time, the DJ had turned the music down a notch. Everyone's eyes were still on us and the room was filled with voices, murmuring and whispering to each other. Everyone was wondering what would happen. I held E-Class for a few moments longer and then relaxed my grasp. Pulling the blunt from my lips, I toked hard on it and then picked up my chair to sit back down.

"Crystal, come get somebody to clean up these fuckin' drinks," E-Class ordered to one of the strippers nearby. She hurried to do as he asked. The DJ turned up the track and people went back to enjoying themselves for the most part. A lot of them continued to glance occasionally in our direction, not wanting to miss a thing.

"That's fucked up, nigga," E-Class started, sitting down back in his seat. "I always tell you shit that I've heard. That's what the fuck I do! But for you to come at me like that about a chick…" He shook his head.

"She ain't just a chick. Like I said, I don't wanna hear shit 'bout her unless you know it's true. I don't play 'bout her."

"Yeah, I see," he said the words with grit and it put me on edge, like he had an issue with LeTavia for some reason. I didn't like it but I left it alone. If he didn't like her, that was okay, but he was going to respect her in my presence and I was sure that now he understood.

A beautiful brown-skinned woman with a short afro came over to us, placed two new drinks on the table, and then began to clean up the mess as I stood up.

"I'll holla at you later. I need to get shit in order so I can make this move." Grabbing the drink, I downed it, swallowing it down in gulps as I enjoyed the burn in my chest. E-Class watched me quietly as he clutched his own drink in his hands and nodded his head.

"Good luck, fam."

I shook my head and forced out a dry chuckle.

"I don't need luck. Never did."

***

Tuesday couldn't come fast enough. I was lounging at LeTavia's crib, watching the football game, as she sat opposite from me wearing some skinny little Victoria's Secret outfit. She had her legs partially open as she polished her toenails, looking sexy, and not even conscious of how badly she was distracting me. It was hard for me to keep my eyes on the game, until my phone rung. I checked the caller ID and it was Shaquita, but for some reason, she was talking in hushed tones.

"There has been a change of plans," she whispered. I could hear music in the background and the cacophony of voices.

"What the fuck you mean there has been a change of plans? We need to make this happen. I need to see you ASAP."

Instantly, I was picked up on LeTavia's radar. Her body did that little jerky motion as she snaked her neck at me with her hand poised over her toenail still holding the polish.

"What the hell? I hope you ain't trying me with no bitch on the phone, DeShaun," she snapped. I ignored her.

"The guy that dropped off the coke, it's like bales of that shit, but they still here drinking and smoking. There are piles of money and guns on the table, and one dude offered me a stack just to eat my pussy! But it's a lot of them here. Too many..."

"A stack just to eat pussy? Damn. How many people there?" I asked, alarmed.

"Uh, about four all together, plus—"

"You talkin' 'bout eating pussy? Gimme that fuckin' phone, nigga!"

I looked up just as LeTavia rushed over to me with feline quickness and then stood right over me, reaching for the phone. I waved her off, frowning hard.

"So, you telling me the plug's plug is still there? The muthafucka Freddy cops his dope from?"

I was excited, heart thrumming like a drum in my chest as I pushed LeTavia back once again.

"Yeah, he is here and I don't like it. I'm scared. Them Haitian niggas is crazy. One dude with a dead eye keeps looking at me."

"Damn!" By then, I was in a wrestling match with LeTavia over the phone. I was barely paying attention to her crazy ass, but she wasn't letting up.

"Okay, look... I'ma give you ten stacks instead. Just hang in there for me until I come through. Can you do that??"

"Uh, hell yea!" she retorted, suddenly emboldened with the sound of all them big face hundreds.

"Okay, I'ma hit you back in an hour. You have that thing ready—"

WHAM!

LeTavia slapped me so hard across my head my phone went flying across the room.

"Fuck you hit me for?!" I snapped and walked over to the other side of the room to retrieve my phone. She had cracked the damn screen.

"I can't believe you tried me with another bitch like I wasn't even standing right here!"

"It's business, Tavi!" I tried to persuade her, gritting my teeth together. I wasn't even fuckin' around, and here she was in my face with all this unnecessary shit.

"Business my ass!" Then she decided to mimic me, contorting her face as she spoke. "Have that thang ready and I'ma give you ten stacks." She made a face like she had taken a big bite out of a sour lemon.

"Man, fall back. You don't know what the bidness is—"

She raised her hand like she was going to slap me and I grabbed it, pushing it down to her side. I wanted to nut up on her ass, but I had to keep my chill so I could calm her down and bounce. Real shit, I had no one but myself to blame for her even acting like this after all I put her through messin' with Quisha back in the day. LeTavia was only a product of the environment I'd created for her. But I knew after a while, she would trust a nigga again, so I wasn't worried. I wasn't fucking around anymore and I wouldn't ever again. She would understand that shit one day.

"Yo, I'll be back."

"Now you leavin'? I swear, DeShaun, if you about to go meet up with some bitch—"

"Just chill," I instructed her, running my fingers down her arm. I went all the way down, soothing her attitude through the tips of my fingers before cupping my hand around her fat ass.

"You gotta trust me. I'll be back."

***

I rolled up to my trap on 19th Street. I had some of my crew hustling out of a two-story brownstone in the hub of the ghetto. It was always easy to tell it was a dope house because junkies loitered out front looking like the walking dead. As soon as they saw me, they scattered. They knew I was going to beat one of their asses like I had did in the past. Junkies were good for business but also bad for business when it came to causing attention from the cops.

I walked inside, right into the smoke den, a section of the house on the first floor with rooms that I let dope fiends use to get high if they spent a hundred dollars or more. It was run by Nene, a crackhead. I had used her ID to rent the place from the owner; she was a junkie but dependable enough. She was an attractive woman with a nice shape, large breasts, with long, black, curly hair, and a cinnamon complexion. She uncannily resembled the singer, Keyshia Cole.

"Where is Nuke and Tony at?" I asked, doing my best not to look at Nene.

Her breasts were fully exposed, in her right hand was a smoldering crack pipe. Her eyes were big and glassy like she had just taken a big hit and was geeking. I hated to see her like that. Truth be told, Nene had a master's degree—she had graduated from Yale. She was married with a daughter, but her addiction to crack made her abandon all that. Her husband used to come by here looking for her and had once even called the cops. But Nene refused to go back home. Instead, she got high and sold her body to support her habit. I had even told her to go back home and she wouldn't.

"They in the back." She pointed to a room and lit up her pipe, the devil's dick, and sucked on it in bliss.

I found Tony asleep on a dirty mattress on his back with his banger in his hand and a hundred pack of rocks on his lap. Lucky for him, Nene had not turned kleptomaniac yet.

"Nigga, get your ass up! I got a big lick planned. Get the AK-47 and the shotgun. Where Nuke?"

I found Nuke on the second-floor tricking with a crackhead, some old lady who looked like she was in her late fifties. The funk coming from them nearly made me vomit. He had his pants around his ankles when I walked in and she was giving him head like it hurt her to even move. She sopped on it noisily, her cheeks caving into her mouth because of the absence of teeth. Disgusting. It was a sight to behold and if I hadn't seen it with my own eyes, I wouldn't have believed it.

"Nigga, bust a nut and get yo' nasty ass up. We got work to do!"

Nuke nodded his head drunkenly and I stomped out the room to let him finish his business. Reaching in my pocket, I pulled out a blunt and lit it up, inhaling hard. I needed something to get that nasty ass image out of my mind.

We rode three deep in an old black Mazda, strapped with four pistols. Luckily, I remembered the address Shaquita had given me in New Jersey to Freddy's residence. What I couldn't remember was her phone number and the damn screen on my phone was cracked. I could receive incoming calls but I couldn't call out, thanks to LeTavia, who had pitched my shit right across the living room. She was seriously tripping but I had to deal with that later on. My mind was on what I had to do, but I couldn't lie and say my current situation didn't have me feeling uneasy.

It was like walking into a danger zone unless Shaquita called before I got to the plug's house. As we drove, my mind frantically tried to formulate a plan. I had none; this was an inside job with the help of Shaquita. But I had to seize the opportunity of a lifetime.

"What we gon' do?" Nuke asked as I drove with the radio blasting, smoke from the blunt swirling around like a tornado.

"We just gon' pull up, park out front so they can't see the license plate, and ring the doorbell. Whoever answers, God bless they ass because we gon' air that bitch out," I replied impromptu, straight off the cranium. It was a crazy idea, but I was the type of nigga just crazy enough to do it.

"I don't think that is a good idea," Tony replied uneasily, holding the AK-47.

"That's why I ain't asking you to think! Just do what the fuck I say!"

That's when I got a call. I looked at my cracked screen but I couldn't see shit so I prayed like a muthafucka it was Shaquita calling with good news.

"Aye, wassup?" I answered, anxiously.

"Nigga, I want your whorish ass to know that your phone got a GPS system. I can follow you to that bitch house if I want to. You not about to fuck around on me no more, DeShaun, I'm not the same woman I used to be. I'll leave your ass after I put my foot in it!"

"Tavi?! C'mon, bae, stop it. I told you I was working on something—"

"Yeah, eatin' pussy and then givin' her ten stacks!"

Frowning, I shook my head. Why the fuck would a nigga like me ever give a bitch ten stacks for some pussy? I had hoes lining up for this dick and LeTavia knew it. She was on one for real.

"Stop this stupid shit, man. Have I ever given you a reason not to trust me, Tavi?"

"YES!"

Fuck. Well, she had a point, but this was the wrong damn time for this shit. I groaned, frustrated, as Tony and Nuke both glanced at me, curious and a little amused.

"It ain't like it used to be, Tavi. I swear I ain't doin' shit."

"DeShaun, you better hear me and hear me good. I'ma shoot you and that bitch with the same gun you taught me how to use if you don't—"

Click!

I hung up the phone and drove faster. I couldn't deal with her crazy ass right now. LeTavia was fuckin' up my mind.

We arrived at the house in New Jersey in the wee hours of the morning. It was definitely not a damn brownstone either. Freddy Black lived in a mansion. A huge beige structure with a large horseshoe driveway and plush yard. There was a statue in the middle of the yard spewing water from a fountain. A gleaming, full moon hung high in the sky, luminous like a bright lightbulb in the night. The driveway was lined with expensive, exotic cars: a Porsche truck, two Lambos, a Bentley Coup, and an older model Benz.

"Who gon' knock at the door?" Nuke asked with a tremor in his voice. Scary ass nigga. I needed to find some replacements worth shit, quick.

"I'ma knock!"

"Cool," they both responded in unison, relieved that they wouldn't have to play crash dummy and risk getting shot first. The thought hadn't even occurred to me. I didn't bust back because I shot first. If I was running up in someone's shit, I was coming with guns blasting before them niggas even had a chance to react. They didn't call me Gunplay for nothing.

As soon as we got out the car and began to walk up the long plush lawn with weapons in hand, wearing ski-masks, I realized a couple things but it was too late. First thing was, there was a camera at the corner building of the mansion that moved as we walked, following us and causing my heart to beat faster. There was a real chance that Freddy and his crew already knew we were on our way in. The second thing was that I realized there was only one way out. We would have to kill everything moving inside if we wanted to get away. The latter, I had no problems with.

Any normal muthafucka would've been ready to run. Tony and Nuke were. I swear I could hear them niggas' knees knocking from behind me. But they were rolling with a savage and I didn't turn back. So, I simply pointed my chin up to the camera and I told my crew to be on point.

I rang the doorbell and heard Freddy's Rottweilers inside, barking like they couldn't wait to tear me apart. Shaquita had told me that she was going to make sure she locked them up but she hadn't. She was already fuckin' up my plan.

I suddenly had an idea and snatched off my mask. Maybe I'd get lucky and Shaquita would answer the door, but even if Freddy was the one that answered, I had an excuse for his ass too. Tony and Nuke waited behind some bushes on the side of mansion. I pressed the doorbell again and prayed like a muthafucka Shaquita was the one who answered.

It seemed like an eternity before I heard the bolts on the door rattling. The door opened with a whoosh and music blared from inside. To my dismay, it was Freddy with his eyes fiery red, his sable skin the color of a black shinny tire. He was holding a .45 military pistol at his side.

"Mon, wha' da-mudda-fuck you dun'in at mi home—"

BOOM!

I shot him in the chest with the Mossberg shotgun, propelling his body backwards up in the air, like he had been shot out a cannon. There was a gaping hole in his chest the size of a football as he landed on the floor with a loud thud.

And that's when the damn dogs leaped at me.

I shot one, hitting him in mid-air causing him to howl in agony. He fell over dead instantly. The other dog, scared as hell and a little smarter than his companion, ran out the door past me as I rushed in, followed by Nuke and Tony, the shotgun still blazing at my side. The mansion was huge inside—lots of spots for muthafuckas to hide. I moved past a white Baby Grand piano and looked up ahead. I detected movement down a long corridor and took off for it without a second thought.

In the dining room, we discovered a large burly man with dreadlocks and a double chin. He was attempting to scoop up a large bundle of cash into an army duffle bag off the table. His brow was covered in perspiration and fear; his breathing was heavy, making grunting sounds. I cocked the shotgun and aimed at his head.

"Please don't shoot me!"

He flailed his flabby arms, face stricken with fear. There were several guns on the table. I couldn't help but wonder why he hadn't picked up one to defend himself. Then I was reminded of something my mama used to say.

Fear is a terrible thing; you never know how somebody will act when they scared.

"Where everybody else at?" I asked, looking around.

"Me dun know. The girl and Mustafa went somewhere to be alone."

"Mustafa?" Nuke repeated.

"Who the fuck is that?" I asked as I stared at over a hundred kilos of packaged cocaine on the adjoining table, piled high.

"He is a hitta. Works for a lot of the cartels, like Freddy and the Mafia at times," Nuke explained. I could see the whites of his eyes through the ski-mask and my intuition told me he was scared. What the hell had I just walked into? Shaquita didn't say shit about no hitta named Mustafa.

"Fuck. Find him."

I lowered my voice as I watched with my lip curled up as Tony ran over to the piles of coke and began to stuff them in black garbage bags that they came in. Greed was a terrible thing. We needed to be taking care of whoever the hell else was up in this bitch and his ass was trying to pack shit up.

"Man, fuck that dope! Go find Mustafa and the bitch he's with."

Tony nodded but didn't move. He was too busy stuffing the last of the dope into the trash bags.

That's when we heard it at the same time—a bloodcurdling scream that echoed throughout the mansion causing a timorous shiver to run down my spine.

Then a shot rang out! The sound was deafening. We all turned at the same time, frantically looking around.

Big mistake.

Blocka! Blocka! Blocka!

Just in the quick second that our attention was drawn to the sound of the horrific scream and gunshot, the fat Haitian had picked up one of the guns off the table and shot Tony in the back twice. He then leveled the gun at me, firing. He barely missed. I ducked in the nick of time as bullets buzzed by my skull. That was when Nuke let loose with the AK-47 and shot the big Haitian in the head. His face exploded like a watermelon, splattering blood, bone, and matter all over the table and me. The shot had damn near decapitated him. He fell on the floor in a heap as crimson blood ran from his body like a river.

"Fuck, Tony! I told that nigga to stop—"

That's when I heard somebody call my name.

"GUNPLAYYYY!"

It was Shaquita. The sound was coming from the next level up, the sprawling circular staircase. I looked up; a palatial chandelier was swaying back and forth, engulfed with gray hue of gun smoke.

She called my name again! This time more desperate. Call me foolish, but I took off up the stairs taking them three at time. To my surprise, Nuke followed behind me.

We padded across the plush mauve carpeting with our guns cocked and ready. There was a bra, across from it was a door, slightly ajar. Both Nuke and I exchanged wary glances; this had all the ingredients of a setup. Was that bitch Shaquita trying to set me up?

"Gunplay, please help me," she called out again from the other side of the door.

"Fuck it!" I muttered under my breath. Walking over, I kicked the door lightly with the tip of my toe. It opened and unveiled one of the most baffling sights I'd ever seen.

"Muthafuckin'-goddamn-son-of –bitch!"

I couldn't believe my eyes.

CHAPTER FIVE

Gunplay

𝒥 walked inside, the floor was covered with clothes, bottles of Alize and Moet. Shaquita lay on her back covered in blood and Mustafa was on top of her. There was a hole the size of my fist with blood gushing from his neck as Shaquita cried hysterically, trapped underneath his heavy dead body. He was still choking her in a dead man's grip. Even though he was deceased, his face was still etched with a frown of pure hatred; eyes still open, large lips in a sneer. It was clear that even in his dying moments, Mustafa had been using every bit of his strength to try and take Shaquita to hell with him.

It took a moment for it to dawn on me what must have happened. There must have been a scuffle over the gun and she had ended up shooting him in the throat. He had died with his hands around her neck, choking her, leaving her in a dead man's grip. I had heard about this shit before but it was my first time seeing it.

It took us several minutes to unwrap his hands from around her neck—by then she was nearly unconscious. On the floor was the murder weapon she had shot him with, his own gun. There was jewelry on the nightstand, an iced-out chain, a Presidential Rolex, a few diamond rings, and bracelets. The value of that alone had to be over a quarter million. I put the items in my pocket. On the dresser was a stack of money, $1,000. Money that the hitta had paid her for her sex.

His lust had cost him his life.

We headed back downstairs with Shaquita stumbling and bumbling. She was nude except for a pair of thong panties, painted red with blood.

We walked up on the horrific sight of Tony sprawled out on the white carpeting, stained with a rivulet of blood, his right hand holding a kilo of coke wrapped in black masking tape.

"Fuck," I whispered, walking over to his body.

Kneeling down, I grabbed his chain from around his neck to give to his moms. Tony and I weren't close, but he was a nigga I knew I could call to help me with a lick when I needed it. He never asked for much after, just wanted me to front him some dope for the trouble. He would be missed. Turning around, I stepped over the other body of the Haitian with his head blown off. Shaquita stifled a scream with her bloody hand covering her mouth, eyes ablaze with terror. There was a stench in the air that was familiar to me. I could never forget it.

Death.

For the first time, Nuke showed panic, his eyes darting around with paranoia as if he were going to lose his mind.

"Man, we gotta get outta here and take Tony with us!"

I shook my head curtly and grabbed up a trash bag.

"We getting out of here but we can't take Tony."

Swiping my hand over the table, I shoveled in bales of money and coke. It was so much, we would have trouble taking it all.

"Why we can't take him with us? We went to school together. His mama needs to bury him."

Gritting my teeth, I tried to swallow my agitation at the entire situation. When you chose the street life, death was a likely outcome. I accepted it when I chose this life and so had Tony.

"His mama gon' be alright. Which one you think she would rather have? A body bag with her dead son in it or a bag of money?"

Nuke gave me a look with a pained expression but he got it. We worked feverishly around the dead bodies, packing up the cocaine and money. Total, we had close to five million dollars in cocaine and two million in cash. It was one of the sweetest licks of my life. There would be no looking back.

I was that nigga and I had everything ready to start making my name ring heavy in the streets. I just needed to finish up and get my ass home to settle things with LeTavia. An empire wasn't shit without my queen by my side.

****

After taking Shaquita to a hotel and getting her cleaned up, I got ready to go, telling her I'd stop by to take her home in the morning.

"You can't stay the night?"

I lifted a brow at her, wondering if she was trying to bait me with pussy like I hadn't just saw the last nigga she tempted get bodied. But one good look at her told me that sex was the furthest thing from her mind. From the look in her eyes and the way her hand continued to shake when she lit up her cigarette, she was traumatized and didn't want to be alone. She was attractive, that I couldn't deny, and I felt bad for her. I didn't want to leave her hanging after helping me out, but there was nothing I could do.

"Naw, I can't stay. I got a woman at home to get back to."

Her eyes lit up and widened in shock. Then she nodded and they dimmed as she looked away.

"Good thing is that you're $11,000 richer," I told her and handed her two handfuls of hundreds strapped up with rubber bands. "This the ten I owed you for helping me out plus an extra thousand for bodying Mustafa. Far as I'm concerned, you earned that shit."

I shot her a smile, licking my lips out of habit. Her eyes went to my lips and I saw the longing that lay behind them. My dick got hard but I shook my head, trying to will it to fall back. I couldn't get caught up in no shit with this girl. I left without saying another word, closing the door hard behind me.

My next stop was to LeTavia but after knocking, she didn't answer the door. My phone had been vibrating the entire time since she last called, but I couldn't tell who it was and didn't want to argue with her, so I'd stopped answering. But now I had to do something since she was refusing to answer the door. I went to the store and bought a new phone just so I could start blowing her shit up. She didn't answer. I thought about copping her a new red Benz and just leaving it parked outside her crib to show her how much I was feeling her. I needed her to know things with me wouldn't be the same as it was in the past. I was done messing with other bitches… that wouldn't ever be a worry for her.

Three days after the lick, I still hadn't heard from LeTavia. I wanted to give her time to cool down so I fell back, but I wasn't about to stay chill for too much longer. I busied myself by getting my folks straight—I bought my mama a new home in a decent neighborhood in the Queens, that was mostly inhabited by Italians and Jews with a sprinkle of middle class Black folks. It was low-key but close enough to me that I could easily check up on her and Imani.

I decided to hit my boy, E-Class's club, to talk numbers. He had been calling me a lot lately to keep tabs on me, to make sure I was straight. He had also been one of the masterminds to help me with the Freddy Black situation and cleaning the money once I had it. Plus, E-Class also introduced me to my new plug, the infamous billionaire Colombian and cartel leader, Mario Falcon. Our first deal was for a hundred kilos of cocaine and twenty in heroine. We were about to flood the city and the good thing was, E-Class had a business savvy mind.

When you were raking in millions in cash, you had to have a way to legitimize your money, and that was where E-Class came in at—he was a fuckin' genius. The plan was to wash all the dirty money through his clubs and other business ventures, including a corporation where we could get tax breaks. He even worked with me to get a customized vault built underground at an old house on the east side of town, where nobody would think to check on it but only I had the combination. He couldn't open it without me.

As soon as I walked in, the club was packed. The DJ was playing Young Jeezy's new joint, and instantly, I was feeling the vibe. The music was pulsating, chicks with big asses were gyrating, dancing to the beat, kissing and touching all on each other... basically wildin' out. As usual, there were more females than dudes on the dance floor. But the atmosphere was hype.

The scent of loud was heavy in the air, and before I could even find my seat, two females tried to get my attention, directing me to sit in a booth with them. One chick at another table boldly grabbed my hand as I passed. She had huge, beautiful breasts. I could even see her nipples were pierced through the sheer, thin black silk material. She was a dime-piece, with long fire-engine red hair. She stuck her tongue out at me; it was pierced and long as a snake.

I'd be lying if I said she wasn't enticing, but I kept it moving past the throngs of people and found a seat in the corner, a few feet from the bar across from the stage where a female danced nude. Her amber complexion glowed like she was mixed with white or maybe Hispanic. Her body had some type of glitter on it that shined in the ambient light as she danced. Her pussy was shaved bald except for a small patch of blonde-dyed hair. For some reason, I found myself staring at her.

With Cutta out the way, E-Class had expanded and opened a club in Harlem. Although he said it was a new venture, the spot was already hot like it had been open for years. Just like his club in my city, E-Class's new Harlem spot was the shit. Already, it was easily one of the hottest hood joints and the perfect place where a lot of capers could be conspired, drug transactions conducted, and niggas' lives plotted on to bring down a timely demise. Strippers owned the stage and everybody who was somebody came to get lit and turn up, myself included. But this time I had other shit on my mind. I tore my eyes away from the stripper who had plopped down on her butt on stage, putting on a pussy exhibition; she spread her legs wide open, pussy galore.

The past few days, I'd still been unable to find out who it was looking for me and had asked where my mama lived. So, I'd started a hunt and destroy mission. Somebody was going to tell me something. I even declared war on all my rival drug dealers. Even if they weren't rivals in the past, they were now if they weren't on my team. I was taking over all territories. I didn't have a choice. I was steadily building my team and doing it consisted of a lot of mayhem and murder.

I finally had enough chips to finance an army of select goons, all my niggas that had come up with me in the trenches. In the span of forty-eight hours, Nuke and our crew of twenty-six goons, had been responsible for thirteen murders, sixteen gunshot victims, three kidnappings at gunpoint, and over a dozen brazen robberies. The message was simple, either you're with Gunplay's crew or you get killed.

Shit should have been lovely; I was a young gangsta on the come up. But I just couldn't shake the feeling—the eerie feeling that I was doing something wrong. And on top of all that, I had chick problems. I missed the shit out of LeTavia but she still wasn't fucking with me. I reached into my pocket and checked my phone again, thinking maybe she had responded to my many texts. I had been doing more begging than Keith Sweat.

Suddenly, somebody was standing over me; the sweet smell of perfume was deep in my nostrils, intoxicating me.

"May I take your order, please?"

I looked up and did a double take, nearly falling out my seat! There stood Shaquita, wearing some type of short, black, sequin skirt, and a matching tank top that barely concealed her gorgeous double D breasts. Her nipples looked like headlights, protruding through the thin, lacy, transparent material. She had a sexy navel ring, and a pink tattoo of a red rose adorned her stomach and then curved and ran down her thigh. She wore six-inch stiletto heels, and in her hand was a serving tray.

"Fuck you doin' here?" I shouted above the music.

She gave me a pixie smile and shifted her audacious hips from side to side making sure her breasts jiggled as she moved the tray from one hand to the other.

"Shit, a bitch gotta work! It costs money to look like this," she replied jovially and patted her long hair weave that was cascading down her shoulders onto her back. It was tinted reddish on the ends and complemented her style well. I couldn't help but break into a smile.

"I heard you been getting active since the last time I seen you."

She gave me a sly look like she knew what I had been up to the last few days. She had thrown the proverbial bone out there, designed to get my utmost attention and make me bite.

I couldn't help it, I did.

"What you talkin' 'bout, shawty?"

Finessing my facial hair, I gave her my full attention. In my mind, I was hoping she wasn't talking about how me and my niggas had been wreaking havoc through the city.

Just when she was getting ready to speak, some tall nigga walked up, drunk. He had on a beige sweater and brown slacks, complaining to her about an order that he hadn't received. I watched them go back and forth, with her trying to be polite and him being an asshole, until finally I'd had enough.

I stood up quickly, accidentally bumping into someone.

"Yo, my nigga, she didn't take the order, go find the chick you ordered from."

"Who the fuck is you?" he barked, slightly staggering in his drunken state. I got up in his grill, real close.

"I'ma be the nigga to get off in your ass and it ain't gon' be nice. Now get some get right, or I'ma make you get right."

We were standing close. Almost nose-to-nose. I reached down and let my hand graze my burner. Shaquita popped her head in between us.

"Gunplay, nooo. Don't start nothing."

Hearing my name, dude sobered up quick.

"Gunplay? You Gunplay??" His jaw dropped like he was in shock.

I didn't even answer; I just continued to grill his ass, maintaining my focus. It was the kind of expression you gave a nigga when you was getting ready to send them packing back to their maker in the sky. He took the hint.

"Man, I apologize. I am so sorry, I ain't know it was you, cuz. My bad."

He extended his hand for some dap. I left him hanging and thought about chin-checking his ass with an overhand right straight to the face, just off the strength that he had tried a nigga. He must have sensed my anger. He quickly turned and walked off.

Shaquita smiled at me and placed her hand on my shoulder. Instantly, I was inhaling more of her potent sweet perfume. I couldn't help looking down her blouse at her breasts. Nudging away my lustful thoughts, I went back to the original question.

"Shawty, what you mean you see I have been getting active?"

My brow was raised tight as I waited for her to reply.

"Nigga, you know the streets been talkin'. Bodies dropping like flies and you know I live in the projects. That shit like the CNN of ghetto news. You and yo' niggas been putting in work. I've never seen so many people faces on the front of t-shirts in my life. Damn, do you sleep?"

All I could do was sit down and wipe my weary face with the palm of my hand. The truth was, I hadn't slept in the last forty-eight hours.

"Word? And you think that was me and my crew?"

I played coy. She shot me an incredulous scowl, like I had just tried her, as she placed a hand on her round hip. I plopped back down in the chair, deflated and full of despair. If she knew it was my squad wreaking terror throughout the city, then it wouldn't be long before the police found out.

I'm moving too fast, I thought to myself.

"Lemme get a double shot of Hennessey and Coke. Naw, take that back. Just bring the whole fucking bottle."

"Baby, I wasn't trying to upset you—"

"Just go get the damn bottle!" Sucking her teeth, she walked off.

As she went to the bar to order my drink, I couldn't help but reflect on the last forty-eight hours. It had been a bloody massacre and I still was no closer to finding out who was looking for me and my mama. Then suddenly, as I watched the chick on stage hang upside down from the pole displaying pink pussy for days in my face, I started to move my chair back and that was when I felt my phone chime and vibrate in my pocket. I checked the number, but it was private.

The text read, *Nigga, you ain't shit and your days are numbered. I'm watching your punk ass right now.*

Frowning, I looked up from the phone, my heart slamming in my chest. The anticipation I got whenever it was time to bust on a punk ass nigga had my shit racing.

Who the fuck was watching me? was the diction in my head as I looked around the club, absentmindedly placing my hand on my banger.

And what fake ass thug was sending texts from a private number? Cowards were running loose, fucking up the code of the streets.

"Shit!"

I scanned the club once more, flexing my jaws. My head was fucked up but I had a reason for that. I had just murdered many men and, at the same time, created many new enemies. Shaking my head, I tried to rid myself of the paranoia that had filtered in like a ghost occupying my brain.

Shaquita returned, somehow her mood had brightened. She smiled at me and then came and stood between my legs, pushing up on my dick real intimately like she was my chick. Once again, I inhaled her feminine scent. Her navel ring, a tiny gold embellishment of some type, sparkled next to my eyes. She had a bottle of Hennessey in her hand, a gold bracelet with lots of trinkets, hearts and stars, sparkled on her wrist.

"Somethin' got you shook up?" she asked with a slight giggle.

All of a sudden, as I looked at her, I had a thought. She placed the bottle on the table to open it, making sure her breasts rubbed against my face, titty-boxing me.

"That was you textin' my phone? What you playin' them games for?"

She stopped and frowned. As she jerked her neck at me, a ringlet of hair fell over her face and she swiped it out of the way angrily.

"Nigga, why you always tryin' to make it seem like I'm sweatin' you?"

I cut my eyes at her, looking her up and down as if sizing her up, asking myself if she was worth the verbal battle.

"Wasn't it your ass sending all them fuckin' pics to my phone? The fuck you mean?"

She tossed her head back and laughed while I ogled her. "You fine and all, Gunplay, but let's face it, you crazy as hell and I don't wanna be in the middle of no drug shit no more unless it's with a nigga who is serious about me. To be truthful, unless you gon' be real with a bitch, the only thing you can be for me is a sponsor."

Looking down at her, I chuckled condescendingly. It was dry and rough, just like the heels of her feet. She wasn't an ugly chick and back in the day, I might've fucked with her, but she wasn't nothin' worth tricking off my cash for.

"Sponsor? Bitch, you got me fucked up! My dick ain't never had to pay for shit!"

Arrogance must have been her aphrodisiac. Her face suddenly beamed with mischievousness, like she was getting a big kick out of pissing me off. She leaned further between my legs, pushing up hard against my dick. I knew she had to feel it resting between my legs when she began to speak in a lascivious tone.

"Nigga, you know you want some of this good, juicy young pussy. I see how you be looking at my ass and shit. I get off at 2:30."

She chuckled and pulled away to study my expression and then sashayed off with her big ass bouncing from side-to-side. Still frowning, I shook my head. That hoe was crazy but she could forget about gettin' dick from me. I had enough damn problems and her gold-diggin' ass wasn't about to be one of them.

The ironic thing was, Shaquita was as hood as they came—straight up hood rat. Most real thugs and gangstas had an affinity for hood chicks like her. She was the key ingredient to ruling the dope game, sitting by a nigga's side with a banging body, fat ass, giving up some smoking head all while knowing damn will she was the poison in the game. Like Eve was to Adam in the Bible, she was a nigga's downfall. Just like she had helped set up Freddy Black and got him whacked, she would do the same to me if the opportunity presented itself. I couldn't be mad at her; this was all part of the ghetto's ecology.

Only the strong survived, something I'd learned a long time ago.

My body was tense when I picked up the bottle. It was already open so I took a long swig, trying to swallow my apprehension and suspicions in one big ass gulp. And it burned like hell all the way down. I took another long swig from the bottle, feeling the alcohol trickle down my chin as I scanned the club dance floor. Paranoia started to be my constant companion as I racked my mind. Who in the fuck had sent that text?

Who the fuck was watching me?

Le Tavia

Biting down hard on my bottom lip, I rubbed at my eyes, urging my tears away as I hugged my brother and sister goodbye. Today was the day they were leaving for Miami and, although they seemed excited about going to a new place, I couldn't say the same. I didn't want to see them go. I'd been staying over at my grandmother's house ever since Gunplay left me to be with whatever bitch he'd been talking to on his phone. Spending time with my family kept my mind off him.

"Will you come and visit for Christmas?" Nori asked me as we stood in the airport, waiting for their flight. "If you could make Thanksgiving and Christmas, it would be dope, but if that's too much, I'd rather Christmas at least."

"Yeah, me too," Peanut chimed in and I smiled, nodding my head.

"I'll do what I can to make it down for both," I promised. The announcer began to say over the loudspeaker that it was time to board and I flinched, not ready to let them go just yet.

"It's time… Please don't forget to call me as soon as you land!" I instructed as they both started to gather their things.

"Stop worryin' so much," Nori teased, rolling her eyes. "We are damn near grown."

Pressing my lips together, I fought the urge to get in her ass about cursing and gave them both one last hug before pushing them away.

"Hurry so you can get on and get settled," I told them and they both nodded, giving me a smile before turning to walk away.

Watching my brother and sister leave was probably one of the hardest things I would have to do. I held myself in a half-hug as I kept my eyes on them, wishing that my grandmother could have been here. Her health wasn't as good as it could be to where she could stand sitting in the airport for hours, but I missed her dearly right then. It was hard enduring this moment alone. If only I could depend on Gunplay…

"I love you!" I yelled as I watched Nori and Peanut board their plane. They both turned, waving to me as I blew them kisses and then, just like that, they were gone.

With tears in my eyes, I ran out of the airport, keeping them at bay until I finally got into the car. What the hell was I gonna do with my brother and sister gone? I'd helped raise them since the day they were born… how could I stay in New York without them?

But I'd spent most of my life caring for them and sacrificing my wants and needs to make sure they were taken care of. It was time for me to live my life. I needed to get things right with Gunplay because I loved him and I didn't want to be with anyone but him for the rest of my life. But first, I had to see what he was up to and figure out whether or not he was cheating on me again.

I called Sonya and asked her to meet me at my place to keep my mind busy while I spied on Gunplay. I was determined to catch his ass. As of late, he had been blowing up my phone, calling and texting. Not to mention the times he just showed up at my apartment before I decided to stay with my grandmother. One time he had the nerve to kick on my damn door like he had lost his damn mind. I let him stay his ass right out there as I packed up a bag to leave.

Now did I really feel like he was cheating on me? Not totally. But I wanted to deliver a strong message to his ass so he wouldn't think about trying the shit ever again. After all this time, I was finally fighting back. But just in case he actually was cheating, I had a trick for his punk ass. Niggas thoughts chicks were so dumb. NOT! My phone had been under Gunplay's name since the time he tried to call me, and my phone was off when we first met. Being an authorized user on his plan meant that I could get all the information I wanted. In fact, when he got a new phone recently, I was even notified by text and that was what started me to thinking.

I grabbed my phone and called customer service to see how I could get the phone records for everything: texts, the dates and times that he made certain calls, the numbers he was calling… I wanted it all. I was determined not to play the fool again! Lucky for me, the woman on the phone took it a step further and told me all about how to use Find My iPhone to actually get the exact location of where the phone was located. She told me how to download some software to get access to texts, voicemails, and even what names he saved his contacts under. It was obvious from listening to the woman that her boyfriend was a hoe too. She gave me an entire course on how to catch a nigga cheating.

I'll admit at first the phone was dry and I started to think I'd wasted my time. Gunplay's phone was filled with drug dealer talk— you know, when they talk in code that makes no sense to the average person. There wasn't even much of that because unless it was someone he knew on a personal level, all his work went to his burner phone.

But then I saw it.

Some bitch had sent him a gang of nude pics with her legs spread wide open, showing him her kitty. There were some other messages going back and forth, but it wasn't anything I really could pick up on. But then I saw that this was the same number he'd been speaking to when he was discussing 'eating pussy' and giving some girl ten grand. I checked the date the photos were sent and saw that they'd come the day after. So, whatever they did that night had her thirsty for more and sending nudes to encourage him to stop by.

Gunplay was fuckin' around on me *again!* I seriously couldn't believe that I'd allowed myself to be caught up with his unfaithful ass again. He had me so convinced that he'd changed but he hadn't changed a thing. I was going to handle him for sure but I wasn't stopping there. I know they always say don't fault the female, but I knew how Gunplay rolled so I knew he'd informed her of who I was and all his rules. So, whoever this chick Shaquita was, she was going to get chin-checked too.

CHAPTER SIX

Gunplay

A chick with a body like a goddess, small taut waist and a plump, fat round ass, walked to my table. She was completely nude except for a pink sarong. Her buxom breasts with nipples ripe—like tiny delicious brown raisins, pointed at me.

"You want a dance?"

Her torso was in my face, giving me a good whiff of her sex and her perfume.

"Naw, I'm good."

I reached into my pocket and passed her a hundred-dollar bill. She looked at the money and her face broke into a large grin. She had beautiful dark skin and pretty ivory white, perfect teeth, dimples, and a beautiful smile. Had I not had LeTavia, I knew I would have made her mine.

"Thank you so much!"

She was giddy. She placed her body on me and wrapped her arms around my neck, whispering in my ear.

"You wanna walk outta here together? I can leave… just you and I, Gunplay."

She called my name and I perked up. The bottle I'd been drinking on behind me nearly fell off the table but she grabbed it quickly. Too quickly… with sharp awareness that came from years of practice watching your own back. Instantly, I was back to my senses and alert. I looked up around the club and saw several other strippers, they were standing back stage, watching me.

Am I trippin'?

"Naw, I'm good, shawty. I appreciate it."

I resisted the urge to ask her how she knew my name. Unmoving, she cocked her head at me so I palmed her soft ass like it was dough and then slapped it dismissively. She caught my drift and walked off, shaking her ass alluringly.

A large shadow casted over me and the table jumped. I was about to reach for my strap when I recognized E-Class and his deep, throaty booming voice. Of course, he was dressed in business attire, a clean ass suit and tie. He could pass for a business man easily when he put on all this corporate gear.

"Aye, I ain't know you was coming out here to chill with a nigga this early," he said as he took a seat. "Good to see ya, fam."

"Nigga, I told you I was coming," I frowned up at him, still agitated from being so paranoid.

"As busy as you and your team have been the last few days, I thought you'd be laid up with your people."

"What you mean by that?"

"Niggas know you've been doing a takeover with a 'no hostage' approach." He chuckled heartily and I cringed.

"Man, I don't want that shit in the streets. Next thing you know them white folks will be lookin' for a nigga."

"Let these muthafuckas talk. That brings respect! You show me a gangsta kingpin that took over an entire city and I'll show you a ruthless gangsta that everybody respects. Respect ain't negotiated where we from. It's taken, earned through the barrel of a gun, son. Man, as soon as you walked into the club, all the bitches in here went crazy. Even the new ones I hired knew who you was! You're like a ghetto celebrity!"

E-Class was all excited and animated but I wasn't feeling it.

"Why the hell you got that bitch, Shaquita, working here?"

"Shit, she gotta eat too. Besides, she earned it. If it hadn't been for her, we couldn't have pulled off the lick so soon. I had to help her out."

"Yeah, but something ain't right."

"What you talkin' about, fam? Shit is lovely! She straight—if anything, she probably trying to fuck her way to the top. Now, who you should be worried about is Rayshaun and that nigga Cutta."

"Rayshaun and Cutta... Why?"

"Cutta filed for some type of appeal since his case went to the Supreme Court. Something about a constitutional violation. And, from what I hear, Rayshaun is trying to work with him. They saying that Cutta is scheming up on something Ray can do to show his loyalty isn't with you."

All I could do was laugh out loud. "Do you know how many desperate niggas be filing frivolous chain-gang motions talking about the arrest is illegal? That nigga done helped fill up the graveyard with bodies. His chances are slim as hell. Besides if he were to come home, I'ma slump him quick with a bullet to his dome. As far as Ray is concerned, I ain't believin' it."

For some reason, E-Class gave me a grim expression, then added, "I know you and Rayshaun tight, but he hit me up the other day talking about there was a hit out on you for a hundred grand. He also asked where your mama lived at… said he went over to her crib but y'all moved."

"What the fuck, man?! Are you serious? What did you tell him?"

"I told him I wasn't down for that fuck shit! It's crazy though… we all grew up together, but I think he might be the one tryin' to get at you for Cutta."

"Damn," I uttered, devastated. Rayshaun was my nigga and this was the last thing I wanted to hear. This couldn't be happening. There had to be another reason for this shit he was going through.

"I ain't know you moved your mama though. Where she at now?"

Dropping my head down, I barely listened to E-Class because my mind was still on Rayshaun. This news was fucking with me for real.

"I set her up in a crib in the Queens to keep her safe."

"Imani too?" he asked and I nodded.

"Yeah, but on some real shit, I'm moving Imani in with me. I got Tavi so I just wanna get on some family shit and take care of my seed so my moms can live her life how she should."

E-Class smiled brightly, patting me on the shoulder. "Nigga, I'm proud of you takin' care of your daughter and shit. Being a family man. That's what's up. I know moms ain't gon' like being home alone, but she'll learn to enjoy that shit."

I didn't say anything right away because my mind was still brewing. Still plotting.

"Damn... I'm fucked up over this thing with Ray though." I clenched my teeth as I spoke, knowing that I was going to have to see Rayshaun over all this I was hearing. And it wasn't going to be a good visit either. However, it was long overdue.

"Greed is a terrible thang," E-Class added, shaking his head somberly. Thinking back on Tony, and now Rayshaun, who had both chosen money over their own life, I had to agree.

"You fuckin' right, that nigga is my daughter's godfather. We slept on the same pissy mattress as shorties. I shot a nigga once for disrespecting him and not just that, that nigga is close with my damn mama. She calls that nigga her son!"

"Dig, I'm just pulling your coat about this nigga. Maybe he has an excuse."

I pulled out my phone and dialed Rayshaun's number. There was no answer. I spent the next few minutes stewing. My mind was elsewhere, thoughts riveting like ping-pong balls bouncing around in a glass. My brain was scattered. Rayshaun was my dude, I loved him like a brother. What the fuck was going on?

I dialed his number again.

No answer.

"Shit!"

E-Class reached inside his coat pocket and took out a sheet of stationery writing paper and studied it in the dim light.

"So, here is the deal," he said, taking a deep breath. His eyes did a quick scan of the club.

"We got a hundred and forty bricks of coke with a street value twenty-eight thousand for each. But if we break each brick down, chop it and bag it, pay workers and overhead costs, we can get eighty-grand off each one—which, of course, we'll split it. So, the math basically goes like this: 140 times eighty thousand. That comes to almost eleven mill, son! We take some of that money to the new plug, Mario. He's going to give us 1,000 bricks. Now, you do the math on that shit! I'ma buy an island or some shit with my half!"

E-Class broke out into a hearty laugh, clapping his hands. I sat, silent and stoic.

I didn't see his humor or his math because, in my book, they were both wrong. I began to feel the pressure in my trigger finger that always accompanied gunplay and violence. I didn't want to have another confrontation over money, especially *my* fucking money. E-Class was my boy but his math was wrong—*terribly* wrong. The kind of wrong that could have got him shot in the back of his own damn club.

"My nigga, I don't know where you got that word 'split' from. It's not 50/50. It's 90/10. That's what we discussed. I get ninety for doing this shit and you get ten for looking out and givin' me the info. Now, I'on wanna beef with you over some chips—"

The smile faded from his face like he had just walked into a grim situation.

"Yeah, but you do understand, homie, I been doin' a lot of the work behind this shit! Just to have that stash spot built cost me a fortune, plus, I came up with the info on the new plug! The Colombians don't even fuck with niggas but I made it happen," E-Class spoke with a tight face.

I stayed silent for a beat. There was so much tension in the air, I could cut it with a dull knife.

"I'm feeling you on that and I respect what you did, but I only got one issue with this shit, my nigga."

"What's that?"

He placed both of his elbows on the table, moving closer while looking at me.

"We had an agreement and that was if I manage to pull off the lick I was to pay you ten percent. You givin' me helpful info, but I'm the brute force behind all this shit. I'm the one putting in the groundwork. You was cool with the ten percent in the beginning and I made moves based on the strength of your word. Now you saying you want half? Come on, my nigga, keep that shit one-hundred."

E-Class just gave me a blank stare and I looked at him right back. He was buggin'! I wouldn't have had any issues giving him the fifty if that's what he'd asked for, but he didn't. I'd already gave a large amount of the money to my new connect so there was no way I could cough up an extra forty percent to him. Silence hung between us as we both stared at each other, knowing that a confrontation was about to ensue.

But who was he?

I moved faster and I saw him began to trot as he looked back at me. I bumped into several people, knocked a drink out of some girl's hand. I was just about up on him as he headed through the crowd. That's when I felt a hand grab me. Instantly, I spun around and came up with my burner.

It was Shaquita. She had almost caught one straight to the chest and didn't even know it. Shaking her off, my eyes returned to the guy. He walked through the crowd and headed to the door, pulling a hat down over his head.

"You're leaving so soon. You sure there ain't nothin' I can do for you?" she queried, giving me a girlish smile. "I was just kidding 'bout that sponsorship thing." She gave me a seductive look, puckering her lips in a way that I knew worked on other lame niggas. I could tell from her haughty expression she figured it would work on me.

NOT!

"Bitch, don't play with me!" I said, staggering as I bobbed my head trying to keep an eye on the guy, but there was a lot of activity going on around me.

Her jaw dropped like she was lost for words. Then she quickly recovered with her witty, hoodrat slick ass mouth.

"Punk ass nigga, I know too much of your business to be talkin' shit to me. Them Haitians would love to find out who killed they hitta, Mustafa, and the infamous kingpin, Freddy—"

Before she could finish her statement, I had my hands over her mouth and pulled her so close to me that if she moved a muscle, we would have been tongue kissing.

"Bitch, I know where yo' mama live at with that ugly ass baby you got. Try me."

Disgusted and a little light-headed, I didn't give her a second glance before I pushed her away. By then, I felt pressure building up behind my eyes and it looked like the lights were getting dim. I returned my gaze towards the door, in immediate search of the guy, only to see he was gone.

Shit!

Running through the packed crowd, I accidentally bumped into several patrons and was even accosted with disgruntled complaints. Still, I rushed straight out the door. My breath fogged in the night air and there was a slight chill. Perspiration gleamed on my brow as I searched through the night. Besides a few guys standing outside smoking and talking shit—parking lot pimping—there was no sign of him.

I continued to walk. Scanning the streets and gritting my teeth, I narrowed my eyes and began to circle the parking lot, looking for anything moving. Then I looked across the street next to a yellow truck and that's when I spotted him. What I didn't see was the person tailing behind me, following me since I left the club.

The guy looked back and saw me, and took off into a sprint past the yellow truck and down an alley. I took off after him.

Big mistake!

About thirty yards into my sprint, the alley seemed to get darker, the fetid stench of garbage and piss was overwhelming. This was more than a simple hangover. I felt like my ass had been drugged. A large rat, the size of a cat, scurried across my foot to take for cover. I was winded; the world had started to strobe around me like the Earth was moving. Suddenly, there was a flash of ardent bright light and I was partially blinded. I reached for my banger.

Too late.

I felt a sharp pain straight to my skull. I was struck upside my head then another crushing blow to my jaw, caused me to fall to one knee. My gun careened across the concrete. I felt somebody kick me in my stomach, knocking all the air out of me. Somehow, somebody had crept up on me from the back.

How?

I could vaguely see several feet as I was being pummeled, kicked, and punched viciously. Somehow, I had walked into a trap. Then I heard a thick baritone voice.

"I told you his dumb ass was going to go for the bait. That mickey that bitch put in his drink helped like a muthafucka! Look at his eyes. Stupid muthafucka. Put a bullet in his dome and make sure he's dead. We gotta get the fuck outta here."

I lay in a stupor, losing consciousness and it suddenly dawned on me that I had been drugged as I struggled to get up. Who had drugged me? Shaquita? That was when I was punched and kicked again. More violent kicks.

More pain. More abuse.

The next thing I felt was the steel of a pistol pressed tight against my forehead. This was the moment I'd been looking out for my entire life: the moment a nigga caught my ass slipping. I pinched my eyes closed and thought about my mama, my daughter and finally, my mind rested on the image of LeTavia's face. Then...

Blocka! Blocka! Blocka! Blocka!

Shots were fired!

Despite all the shit I'd done, plenty of which was worthy enough to make me a legend in the streets, I'd died like a fuckin' junkie. In a back alley, next to a stinkin' ass dumpster full of rats, laying on pissy concrete.

I was dead.

"Bitch, I didn't tell him who I was! I sent the text from the app a chick suggested to me."

"Oh! Well damn, it must have worked. That nigga head done turned all the way around on his neck looking for somebody." She cracked up laughing. I didn't see shit funny. Gunplay should have been mourning about losing me but instead his ass was in the strip club talking to some big booty bitch with a head full of fake ass weave.

"Ohhhh, look at that nigga over there!" She nudged me with her sharp ass elbows again. "He's fine as hell…"

"Ya-Ya, would you PLEASE stop elbowing me!"

"Well damn! You ain't gotta get all in your feelings over some nigga and take it out on me. It ain't like you didn't know what you was gettin' into. Look at him, girl—he a damn thug."

"Just shut up!"

Frustrated, agitated, and utterly annoyed, I turned back around and watched as Gunplay sat by the stage watching some chick straddle the pole with her legs wide opened. She was positioned right at him as if he was the only one in the room. But what got me, was that he had the audacity to actually seem like he was having the time of his life watching her. The past few days without him had been miserable for me, but he wasn't bothered at all.

Then the first chick with the big ass returned and it became apparent that she was a waitress since she had drinks. I relaxed. That made it better… at first. Then the bitch pushed up on him, all between his legs with her big ass double Ds in his face as she stood between his legs. She leaned in further between his legs and I just knew she was grinding up on his dick.

"Uh uh! Oh, *hell* naw!"

I hopped out my chair. I was about to rush over there and confront both their asses until Sonya grabbed my arm and talked some sense into me.

"Girl, don't bust his ass yet! He might take that hoe home with him then we got some real incriminating shit on him," she explained, and I had to admit that she had a valid point.

I sat my ass back down, breathing hard through my nostrils, completely mad as fuck. I was going to get his ass! I wanted it so bad that I couldn't even sit still, so I began to rock back and forth in my chair. But even as I sat, I thought about going outside and throwing a brick through his car window.

"Niggas ain't shit! When we leave, I'ma throw a brick through his windshield," I vented as I watched the chick stand between his legs, boxing him in the face with her tits.

"Ugh!!"

Then she walked off. Something dramatic must have happened because she left in a hurry, only for another bitch to come up. This one was nude and pretty just like the last one. What was it about Gunplay that had them acting like his ass was the only decent lookin' nigga in the fuckin' club?! He wasn't that damn charming!

Gunplay and the girl spoke briefly, then he reached in his pocket and gave her some money. She took it and then reached over when he wasn't looking and placed something in the bottle right as he palmed her ass.

"Bitch, you saw that?!"

Sonya and I turned to each other and both said the words in unison, like friends that know each other often do.

"What the fuck?! Did that bitch just put something in his drink?"

Sonya looked from me back over to Gunplay but my eyes were still on the chick.

"That skank ass bitch," I hissed. "I don't know what she did but I saw him touch her ass. Can't stand that nigga."

"Girrrl, you think we should warn him and let him know?"

I debated Sonya's question in my head for less than a nanosecond.

"Fuck him, with his cheating ass! Them bitches setting him up and that's what his ass get. I damn near had to be wifey before he even dropped a damn Michael Kors purse on my arm but he out here just giving bitches money. Fuck him!"

"Tavi, look at his ass!" Sony exclaimed, gesturing towards Gunplay, but I shook my head, refusing, until she grabbed my arm and pushed me back towards where he sat. By then, I was so angry I had misty eyes. I was a gale of emotions, fighting back tears. To think I was fool enough to believe Gunplay loved me and me only.

Finally, the stripper chick strolled off with a fist full of money and some big dude came and sat down at the table with Gunplay.

"I know him!" Sonya piped up, a little too loud, but I could tell she was feeling the effects of the liquor. "He owns this place... I used to flirt with him a while back. Maybe I should get his number again. Business seems to be doin' good."

"He's one of Gunplay's dumb ass friends… Seems cool."

I hadn't seen the guys Gunplay hung with often, but I recognized this one as one of the few he said he was really tight with. They talked the entire time and I just zoned out. I couldn't remember feeling so humiliated in my life. My grandma had an old saying: *Be careful what you look for because you just might find it and it may not be what you wanted.*

As I looked around at all the women, I saw that most of them were dressed fly with designer gear. I began to feel self-conscious about myself, my body. But then I nipped that shit in the bud. I may not have been the finest woman in the world, but I was far from ugly. My body wasn't stacked like a video model, but I still had ass, tits, and nice hips.

So, why was he cheating on me?

I had seen enough. I was frustrated and devastated. I couldn't wait to throw a brick at this nigga's car window. He loved that damn car and would probably cry real tears. I felt a sharp cramp in my stomach and I winced. I knew they were associated with the abortion I'd had. Lucky for me, the cramps soon subsided and went away.

Then suddenly, some guys came and sat at an adjoining table across from us. And one of the guys looked so familiar that I felt a chill run up my spine. Sonya saw me staring and the first thing that came to her mind was I was attracted to him.

"Yeah, bitch, I see you over there looking at them niggas too. Ain't they fine? Want me to go holla at them for us? Shit, they might buy us some drinks…" She paused and took a sip out her glass of Patrón.

I continued to stare at the one guy. I knew him from somewhere…

someplace.

But where?

That was when the chick with the nice body came over, the nude stripper that had been at Gunplay's table, who he'd blessed with a few dollars. She sashayed her ass over to the guys at the next table and bent over. They whispered and conspired as I watched, staring at her and then back to the first guy. Then it became crystal clear. I gasped, inhaling a sharp breath. It was the guy that had the phone who was watching me at the store. He was all animated, pointing, giving orders, and gesturing towards Gunplay. One of the guys got on a phone and was talking to someone from across the club on his phone. I picked up on it because they kept glancing at each other. Once they were done, the stripper then strutted over to the other guy's table.

Then it happened. Gunplay was on to the guy with the phone, I could tell by how he was watching him. When the guy got up to leave, so did Gunplay. He began walking in a hurry but he was staggering badly, moving like his legs had bricks on them. Just as he got up, so did the guys at the table by us. They were following Gunplay as he followed the guy.

They were going to do something to him!

"Let's go, girl!" I shouted to Sonya instantly.

"Go where, bitch? I just ordered another drink and, besides, I like this spot!" she complained.

Ignoring her, I stood up to leave. Watching the guy following behind Gunplay, my heart leaped in my chest. I knew that they were going to do something bad to him and even with all feelings of hatred I had felt only moments before, I couldn't imagine seeing him hurt when I could possibly stop it.

"Tavi, where are you going?" Sonya shouted in disbelief.

"To Gunplay! I gotta save him, I can't let nothing happen to him." My voice was a plaintive plea. Sonya hadn't been paying attention and didn't have any idea what I was talking about. She narrowed her eyes at me and furrowed her brow with contempt.

"Bitch, you was just talking about throwing a brick through this nigga's windshield and fuckin' him up. Now, you wanna save him from these bitches? You bipolar or some shit? I'm not about to let you fall for this nigga again after he done made you look stupid."

"No, Ya-Ya! Them niggas sitting by us finna jump on him."

I pointed at the guys who had been at the next table and were now trailing him out the club. Sonya didn't have a clue as to what I was talking about; her sordid facial expression said it all. I didn't have time to explain. I reached down to pull her arm but she snatched away. My arm accidentally hit a chick who was walking back to her table with bottle, wearing a short white dress that damn near showed her booty cheeks. The bottle fell to the floor and exploded, champagne sprayed everywhere.

"Oops! Sorry." I plastered my hand over my mouth.

"'Oops' my ass! Bitch, you gonna pay for that."

"Who you calling a bitch?"

"Yeah, who you calling a bitch with your skinny ass?" Sonya cut in. She was standing right behind me. As usual, she had my back.

The woman's eyes drew wide as she began to get loud. Several of her friends out of her entourage walked over and soon there was a shouting match with people pushing and shoving. I cut my eyes at the door while Sonya went in on them all.

Gunplay was gone!

And so was I.

I pulled Sonya along, towing and plowing through the crowd as the girl I'd bumped into shouted her anger. She even accused me of running from her, something I'd never do because I damn sure wasn't scared, but I just didn't care. I had to get to Gunplay.

Le Tavia

Outside, the temperature had dropped. I felt a sudden chill in the air as I looked around wide-eyed for Gunplay. Several dudes tried to holla at us, one guy actually tried to grab my arm.

"Come here, baby. Let a nigga holla at you a second."

"Nigga, get your fuckin' hands off me," I said and pulled away, turning around. For a fleeting second, I could have sworn I saw somebody duck off in the alley across the street.

Gunplay?

"Come on," I hissed to Sonya and took off across the street.

"Where we going?" Sonya's heels were scraping across the concrete; she was nearly out of breath.

"I think Gunplay 'bout to walk into an ambush. Them niggas getting ready to do something to him."

"Well, shit, don't we need to call the police or somethin'! My ass ain't walking into an alley chasing after some no-good ass nigga who you just said ain't shit!" She stopped in her tracks.

"Come on, girl!" I reached into my purse for the .9 mm Gunplay had taught me how to shoot. My hand was shaking so badly that I almost dropped the gun. Sonya saw it too.

"Uh-uh, Tavi. I may look like this but I ain't stupid. I'm not takin' my ass in there," she said, wagging her head from side-to-side emphatically.

I continued to walk with the gun in my hand. At first, all I saw was the silhouette of bodies enshrined in bright lights with what looked like Gunplay withered on the ground. Some guy had a gun pointed at his head.

Sonya could make out what was going on before I could.

"Let's go! They done whooped his ass and it looks like somebody got a gun to his head!"

"Oh my God!"

That's when I heard footsteps, high heels striking out across worn concrete. I looked over my shoulder and Sonya was booking it down the alley, but I couldn't go anywhere without Gunplay. Like a dose of high octane fuel was dumped into my veins, I closed my eyes, pressed my finger to the trigger and just started firing!

Blocka! Blocka! Blocka! Blocka!

Shots were returned!

A body dropped and somebody screamed out in pain. People started running, scattering like roaches with the lights on. A car sped off in the opposite direction. My eyes were planted on the last spot I'd seen Gunplay. With tears in my eyes, I ran over to him. There was a body lying on top of him and they were both covered with blood.

"Oh God!" My voice cracked with a quiver as I managed to roll the body off Gunplay with all my might. The dead man's eyes were open, wide. There was a hole in the side of his head, spewing blood.

Blood was on my hands from the dead man. I cringed with disgust as I reached for Gunplay as he lay on the ground all battered and bruised.

As soon I reached out, grabbing his hand, his eyes opened in a flash. I could tell he was not all there, but he had the sense to hold my hand as I hoisted him up. Then we heard the boisterous wail of a police car siren or maybe it was an ambulance. Whatever it was, it got Gunplay's attention. He helped me raise him up, even though his eyes were rolling around in his head. He was obviously drugged. We made it out the alley with me partially carrying him, only to find Sonya standing with throngs of people, gawking at us like they were watching some supernatural beings.

Sonya had the nerve to run her scary ass over to us to help. At the time, I didn't know if Gunplay had been shot or not because his face had an ugly gash in it and his clothes were covered in blood. But what I did know was that his ass owed me an explanation—if he survived.

****

"Ouch, man! Shit! What the fuck wrong with you?!" Gunplay yelled, complaining as he squirmed. He was stretched out across my bed, semi-unconscious, when I doused his ass with a bucket of ice water, enjoying every single minute of it. He wasn't shot, not harmed at all, so now it was time for him to talk.

"You have some explaining to do," I said in a sharp, clipped tone, still holding the bucket in my hand. I wanted to clobber his ass over the head with it for trying me the way he had.

"Explain what?! Somebody tried to kill me."

"And I saved your life!"

"You saved my life?" He squinted and partially sat up, drowsily holding his head to the side. The effects of the drugs hadn't yet worn off.

"Yes... I shot somebody and I'm scared. I think I killed him! I'm involved in another murder and it's all because of you!" On the brink of tears, I narrowed my eyes and pointed my finger towards him. "You... you used my body, my mind, took advantage of me—I can't believe you're still cheating on me with other bitches! And all I've done is stood by your side and love you!"

Gunplay screwed his face up at me.

"Man, what you talkin' bout? You buggin'!"

Tossing his legs over the side of the bed, he tried, with difficulty, to get up by grabbing onto the side of the dresser. He wobbled and shook his head forcefully before blinking hard as if to steady his vision. Then he fell back on the bed with an exasperating sigh, rubbing over the bandage that was covering the deep gash on the side of his head.

"Tavi, all I know is one minute I'm in the club and the next minute, I'm following this fuck nigga, tryna figure out how he texted my phone. Then BAM! I'm knocked out on my ass being kicked and punched—"

"Nigga, that was me who texted your ass! And whose picture is this?!" I raved, jumping on the bed, showing him the picture of the big booty chick in his phone. The chick who just so happened, was the same bitch in the club, rubbing all in between his legs.

"You texted me? And how did you get that picture?" he asked, dumbfounded, as he massaged one of the knots on his head. "So, you telling me you think I changed the phone just to spin you and knock you off track. Really?"

"Really! And I saw you with this same chick last night. Had her ugly ass all up between your legs."

"Man, you trippin'! That chick helped me pull off a lick. Yeah, she diggin' a nigga but I'm not feeling her like that—"

"And I saw you feeling on her and some other big booty bitch in the club."

His jaw dropped like old folks with no teeth.

"You was in the club?!"

"You damn right I was in the club! I was with Ya-Ya, and we saw that ugly, big booty, horse-face bitch place a drug in your drink. The one you gave all that money to after she hugged all over you."

"Word?" His mouth formed a big incredulous O before his eyes narrowed into a frown. "So, it was *that* bitch who did it."

"Yeah, and I was gonna leave your ass hangin' but I saw the guys following you out the club. I had my gun so I did what you taught me to do. But try me again and I'm leavin' your ass for dead." I cut my eyes over to his face but he was looking at me in awe with a goofy grin on his face.

"Man, that shit sounds gangsta as fuck! You saved my life, Tavi. I owe you one for that." He tried to hug me but I slapped his hands down. I really wanted to slap him, but I held it back only because he'd gotten his ass beat already.

"Bae... on err'thang a nigga love—I was just messing with them bitches! They can't fade you."

Silence. I wasn't feeling it.

Gunplay bit down on his swollen lip and then began to talk, slow and pathetic. His words were slurred.

"Bae, I was caught up in the moment. I was wrong for that but on err'thang, I swear I ain't never fucked none of them bitches. I love you and you only. Shaquita helped me pull something that got us a lot of money. We rich now, bae! I got about two mill stashed and close to about five mill in dope. I started to buy you a candy apple red Benz and park that bitch right in front of your crib!"

"Humph."

"I wasn't even supposed to see her ever again!" he continued to explain with his hands up. I tried to keep quiet, knowing that if he was bullshitting, sooner or later he'd tell it if I let him talk long enough. People told on their own damn selves that way.

"I wasn't even supposed to see her again. It was just a coincidence, my nigga, E-Class, who owns the club hired her because he just opened up that new club. I was just chillin' in the club and that's when that bitch popped up!"

"Just opened up? You must think I'm stupid, nigga, that club been there for a minute!"

Gunplay blew out a harsh breath. "Whatever, yo. All I know is I ain't do shit."

With my arms still firmly folded across my chest, I gave him a curt roll of my eyes. But really, I was being hard for no reason. I believed him. The story seemed so wild it could be true... and that's how it always was with Gunplay. The craziest shit always happened to him as if he were drawing it in like a magnet.

"So, you go into your homeboy's club, a bitch put a drug in your drink, niggas try to kill you—"

"And you come to a nigga's rescue on some Bonnie and Clyde type shit," he finished for me, and then reached out, pulling me into his arms. I resisted only for half a moment before melting in his arms. Settling in snugly on his chest, I listened to his words along with the palpitating beat of his heart.

"I don't know what's going on but I'ma get down to the bottom of this." He paused. "But first, I need to get you out this dump—"

"Dump? It wasn't a dump when you was over here every damn night, fallin' asleep in my bed before I do!"

Chuckling, Gunplay kissed the top of my head and held me even closer on his chest.

"Tavi, you too damn sensitive! I'm just saying... I wanna do something nice for you, put you in a nice place. Go look for a house for you and my daughter, make it some big ass shit! You want a whip too? Any make and model—Benz, BMW, Porsche... whatever, bae! I'ma do that shit for you. I never wanna hurt you—I love you."

We stayed there in silence for a little while, both of us enjoying the feel of the other. And then he sighed and began to shift, reaching out to grab his phone. I slid off his lap and he stood up, dialing a number as he walked away.

"Who you calling?" I asked, unable to hold the tremor of worry in my voice.

"I'm trying to reach Rayshaun," was all he said and I relaxed only somewhat.

He seemed to sense it and walked over, held me tighter in his arms, and whispered in my ear how much he loved me and how thankful he was to have me in his life.

That was it, I was like butter. I melted in his arms. Then I was reminded of something.

"Oh! He came over here while you were gone. He asked me where you was at and I told him I wasn't letting you in here so you was probably at your moms. Then he left."

Gunplay turned to me, dropping the phone from his ear. "He came over here?"

Frowning, I nodded my head, wondering why he was getting so upset about it.

"I told him he could either find you at your mama's house in the Queens or the club. Did I do something wrong?" I tensed up even more when he didn't answer right away.

"It's okay, bae," he said with love in his eyes. "You didn't do anything wrong. You're good."

That morning when I awoke, he was gone. There was a pile of money on the dresser, along with a note. His scent was still on my pillow... so was his blood. A pang of sympathy filled my heart. He was in no condition to walk, much less go do what I knew he was going to do. If I knew Gunplay like I was sure I did, I knew he was going on a 'seek and destroy' mission for information on whoever it was that tried to murder him at the club.

God, watch over him, was all I could pray.

CHAPTER SEVEN

Le Tavia

"*N*aw, bitch, them niggas was shooting with real bullets! And I saw that shit on the news. Several people got shot and one of them is in critical condition. There is a reward out for the shooter. I bet this is all because of Gunplay. Word is him and his niggas been lighting up the damn city and those niggas were retaliating on his ass."

"Who told you that?!" I scrunched up my nose and looked at Sonya.

"Remember the nigga who is friends with Gunplay? The one I told you I used to flirt with back in the day?" I nodded my head and she smirked. "Well, kicked it a little bit that night at the club after y'all left. But he told me Gunplay was emptying rounds off in niggas without askin' questions."

"You talkin' to Gunplay's friend? I thought you and Trent was still messing around."

Trent was the guy that she had hooked up with the night that Cutta raped me. With Cutta gone, Trent was still hustling on his own

175

with Sonya as his leading lady. She didn't talk about him much and I was happy about that because thinking of him reminded me of that night.

"I am still with Trent. I only flirted with E-Class to hear some good gossip and moved on."

Sonya lay across my bed with her eyes to the ceiling as she thought on what she'd just said. I sat by quietly, still thinking on what she said about Gunplay. Rolling my eyes, I sighed and shook my head, trying to stay calm. The truth was I was on pins and needles the more I thought about Gunplay.

"I know something has been going on and I am concerned because that nigga crazy."

"And your ass took him back after all the shit he's done? Girl!" Her voice had an irritating screech that annoyed me.

"Yes, he explained it to me. So we're good."

"And you gave him some too—didn't you, bitch?" She smirked. I tried to bite back the smile that began to rise up on my face.

"No but I thought about it!" We both broke out laughing.

"And I know you ain't the one talking! What's that? A new ring on your finger already? You been doing a lot of work to get that nigga to buy you diamonds and shit, huh?" I teased her with a smile.

Ducking her eyes, Sonya blushed under her butterscotch skin and shrugged her shoulders.

"This shit probably not even real," she said, even though I doubted that she actually believed it. "He's moving fast but I just wanna take shit slow... He's perfect, treats me right, too. I really don't have any complaints but I just want to take my time."

"Shit, I can't tell!" I grabbed her hand and pointed at the ring on her left hand. "You ain't gave up this ring so you might as well have told that nigga he owns your ass!"

Smiling, Sonya shrugged and twisted the small, diamond ring on her finger as she looked somewhere behind me. Then for some reason, her smile melted away and I could nearly see her thoughts cycling in her mind. But in the next second, the smile was right back on her face.

"Yeah... it's nice, ain't it? But—I don't know."

"You want me to ask Gunplay if he knows anything about him?" I queried with a raised brow. She shook her head.

"No, it's not that. I just—I haven't dated anyone seriously since before my father died. It's crazy continuing with my life as normal without him here."

I nodded slowly, realizing that this had nothing to do with the man and everything to do with the absence of her dad.

"He would want you to be happy. It's okay to go on with your life, Ya-Ya. You shouldn't feel guilty about allowing someone in your life who can make you happy," I told her but she only gave me a forced smile.

"I'm tryin' to work myself through it. It's just so hard."

"I know."

Reaching out, I pulled her into a hug that I felt was much needed and held her tight. Truthfully, I probably needed it more than her. I was dealing with stuff she didn't even know about. Her phone began to ring at the exact time there was a knock on the door. Sonya jumped and grabbed it quickly, answering it before I could even get out of the bed. There was a strange look on her face right before she answered and I knew then who it was.

"Hey…" I heard her say just as I walked out of the room.

Pulling the edges of my short shorts down to just barely cover my ass, I walked to the door as I tried to steady the beating of my heart. At this time of night, the only person it could be was Gunplay and that meant it was time for me to have one of the most difficult talks of my life. I wasn't sure I was even ready.

Hell, actually I *knew* I wasn't ready but it needed to be done. Although his mother had told me to keep my secrets away from him, I just couldn't see how being in a relationship with someone I couldn't talk to was beneficial to either of us. I wanted to come clean and I felt like we both would be a better couple for each other in the end. Thinking about living with that lie hovering over us disturbed me.

Right now, I was just happy he was back home and safe. Hopefully, there would be no more bloodshed. After thinking on everything, I even wanted to take him up on his offer and go look for a new place. I wasn't going to break his pockets but I did want to move into a nice condo or somewhere where I felt safe when he wasn't around. Bruce's ass still creeped me out.

Suddenly, a sharp pain went through my abdomen and I winced, stopping for a minute to catch my breath. Although the nurse at the clinic had warned me about the cramping after the miscarriage, she had told me it would be gone by now. But even though there was no bleeding, the pain remained. If anything, it had seemed to get worse by the day.

I composed myself before I opened the door; lucky for me the cramps had died down. With a small smile on my face, I turned back to the door. I had on Gunplay's favorite pair of shorts out of the ones I owned. He was always talking about how he loved them because of how it showed my camel toe. I rolled my eyes every time but I loved the way he reacted to my body. I couldn't help but chuckle thinking about it as I opened the door wide.

But the smile on my face died instantly when I saw who it was.

"Bruce, what the hell do you want, boy! Are you a fucking pain freak or something, nigga?" I screamed at him and peeked out the door making sure Gunplay's car had not pulled up. My heart was beating a mile a minute.

The entire time, Bruce just stared between my thighs. He licked his lips seductively but I felt absolutely nothing but disgust. And to make matters worse, he reeked of alcohol.

"I just wanted to come over and apologize. I was wrong—"

Before he could finish the sentence I cut him off with my jaw clenched tight. Was he crazy? What the hell was he doing showing up this time of night?

"Dumb ass nigga, you gon' get both of us killed. Are you crazy, stupid or both?!"

"Since the incident with your friend, I've been going to church. I found Jesus. So I'd like to apologize to your friend too but I definitely

179

don't fear him."

I was caught off guard about this nigga actually mentioning that he'd found Jesus. He had lost his damn mind.

"You may have found Jesus but if my *boyfriend* finds you here again, he gon' knock a patch of hair out of your head with that .44! You gon' need Jesus to help get him off your ass."

"The good Lord says that He will protect me from all—"

Rolling my eyes, I stepped back a few paces and narrowed my eyes at him.

"Okay, how 'bout I call Gunplay now?" I threatened. Bruce stopped and thought about it a movement, his common sense seemed to finally start working.

"No, no. On second thought, don't call Mr. Gunplay. I'ma go pray some mo—"

"Yeah, you do that. And don't bring your stupid ass knocking on my door anymore. Mess around and get us both fucked up messin' with Gunplay's crazy ass!"

I slammed the door in his face so hard the window frames in the apartment rattled. But I was serious. I had enough going on to threaten my relationship with Gunplay as it was. I definitely didn't need Bruce bringing me any additional problems.

I turned around and there stood Sonya, with a hint of a smile on her face. Her eyes were still a little cloudy as if she'd shed a few tears but the smile was genuine.

"I'm going to go meet up with Trent now. I'll try to take your advice," she said as she walked over and gave me a quick hug.

"Just relax… let go and be happy. Unapologetically happy." I searched her eyes for a while to make sure she was really okay before letting her go.

"I'm good," she told me with certainty. "I'll call you tomorrow."

Without saying another word, I watched as she walked briskly out of the door and then jogged over to her car, a brand new BMW, and jumped inside. I didn't close the door until she tore off down the street, farther than I could see. I couldn't help but notice Bruce standing in front of his apartment, still watching me. He was going to get his ass killed trying to play dumb.

After locking up, I walked back inside of the house and thought about Gunplay and what Sonya had said. He had been warring with everybody. I knew what he did for a living and I wanted no parts of the type of shit he busied himself with every day. I bit my lip as I went over what I planned to confess to him again, wondering if I should save this conversation for a better time. But there was no better time to tell him that Cutta had raped me and I'd gotten pregnant from him. I had to get this over with.

I needed to tell him now.

The problem was how would he react?

Gunplay

I hobbled back into LeTavia's cramped apartment, toting an AK-47 slung over my shoulder, and a duffle bag full of big-face hundred dollar bills. To be exact, it was a cool one million in bloody money. I still had a black eye and a deep ass scar on the side of my head like somebody had hit me with a hatchet, and my body was in painful condition. I walked with a noticeable limp.

I dumped all the money out the duffle bag and propped the AK-47 up in the corner next to the door.

"Oh-my-freakin'-god," LeTavia gasped with both her hands plastered over her face in shock.

"I told you I hit a lick… this the money from it. We eating good for life. I promise I got you, ma. You just gotta trust me. This shit is just pocket change compared to the mothership of money coming," I said, smiling hard even while sporting a black eye.

I got my ass beat, walking into an ambush, but it was definitely about to be the last time some shit like that happened. I was alive and rich as hell, so there wasn't much that could fuck up my mood. But then LeTavia said something that completely caught me off guard.

"Is this the money that came from all them killin' sprees I heard you been involved with or is this money the reason they tried to kill you?" she asked, nervously wringing her hands together. She was a bundle of nerves.

"Bae, come on, man! Real niggas don't talk street shit to they bitc—I mean, lady! Besides, I got that shit handled," I tried to assure her.

The truth be told, that morning in the wee hours, I woke E-Class up right out his damn bed before the sun was even out. I was in search of the chick in the club... the stripper that had placed the drug in my drink. Of course that bitch was missing. But later that day, I found out her body had been discovered. Somebody had shot her in the head and dumped her body in the back of a school playground.

Still, I was tense as fuck when I walked into LeTavia's spot, knowing damn well that I should've continued my manhunt for whoever it was trying to kill me. And there still was no word on Rayshaun. His phone continued to ring without even going to voicemail. I couldn't wait to get my hands on him. I'd stopped by his mom's house but she told me she hadn't seen him in a while. I didn't want to get rough with his mama for her to give me the info but if it came to it, I would.

Ain't nothing get me heated more than feeling like I wasn't on top of my shit and that's exactly what was up right then. But instead of going to my apartment to cool off, here I was at LeTavia's battered and bruised, hoping that she could just do her thing and help me get my mind right. If there was ever a time I needed a woman's touch, her touch, it was now.

I glanced over at her and saw that her eyes were still darting between me, the money and the AK-47. There was a weird look about her, like she was afraid, and it confused me. She looked away when my gaze met hers and I watched as she shifted nervously under my stare. Damn. I really couldn't take much more bullshit.

"What's up, mama?" I asked her, using a tone much softer than what I'd felt. I felt like maybe my mood was messing with her and I didn't want that.

"I need to talk to you about somethin'," she started, her eyes ping-ponging everywhere in the room but on my face. She was nervous about something and it put me right back on edge. Whatever it was she was about to say, I could tell that she knew I wouldn't like it.

"What is it? I hope it ain't about that nigga you shot 'cause he had it coming, bae," I said to her, now my tone much coarser than I'd intended. She shrunk back away from me. She was losing her courage so I sighed and sat back on the arm of the sofa to appear less threatening.

Tactfully, I tried to change the subject. Normally for some reason whenever I talked about my relationship with my little girl or my mama it brightened LeTavia's day. She'd give me that pretty ass smile and throw them dreamy eyes on me… that shit made a nigga like me feel too good.

"I bought my mama a car… A BMW. She was so happy she cried. I got Imani's spoiled ass a black Barbie with a big ass dollhouse."

I stumbled over to chill next to her, waiting for her mood to change. She just huffed and shifted her weight on her feet, disconcerted.

"Bae, what wrong? Whatever it is… you can tell me," I added, gently. "It ain't shit you can't tell me, love. Whatever it is, get it off ya chest. If you're worried about my lifestyle or the body, stop that shit. We good and I'm makin' sure of that, na'mean?"

I began to caress her back, trying every damn thing I could think of to relax her. She moved away from me, bit the corner of her mouth and then stepped closer to me but didn't sit. She was still unsettled but wasn't shit else I knew that would calm her down. Well… besides my dick. But it didn't seem like the right time.

"I—I…Um. Well, remember when we had stopped talkin' after I found out about you and Quisha…" She paused. Her eyes darted to the side before she began again. I edged up in my seat, feeling my temperature already begin to rise as I remembered what E-Class had told me he'd heard about her. If this story ended with her confessing to fuckin' some nigga on Cutta's team, a lot of bodies would be falling tonight.

"I—I went to a club with Ya-Ya. It was at a club out in Harlem and…"

Her voice trailed off again I took a deep breath, trying to calm my temper. But it had flared up as soon as I heard the words 'I was at a club out in Harlem'. The *fuck* was LeTavia doing partying right in the middle of Cutta's stomping grounds? Back when we had broken things off, Cutta was out and Harlem was his city. The fact that she even tried me like that had me ready to spazz the fuck out but I clenched my teeth and stayed silent.

"I was there and I saw Cutta…" she continued and then paused, staring at me.

I shifted my weight from foot-to-foot as I took another breath, trying to stop myself from punching my hand through the muthafuckin' wall as I waited for what was to come next.

"...Ya-Ya was talkin' to a guy and I was alone. Then Cutta came over to me and—"

"FUCK!" I screamed, unable to hold it in any longer. "I know you ain't 'bout to tell me you fucked that nigga, Tavi!" I shouted, making her jump almost twenty feet in the air. "Please, tell me you not 'bout to say that shit!"

Her eyes clouded up immediately and her bottom lip began to quiver but I wasn't seeing none of that. If she had fucked around with Cutta just because she'd been in her feelings, she'd have more to deal with than she'd prepared for. My eyes narrowed in on her as I watched her stutter to respond. Briefly, I wondered whether or not there was room back in the spot I'd dumped Quisha's body. I chopped her up and buried her but there had to be space there for two.

Fuck... was I really thinking about LeTavia? I loved her and would never thought I'd consider hurting her. But the problem with me was when I got angry, another nigga took over. People had been calling me crazy for as long as I remembered. In the hood, it seemed like a term of endearment or a joke. But the joke was always laced with a little hint of realness because they knew the truth. I was crazy. No nigga could do all the shit I did and not have any setbacks because of it. I had plenty but they all helped me become the kinda nigga I was... one whose mind was set on owning the streets no matter what it cost me.

I would die being a street nigga and my level of thinking came with only anger... no fear. And I knew this same anger would be uncontrollable even for me if I found out LeTavia had betrayed me. I ran my hand over my face and took a deep breath, struggling to extinguish the fire burning inside of me. But it only provided the oxygen needed to grow the flame to a dangerous level.

I fuckin' *snapped.*

When LeTavia took too long to get another word out, I took off, stomping towards her, ready to hem her ass up against the wall until she told me what the fuck was going on.

"NO!" she screamed, backing away into the edge of the wall behind her. She hit the back of her head hard but she was so focused on getting away from me that she barely seemed to notice. Freezing, I planted my feet firmly in place and steadied my gaze as I waited for her to continue, mentally urging her not to say some shit I didn't like.

"I didn't—I... I... he—" she stammered. Her body was shaking too much for her to even get her words out.

"I didn't!" she finally spat out as tears flooded from her eyes. Closing her eyes, she shook her head forcefully and then said it once again, more steadily this time.

"I didn't... he—he tried to but I didn't. But I didn't know *who* he was," she continued on, her voice wavering a little more as she kept speaking. "I—I didn't know about the history between the two of you. Ya-Ya told me later but I'd already blown him off. Nothing happened between us. I... I just thought that you should know. I wanted to tell you everything before we moved on and shit got serious," she finished.

Staring at her, I knew that she was lying about something. There was more to the story but she wasn't talking and wasn't going to say shit else either. To be honest, I was starting to feel like I couldn't believe a damn thing coming out of her mouth.

"What the fuck happened between you and that nigga that you ain't tellin' me, Tavi? Don't fuckin' lie to me!"

It wasn't until I noticed her eyes drop to my right hand that I realized I was clutching my pistol tightly in my fist. I hadn't even noticed it was in my hand. That was how it was with me. I didn't think, didn't rationalize… I just reacted.

LeTavia's eyes widened and her breathing stalled as she looked from the gun up to my face. I could see her thoughts almost as vividly as if they were mine. She was wondering if I would really shoot her ass if she told me she had been fuckin' around with Cutta. The reality of the situation was that I didn't even know. And, if I did, once it was over and I realized what I had done, it would fuck me up inside. It would *destroy* me. But I was so heated to the point that I was beyond reasoning, beyond thinking. I was working off of pure emotion and that's when I was my most reckless.

They say hate is the closest thing after love and I felt like I was there.

"I said nothing happened!" she screamed with pleading eyes but I saw the desperation behind them and I knew it wasn't the truth. She still couldn't even look me in my eyes. She was still lying to me. Fuck! Why the hell was she always making me do crazy shit? Didn't she know the type of nigga I was? Didn't she know I couldn't control this shit… couldn't fuckin' control myself?

Lunging forward, I grabbed LeTavia by her arm and pushed her body backwards, pressing her hard against the wall. She groaned and winced from my firm grip but I didn't loosen it. In the back of my mind, I could hear a small voice telling me that I was fuckin' up but I couldn't contain it. In fact, I went even further, twisting her arm and pressing it hard against her chest to hold her in place. I swear, I was ready to break that shit off if she told me the wrong thing.

"Look me in my fuckin' eyes and tell me you didn't do anything with that nigga!" I gritted, pressing my face so close to hers that our noses nearly touched.

With no other choice, she had to look me in the eyes and answer me honestly. There was no way I was letting up until I found out the truth.

Suddenly, LeTavia's face twisted up in pain right before letting out a shrill scream as she dropped her body and bent over forward. Seeing her like that jolted something in me and I was able to focus… able to actually think and realize what I was doing. I felt my blood ice up in my veins. Loosening my grip, I stepped back and stared at her with wide eyes, suddenly scared as shit that I'd hurt her even though, only seconds before, I swear I was prepared to kill her ass. I know I hadn't been holding her that damn hard. What the fuck was wrong?!

"Tavi?"

Letting her go, I stepped back a few paces and watched as she dropped to the ground and balled up on the floor into fetal position, clutching her stomach as she screamed in pain. Dropping down to my knees, I reached for her just as she began to roll and writhe on the ground, screaming out like a banshee as if she'd been shot in the stomach. I snatched her shirt up, fully expecting to see an alien or some shit growing from out of it based on how she was acting. But nothing was there.

The hell was wrong with her ass?

Lifting her up, she cried as I cradled her in my arms and walked her back to the room. I had a lot of shit on my mind and still wanted to know what happened between her and Cutta but she sounded like she was about to fuckin' die. I felt helpless as hell on what to do to help her. Maybe it was cramps or some feminine shit. Hell, I ain't know… in my experience when I nigga yelled like that, I just put a hot one in him and put his ass out of his misery.

"It hurts… Oh God, it hurts…" she began to whine once I laid her on the bed as big ass tears fell down her face.

"What hurts?" I asked her. "You want me to call the ambulance or somethin'?"

She shook her head as she continued to moan softly and cry into her hands. I just stared.

"You want some Midol or some shit?"

She shook her head.

"Some dick?"

"Noooooo!" she moaned and I gave up. Shit, I didn't know what the fuck to do. Then, something occurred to me and I cocked my head to the side, giving her a narrowed look just as another thought came to my mind.

"You ain't fakin' just because I was about be a problem up in this bitch, huh?" I asked.

She swung at me, hard—like she was trying to pop me upside the head. Luckily, I ducked.

I guess that answered my question.

CHAPTER EIGHT

Le Tavia

*I*f I could breathe… could even get a full sentence out, I would have fought Gunplay for even suggesting that I was playing around in order to avoid his questions about Cutta. Yes, he'd scared the shit out of me. No, I didn't want to have to answer his questions about what had happened between Cutta and me. But *hell no*, I wasn't pulling no stunt just so that he'd leave me alone.

"No, I'm not fakin', DeShaun. This shit hurts…"

"You want me to rub your back or some shit?" Gunplay asked with a boggled expression on his face as he stood ahead of me with his hands stuffed in his pants pocket.

He had absolutely no idea how to handle what was wrong with me and it showed. Who sees someone in absolute pain and asks if they wanted some dick? Only Gunplay's ass. But I didn't even know what was wrong with me so I couldn't blame him. All I knew is that I had the most excruciating pain going through my body and I needed him to leave. I didn't want him anywhere near me.

"Just leave… please," I mumbled as I rolled on the bed and pushed my head into the pillow beside me, squeezing it so hard that my fingers hurt.

Gunplay hovered for a few minutes above me, and then finally I heard his feet shift around as he began moving towards the door.

"Okay… I'll check on you later," he said, and I moaned. Then I heard his steps come to a halt.

"If you keep cryin' and shit, you need to get up and take yo' ass to the hospital, a'ight? I'll even take you, bae. But you gotta just cut this shit out! You got me buggin'."

Despite my pain, I almost wanted to laugh but I could only cry harder. Of all the men to fall in love with, I had to choose the one who was insane. The one I couldn't predict and couldn't bet on. He was unpredictable. On one side was the Gunplay with the bad temper, fucked up attitude, no filter, and no manners. Then on the other side, his ass was acting like a sensitive thug, attentive, and caring about me. I couldn't even blame him for that either because love is an experience. It's a learning process and we were both finding that out.

All of a sudden, his phone chimed. He looked at it and, for the first time in my life, I saw fear register in his face. His skin seemed to go pale right before my eyes as he read the screen on his phone.

"Ohhh fuck naw. I gotta go!"

"What's wrong?" I asked just as another sharp cramp hit me. I winced only subtly, barely noticing it because I was so focused on him.

"It's my mama," he blurted out, not really paying me the least bit of attention. I watched as he dialed her number.

There was no answer.

Instantly, his face was etched with mistakable dread. "I gotta go!" he forced out through his teeth, his face tense with anxiety. For the first time in my life, it looked like Gunplay was actually scared. No, *petrified*. Something was very wrong.

He rushed out the door, holding his big ass AK-47 that he'd stuffed inside a duffle bag. Seconds later, I heard the loud roar of Gunplay's car as the tires screeched on the concrete when he peeled off down the road. Biting down on my bottom lip, I prayed that everything was okay but my innermost feelings were telling me differently. At the time, I had no idea just how bad things were, or that they would get worse.

Much worse.

In the meantime, I didn't know what was wrong with me but I hoped I would be okay.

Gunplay

I left LeTavia's crib with a heavy heart and my mind tormented after I received a text from my mom's. All it read was "Help!" When I called and texted her back, there was no response, so I hopped in my bucket and hauled ass at breakneck speed doing over a hundred miles an hour. The problem was not just that I was speeding, but I had that rocket in the backseat, the AK-47. If the police pulled me over, there was more than likely going to be a confrontation in the form of a deadly shoot-out. At the time, I didn't care.

I pulled into the driveway, relieved somewhat to see the new car I had bought my moms. I hopped out with the AK-47, leaving the door open and the engine running. On the walkway was a pink bicycle that, I guess, my mom got for Imani. A balmy breeze blew from the east and the sun shined bright like an orange ball of fire as I visually did a sweep of the house with my eyes.

I was walking briskly and suddenly, there was a loud noise behind me, a large locomotive combustion of some type. Instantly, I spun on my heels, ignoring the sharp pain that was ricocheting throughout my body. And just when I was about to come up blasting with the AK-47, I saw the noise was only a United Parcel Service truck, stopping at the neighbor's house across the street. I expelled a sigh of relief as I watched the driver, dressed in a shitty brown uniform, walk over to the house.

With my heart racing in my chest, I approached the screen door, looking at my mom's crucifix of Jesus that she'd hung on the metal frame next to the door handle. Inside, I heard the murmur of a voice… a woman's laughter.

Mama?

A smile tugged at my cheeks. How foolish of me to think something bad had happened to her. Instantly, I became self-conscious of my appearance. My face was badly bruised and I was walking with a terrible limp. My mom was the female version of Inspector Gadget, so I knew she would pick up on it and began to worry. That was something I didn't want to happen.

Adjusting my clothes, I made up a story for when my mama and Imani asked what happened to me. I looked and felt like I'd gotten hit by a truck so that would be my excuse. I couldn't do anything but chuckle to myself as I opened the screen door. It was then that I remembered I was holding the chopper and needed to hide it in the bushes. But before I could do it, something stopped me in my tracks.

The front door was already partially opened.

I walked inside and I saw blood, sanguine red. It stained the caramel shag carpeting like an animal, or perhaps a human being, had been unmerciful slaughtered.

"MAMA! MAMA!! IMANI!" I yelled, my voice echoing loudly in my ears like I was in the Grand Canyon.

The putrid stench of blood was heavy in my nostrils, filling me with so much despair. My heart beat in my chest like a sledgehammer, my legs felt weighed down with concrete bricks. I took out the .44 I had stashed in my waistband and ran through the house, frantic like a maniac.

"Mama! Mama!" I shouted again and again, as I followed the grisly trails of blood. Its smell overwhelmed me in a way that I would never be able to describe. Passing through the living room, I saw the wall was smeared in blood and what looked like Imani's bloody handprint.

"Imani?! Imani?! Mama!!"

I stalled briefly, wondering if I should continue on. Wondering if my daughter and my moms were dead in front of me. If that was the case, I didn't want to witness it.

I had done some terrible, despicable things in my life—things I couldn't even remember until after they were done—but I never harmed an innocent child.

"Please, God, no."

More blood. A chair was overturned, the TV blared loudly. It was on the Christian station, the 700 Club. A female was laughing heartily about something going on, on the show. My heart nearly crumbled to pieces in my chest. That was who I'd heard laughing.

I continued with my gun in hand, heart racing, palms sweaty. Then I turned the corner entering the kitchen and my heart sank. My chest tightened, nearly shriveled up like a prune. I was having trouble breathing. There, on the kitchen floor, was my mother laying in a puddle of blood.

"Mama!!"

I rushed over and fell to my knees. There was a bloody cleaver hatchet on the floor next to her. She had been butchered with it.

"Aw, fuck! Mama, noooo!!"

I broke down completely. Her throat had been slashed from ear to ear. There were gaping holes in her chest and slash marks on her arms as if she had put up a fight. She had been butchered and hacked violently by her attackers in the worst way. They left her alone on the floor to die, discarding her like trash.

I quickly picked her up in my arms. She was still warm and breathing but just barely.

"Mama? Mama? Who did this to you? Where is Imani?" I asked in a choked voice as tears stung my eyes.

There was no answer.

Then suddenly, her mouth moved as her right hand twitched involuntarily. She tried to speak; her whole body went into convulsions, her eyes flashed wide, rigid with fear. The sight of seeing her like that was unbearable. I fought back a sob as I reached into my pocket for my phone to dial 911.

The emergency operator came on. It was some female with a nasally voice and not enough patience for her job.

"I need help. My mom has been hurt bad..."

"What is wrong?"

"Her throat has been cut and she has been stabbed. Hurry, can you send an ambulance?! PLEASE?!"

I squeezed my eyes shut as I clutched my mom in my arms. By

then, I was sobbing uncontrollably.

"Sir, I am going to need for you to calm down. Now can you tell me what happened? Is the victim—"

"Bitch, send a fuckin' ambulance! I don't know what happened. I need an ambulance in a hurry!"

Suddenly, my mama expelled a deep protracted breath as her body abruptly stopped shaking. Her eyes were still open as if she were staring at something only she could see.

She had died in my arms.

"Sir…? Sir…? Can you give me your location? And is the victim conscious…"

Clenching my teeth, I squeezed my eyes firmly shut in torment. I bowed my head on my mama's bosom and cried like a baby, still holding her unmoving body in my arms. The pain was too immense for my mind to comprehend. There was no way this could be happening. Who would resort to this? Who could mercilessly murder an innocent grandmother and child?

Imani!

I sprung up, coming to my senses. Where in the fuck was Imani? Instantly, my mind flashed back to the tiny handprint on the wall I had noticed when I came in.

"Sir, an ambulance is on its way…." I heard the faint voice of the 911 operator right before I took off down the hall. I bolted right up the flight of stairs and straight to the second floor to Iman's room. My chest was about to explode. I was about to have an anxiety attack. But my only care was that Imani was safe, so I couldn't think of anything else. I nearly knocked the door down as I entered her room, completely winded.

"Imani! Baby, where are you? It's Daddy. Where are you?!" My voice was crescendo of fear. My heart pounded in my throat so fast I had trouble breathing. Then I heard a noise—a thump. Something coming from down the hall.

The killers were still in the house.

I walked back out the room, using my ears as guidance. With my gun in hand, I padded back down the stairs, ready to start blasting. Right as I passed the small bloody handprint on the wall, I heard a siren in the distance, blaring. Then there was the sound of the thump again. But this time I realized where it was coming from: the bathroom. I cocked the .9 mm, placing one in the chamber, and then kicked the door open slightly with my foot. The neatly kept bathroom was barren except for a few decorative towels and other items and the shower to my left.

"Who the fuck in here?"

Silence.

The shower curtain shifted, only less than a hair, but my trained eye picked up on it immediately. The killer was inside. I could barely make out the silhouette of a person but that was all I need to see. I was about to peel the curtain back and squeeze on whoever the fuck it was stupid enough to hide in the shower.

Then the shower curtain moved again. I was about to start blasting right before something occurred to me. I tucked my pistol behind my back and snatched the curtain open, erupting a craze of emotions through my body. There was Imani, with her pretty face dotted with splotches of red; she was nearly covered in blood. All I could see was terror in my child's eyes.

"Imani, come here. I got you. Are you okay?" I asked plaintively, with my heart on my sleeve but my mind still being tormented.

"Daddy!" she wailed as she stumbled out the tub, slipping when her bloody feet touched the tile floor. I rushed over and grabbed her in my arms.

"Th—th—they hurt Grandma! And I was scared, but I didn't want them to hurt me too!" She cried some more as I held her tight in my arms. I swallowed hard, trying to rid myself of the lump in my throat. All I could see was red… my anger and my revenge. Someone was going to pay for this. I wouldn't stop until I found out who was responsible.

"Shhh, everything is going to be okay."

Still holding her tight, I caressed Imani's hair. She continued to cry quietly against my chest, her tears intermingling with my mama's blood.

"I hid here when I heard the shooting. But after they shot Grandma, I heard one of them in the house… looking for me, calling my name. He left when I didn't come out. That's why I didn't come out when you called, Daddy! It sounded like you but I wasn't sure! I was so scared!" Her lip trembled and she let out a long wail. "Aft—after it was quiet, I went downstairs and tried to help Grandma. H—her blood is on me! When I heard you at the door, I tried to run, but I slipped and fell in her blood. I was so scared!"

Her sobbing became heavier but my mind only ran through the details of what she was saying as I tried to piece it all together. I thought about the bloody handprint on the wall. It must have happened when she heard me enter and ran back upstairs. I remembered the feeling of sorrow and dread that I'd felt when I saw it, thinking that had been Imani's blood. I would fuckin' lose it if anything separated me from my daughter.

Then it suddenly dawned on me, as I listened to Imani with the sound of sirens wailing in the distance. If the cops came and discovered I had weapons on me, they would take me to jail and take her to foster care. I couldn't let that shit happen.

"Damn!" I hissed, pulling away from Imani to run back downstairs. I picked up the chopper and ran for the door.

Too late.

The authorities had arrived and there I stood with the weapons. This had to be the most fucked day of my life. But I knew one thing—there was no way I was going back to prison. I was prepared for a shoot-out. I would rather die in the streets before I ever went back.

***

A platoon of white faces, all dressed in blue, were piled up outside my mom's door as soon as I opened it. Just when I was about to come up shooting, it occurred to me that these were not cops, they were medics dressed in sky blue uniforms. My mind was so fucked up, I was trippin'... 'bout to blast on a team of EMTs thinking it was Five-Oh. I couldn't even process everything that was going on. Shit, I needed

LeTavia with me.

"She's in the kitchen." I gestured with my hand to the inside of the house but I stayed outside. I couldn't bear to see my mom's body again. Out of the corner of my eye, I saw Imani bawling in a corner. My gut twisted and I grimaced my evil thoughts away.

"Do you need medical attention?" a female EMT asked but I ignored her and pushed past them all as they rushed inside.

With the AK-47 in the duffle bag at my side, I made a quick dash to the side of the house and stashed it in a small nook under the back porch. It was safe there because you could only find that spot if you knew it was there. As soon as I walked back to the front of the house, I saw a blue and white patrol car headed directly towards me.

Gunplay

Hours Later...

My mother's home was teeming with cops, forensic people, and one child psychologist recommended by the police department to deal with trauma. Then one of my worst nightmares walked in the house to aid in my misery and pain. I had been questioned by the third cop for the umpteenth time and the only thing stopping me from losing it in that bitch was the fact that I couldn't deal with my mama's murderers if I was in prison. So, I played it cool even though I looked suspect as hell because of all the bruises on my body, not to mention, I was covered in blood. My mama's blood. My mind was frantic... all I could think about was how badly I needed to find the niggas responsible for this shit.

And then my day showed me it could get even worse.

The homicide detectives investigating Quisha's murder—the ones who had beat my ass the last time I encountered them—walked into the house. A sergeant dressed in a white shirt, broad shoulders, with all kinds of decorative badges and shit, pointed them in my direction. He leaned over and whispered something to them with his eyes plastered on me. Same shit as always... I was a Black man, a street thug. Them muthafuckas were trying to figure out how to pin all this shit on me.

The black detective, Jefferson, casually strolled over. He was dressed in a brown trench coat and suit with a matching wide brim hat and tie. He was the same damn cop that had sucker-punched me so hard that he bust my lip and pulled one of the locs out my head. I snarled and narrowed my eyes in on him. If they still wanted to get a rise out of me, today was their lucky day.

"The fuck you want?" I snarled, looking directly at Jefferson

His partner, Mike, just looked at me bug-eyed at first. Then he snorted his contempt and cocked his head to an angle, smirking like the pompous asshole he was. Leaning forward, he decided to remind me about his lame ass joke.

"Don't forget our motto, B.A.W.M. Black ass whoopings..." He made a gesture with his hands, clapping them together in a suggestive way.

It almost looked like he smirked at me while he did it. And there was a mischievous twinkle in his eye. On the other side, Jefferson placed his hand to his mouth like he was suppressing a cough but he was actually disguising his laugh.

"Fuck ass pigs," I muttered loud enough for them to hear.

"We need to ask you some questions. First, what happened to your face?" Jefferson pointed at the place where LeTavia had placed a bandage on my head. "And where did all that blood come from?"

He stood stoically, eyes sternly searching mine as he waited for my answer. Behind him, forensic experts were dusting for fingerprints. Then I saw Imani standing to the side. Her eyes were filled with sheer terror as she took a timid step back, her mouth opened. Her face was puckered with daunting fear as she suddenly stopped talking to the child psychologist. I followed her eyes and it soon registered why.

A medical examiner dressed in all black slacks and jacket, stormed towards us. His skin was weathered, old, placid white like a sheet. He had a long beak of a nose with a web of green veins spreading across it. He donned tiny spectacles, so thin they looked rimless, and they sat on the edge of his nose, unmoving even if he did.

But what ripped me into two was what lay in his hands.

He was pushing a gurney, with a white bloody sheet covering it. There was a body under it... my mama's body. The back of my eyes began to sting and I felt my throat close. My joints began to throb in pain as I repeatedly flexed and then relaxed my hands. I was trying to be strong for my daughter, trying to keep the last facet of my sanity, but I was breaking down. I swallowed the dry lump in my throat with difficulty as instantly my eyes watered.

Mike called out to stop the medical examiner and then looked underneath the sheet at my mother's body and frowned. He turned to Jefferson and leaned over to whisper.

"Damn, they slaughtered that bitch like a hog."

That was it! I completely lost it and lunged at Mike's throat. I just needed to get my fingers around his neck and choke the shit out of him. In a split second, his partner and the sergeant intervened, along with several other cops. But I was still able to grab his suit coat as they tried to pull me away. Clutching it in my fists, I squeezed hard as I could, trying to pull him close enough to wrap my fingers around his neck.

"That's my mama, you stupid ass muthafucka! Watch who the fuck you calling a bitch, you fuck ass cracka!"

I pulled harder on his coat and heard something tear. He wailed out loudly in pain and fear. Someone placed their arm around my neck in what felt like a vice grip. I heard the staccato of guns being cocked as somebody hit me in the back. From the stampede of footsteps thundering in my ears, I could tell that several cops had rushed over. But what I heard the loudest was a piercing sound of a child's voice.

It was Imani. My daughter's voice brought me back to reality.

"Daddy, noooo, STOP it!"

I froze, locked eyes with hers. She let out a long sob and then took off running towards me, not stopping until she had flung her arms around my waist.

"Please don't hit my Daddy. Please don't hurt him."

Mike's frown deepened as he looked between Imani and me. He gave me a dastardly stare but then in the next moment relaxed a little and made a clicking sound with his tongue.

"Calm down, everybody. It was my fault. Everyone just go back to what you were doing and leave him alone."

Even as he spoke, he never took his eyes off me. I was too torn up to fight anymore. My head was spinning; my chest felt like it was caving in. My mama was gone... killed because I wasn't there to protect her. I should've done more to protect her.

FUCK!

I released my grip on Mike's coat and hurt prevailed. Crumpling to my knees, I opened my mouth and roared loud, pairing a horrific sound with my pain, sounding almost bestial like a wounded animal. With tears in her eyes, Imani ran over and wrapped her arms around me. I grabbed her and held her tight in my arms as she cried. But where the fuck was LeTavia? I swear I needed her with me. I couldn't think… felt like I couldn't fuckin' breathe without her.

My mama was all I had. My heart felt like it had burst. It was bleeding out and I couldn't help it. There was nearly complete silence in the room; the only thing that could be heard was Imani softly crying. In the backdrop was the sporadic crackle of police radios. Somehow buried deep in my bereavement of pain, I summoned the energy to raise my head, then my body. With my shoulders squared, I pushed away my grief and told myself to get it together. The quicker I could get these muthafuckas out of here, the quicker I could get to doing what I needed to do.

"Imani, you and your daddy are going to be okay, sweetheart." The child psychologist reached out and patted her on the shoulder kindly. She was smiling but her eyes were sad. I was surprised when Imani sniffed and then took her hand, grasping it like it was her lifeline. But the she blew my mind with what she said next.

"Daddy… I saw what one of the men looked like. H—he was your friend."

My breathing stalled and everything in front of me melted away. The only thing I could focus on was Imani's words. Lifting my head, I stared at her right in her face, eyes crystal clear, and heart barely beating. It couldn't be true.

"Whaatt?!" I snapped, wondering if I'd misunderstood her. "What do you mean he was my friend? What else do you remember about him?"

Her bottom lip began to tremble as her eyes cut to the left. I knew I was pushing her a little too much, making her remember something that she most likely wanted to forget, but I needed to get whatever information she had.

"W—when he hit Grandma, he didn't know I was in the house and h—he was talking to her. He said the man on his shoulder was coming to get her. He said he was going to add a tear to honor her death... wh—what does that mean, Daddy?"

Clenching my teeth, I closed my eyes and forced out a deep breath. I knew Imani needed me to console her but my mind was spewing thoughts of murder. I didn't know anything about the first half of what she said, but I understood the rest. Rayshaun, a street nigga just like me, and one of the few men who I ran with to ever lay eyes on Imani, had a whole side of his face decorated with teardrops to signify innocent lives lost of people who he said meant a lot to him.

"It doesn't mean anything, baby," I told Imani, squeezing out the best sentence I could make at the moment. "Relax. We just have to do what we need to do right now and then we're getting out of here."

***

I sat in the police station racking my brain as Imani worked with a police sketch expert to get a sketch of the guy who had murdered my mama. From what I saw, there was a drawing of some black guy with a skinny face and a tattoo on his left arm. The entire time, I sat with the investigators answering questions and being grilled like I was the culprit. What helped me was there were footprints and latent fingerprints, but none of them matched mine. Jefferson kept giving me a look whenever I glanced towards Imani and the sketch artist. I could tell by the look in his eyes that he knew what I was going to do once I found out who was behind all this. I did nothing to try to persuade him otherwise.

And as hard as my daughter tried to make me remember the killer, the only person I could think about was Rayshaun. It had been years since Imani had last seen him or anyone else I ran with. He was her godfather, but the last time I could actually remember her seeing him was back when I was still with Quisha and used to hustle loud outside our apartment.

Either way, I wasn't saying a word about my suspicions. Never would I put the cops in the middle of my business. If there ever was a case where street justice was necessary, this would be the one. I needed to avenge my mother's killer and I had an idea where to find Rayshaun, it was the one place all hood niggas went.

But first, I had to drop my daughter off at LeTavia's crib. It was getting late and I still hadn't heard from her even though I'd been blowing up her phone. I couldn't focus, I was paranoid. Not being able to contact her had me thinking some crazy shit had happened. Fuck, I should've moved her out of that apartment as soon as I thought about it. Niggas was on the street getting too bold for comfort, finding themselves courageous enough to make moves on my family. This shit was serious but they had fucked with the wrong one.

CHAPTER NINE

Le Tavia

As I sat on the metal table waiting for the doctor to return, I tried to relax but I couldn't. I didn't need anyone to tell me something was wrong. I already knew something wasn't right. But I was afraid of what that something was and to compound matters, I still had this gnawing, terrifying feeling something bad was happening with Gunplay. I prayed I was wrong but in my haste to leave and get to the hospital, I'd left my phone. I couldn't reach him or Sonya and I felt like I desperately needed one of them with me.

The door to the room opened and in walked the doctor they'd assigned to me. The look on her face told me that, although she might have been great at what she did for a living, she definitely wasn't a people person. Her eyes barely met mine the entire time she'd been in earlier; instead, she'd kept them either pinned to her clipboard or on whatever part of my body she was inspecting at the moment.

But as she strode in this time, I noticed that she appeared different; her eyes were softer and more caring. Instead of her face being perpetually pointed at my chart as she'd done earlier, this time she was staring directly into my face with an expression that immediately made me uneasy. I could tell she was trying to appear kind and gentle, but that fact alone assured me that something was extremely wrong.

"I apologize for how long you had to wait. I was checking over the tests that were ran and grabbing some opinions from other doctors that are very good at what they do." She paused and cleared her throat. I could feel my heart beating in my throat. Every second she made me wait was pure torture. I needed her to just get this shit out so I could be on my way.

"Something's wrong," I told her, wanting to rush her along. "I already know that. Just tell me what it is without all that extra bullshit."

Clearing her throat, I saw all the emotion drain from her face and her blank stare returned as she prepared to speak.

"The abortion you had led to you developing an infection. Because of the infection, there has been significant scarring to your uterus as well as your fallopian tubes, and also, we found something else..."

"Oh my God. What is it?" The words came out jagged and desperate like when you can sense something is life threatening. The doctor continued to look between her clipboard and me.

"We saw a mass... a few of them. So, I just want to run some tests to make sure it's not cancer."

All the blood drained from my face. "What do you mean cancer? I am only twenty-two years old!"

She nodded her head, a grim expression crossing her face. If she was trying to keep me from panicking, she was failing miserably.

"I know. First, we are going to run some tests to be certain. It could be something benign. There is no age cut-off for cancer but the good thing is, if we catch it early enough, we have a good chance to beat it."

I mopped my face with a weary hand, my entire body was shaking. A light sheen of sweat had started to form on my forehead. The doctor flipped through some pages on her clipboard and continued with a sigh.

"Additionally... and I'm sorry to have to say all this to you at one time. Based on the scarring to your fallopian tubes, it would be nearly impossible for you to get pregnant again. There is just too much damage. You do have other options for this that we can discuss at a later date. Right now, I want to get moving on the tests to make sure we aren't also dealing with cancer."

Her words nearly took the air out of my body. Thinking that something was wrong was one thing but hearing it confirmed was another. First cancer... and now I couldn't have another baby, ever. But as I ran her words over in my mind, a small ray of hope surfaced.

"You said *nearly* impossible, so that means—"

"There is about a less than 1% chance that you could but the probability is extremely low... I wouldn't—"

"Get my hopes up," I finished for her and she nodded her head. Sighing, she gave me a long look and then started to fidget with her white coat. I began to cry silently, sobbing so hard it rocked my shoulders. I could tell it made her uncomfortable that I was now unable to control my emotions.

"I'm fine," I whined out in a strained whisper. "You don't have to stay. I understand."

"Keep a positive attitude and try not to worry about it. As soon as the results come back, we will let you know." She reached out and affectionately patted my knee before turning to leave.

I stared at the space she'd last been as my mind churned with apprehension and dread. I was only twenty-two years old and faced with the reality that I was not only barren, but I could be also dying. I felt cold and alone in the world… the same way I had felt in the abortion clinic.

I couldn't keep dealing with this shit alone. I needed to figure out how to explain this to Gunplay.

Gunplay

It was the wee hours of the morning by the time we left the police station. The streets of New York were deserted like a no man's land; desolation was everywhere as I drove with my hand on my strap and my mind ruminating with wicked thoughts. I was a man on a serious mission of search and destroy. I needed to find that nigga, Rayshaun, and anybody that could be remotely associated with him. I had to make an example.

Before leaving, I had called both of my lieutenants, Gunna and Ron, and issued a hit on all rival major drug runners who even showed the smallest resistance to our takeover. So far, my squad had amassed over a hundred cutthroat killers and armed project gorillas. It was like urban warfare in the hood. I was about to make the street bleed like a virgin who had first got her cherry popped.

Imani appeared to be sleeping in the back so I didn't hesitate to get down to business. Street lights strobed my car as I drove, talking nonstop to both of them on the phone.

"I want to find this nigga, Rayshaun… dead or alive. If we can't find him, we runnin' up in his house and grabbin' that nigga's mama and that cross-eyed bitch that live up in there with her."

"What you want me to do wit' 'em?"

I snapped, "I don't give a fuck! Cancel his ol' girl out quick and y'all boys can have your way with the other one. But I want that nigga dead in less than twenty-four hours, fam."

Imani stirred in her sleep, making me glance at her through the rearview mirror. She was looking at me with her doe eyes sparkling.

"Daddy... you kill people too?"

Yes.

Clenching my teeth together, I shook my head.

"No, baby girl. I was talking about a movie."

"Huh? A movie?"

"It's a movie and I'm going to put you in it too. Daddy would never hurt anybody."

The lie came out like smooth butter and she sopped it up. I reached back and caressed her hair. She looked so much like her mama it was eerie. Refocusing back on the road, I was about to continue my conversation with Gunna and Ron, when she spoke up again.

"Is Grandma going to be in the movie too?"

My thoughts merged.

"Aye, let me call y'all back," I said into the phone, my voice wavering so subtly only I noticed it.

"A'ight. We gon' move on yo' command. We already in the streets, 'bout to start knockin' on doors," Gunna assured me with confidence.

"That's right. Get up wit'cha later, GP," Ron added and I hung up the phone.

I couldn't help but pause for a second as my hands gripped the steering wheel so tight my knuckles paled. Once again, Imani had said something that rendered me speechless, completely at an utter lost for words. I was stuck like I was doing the fuckin' mannequin challenge.

"Grandma's...sh—she's in Heaven now," I managed to say as I pulled onto LeTavia's street. My eyes scanned in the front of her building and my chest contracted. All her lights were off.

"You mean she in Heaven with God? Will I ever be able to see her again, Daddy?"

Silence.

"Yes, baby. But not any time soon. I promise Daddy will protect you," I gritted through my teeth, trying to keep it together. My eyes were burning from my anger and anguish. My pistol felt hot on my thigh. I needed a release. I needed to be making my moves in the streets. I was about to fuckin' lose it.

"But why I have to wait? I miss her and I miss mommy, too! I wanna see my mama and grandma soon."

Imani began to cry and I released a deep sigh of bottled-up frustration as I parked the car. There was a flutter of movement to my side and my eyes fell on LeTavia's weird ass neighbor, standing in the bushes, watching me like a fuckin' creep.

"Shit!" I blurted out as soon as I saw him peering through the bushes. "I mean shoot," I corrected myself, remembering Imani was in the car.

Pulling my top lip up in a sneer, I stroked the top of my pistol as I stared at Bruce who was now pretending like he didn't see me and was looking for something on the ground. Letting go of a bullet right into his skull would be the perfect release for me until I caught up with Rayshaun.

"What's wrong, Daddy?"

"Nothin, Imani. We finna get out the car. I want you to stay close to me."

"Why?"

"Don't ask now questions just do what I say!"

My anger was getting the better of me and I was losing control. I glanced back over at Bruce, feeling the demons in me begin to rise up. I could barely see straight, everything in me was pushing for me to kill. I needed to give pain in order to relieve mine.

By the time I got Imani out the car, Bruce was gone. However, I still had a feeling I was being watched as I walked up the stairs carrying Imani in my arms. As soon as I walked into the door, I knew something was wrong. It was dark inside and the smell of loud reeked in the air. My breath caught up in my lungs and I reached out, cutting a light on quickly while balancing Imani in my arms.

The living room light illuminating, shining a spotlight on LeTavia who was sitting at the small dining room table, glassy-eyed with a halo of smoke hovering over her head. Her low, narrowed eyes widened when they fell on Imani and me. We were still in our bloody clothes, looking disheveled and dispirited. LeTavia got up from the table, knocking over a glass that in turn shattered. Her eyes were swollen and red as she rushed over and hugged me tight. Feeling her body close to mine erupted a whirlwind of emotions inside of me that only she could have brought about. The voices of the murderous demons that had been shouting in my head for me to kill, were reduced to a soft whisper as I inhaled her scent.

"Baby… please, tell me what I can do!"

Her arms were around my knock, her maudlin tears staining my clothes. She knew what had happened. I had called her when I was released from the police station and told her every last detail when she finally picked up and told me that she'd misplaced her phone.

"I'm good," was all I could say with a pained expression, as I stood stoic, impassive.

All of a sudden, she pulled away from me and cast a loving glance at Imani. At the time, Imani looked like one of them war-torn children you saw on the news in one of them third world impoverished countries. My family was falling apart. All I was supposed to do was protect them, but my mama was dead and my daughter had seen much more than her seven-year-old eyes should have ever seen.

"Hi, Imani." LeTavia squatted down to her height and caressed her cheeks. "We're going to get you cleaned up and give you a nice bed to sleep in. Are you hungry?"

She nodded her head and looked up at me for approval before responding in barely a whisper.

"Yes, ma'am."

Polite, just like her grandmother had taught her, even though I could see her bottom lip trembling. I knew she was still devastated.

"Okay, we gon' get you cleaned up, I have a nighty my baby sister, Nori, left here. I also have some of her clothes… they are a little big but it should be fine for now. Then we can eat! Do you like leftover pizza or you want me to cook you breakfast since it's almost that time?"

LeTavia forced a smile out but I could see it was fake... a distraction to shield the hurt that lay beneath. Something else was going on with her. I took the opportunity to really look at her, focusing my eyes on every part of her body that I knew so well. Her nails were bitten down to the quick, her hair was stringy and tousled over her head as if she'd been constantly running her hands through it. Her lips were dry and her eyes were dim. This wasn't the woman I was used to seeing. She appeared to have aged in only a matter of hours due to stress. What the hell was going on with the people around me?

Imani looked up at me and I could have sworn a smile tugged at the corners of her mouth when she responded, "Pizza? I love pizza!" Her face lit up with delight. She almost got a smile out of me.

"Okay, pizza it is," LeTavia beamed brightly, but her eyes were sparkling with tears. "Let me get this broken glass up off the floor." And that was when she padded away barefooted to get the broom and I noticed a crumpled-up piece of paper on the table; it was from the clinic. That reminded me about earlier that day she had been violently sick with something.

As LeTavia bent down to pick up the bigger pieces of glass that she had broken, I remembered something she had mentioned on the phone.

"You had to go to the clinic... Did you find out what was wrong with you?"

She stopped, froze like she was frightened out of her wits. Then she sighed and hung her shoulders somberly.

"Yeah..."

"What?"

"I'll tell you about it later."

My teeth clenched and I swallowed hard before responding.

"Is something wrong, Tavi?"

She shook her head but her eyes still would not meet mine. I saw her bottom lip quiver. She was lying.

"I dunno. Let me get the baby situated. We can talk about that later," she pled, finally glancing into my eyes, silently begging me to drop the subject. My instincts told me not to pry just yet. I happened to glance outside the window and saw a fuchsia colored sky making its miraculous appearance, washing away the luminous moon only to beckon at the ardent sun to take its place. This was a beautiful day. I was going to make it a beautiful *last* day for some.

My phone chimed. I looked at the caller ID and it was Gunna. I stepped away just as I heard my daughter ask LeTavia to use the bathroom.

"What's good, nigga?" I asked with bass in my voice as I glanced out the window. Even as I spoke, my mind was deliberating, formulating plots, and counterplots on the next moves I would make to draw Rayshaun out so I could end him.

"Man, I'm sorry. I just heard 'bout what happened to your ol' girl—"

"Nigga, fuck that! Did you find Rayshaun?" Then, before he could get a word out, I suddenly thought about what he said. I had called him and Ron earlier but I never mentioned anything about what happened to my mama or Imani.

"And how did you find out what happened? It made the news?"

He responded, "The streets is talkin'. You know muthafuckin' cops can't keep they mouths shut. As soon as niggas found out some shit wit' yo' name in it, the shit spread."

"Hmmm, okay." I was pissed. The more people talked, the harder it was going to be to keep a low profile. The entire city would be looking out for me. I had to move quicker. Much faster.

"Anyway tho', we caught that nigga Kato from Harlem. He is Cutta's cousin so he may know somethin'. They real tight... he been movin' a little weight for him."

"And?"

"He had blood on his shoes and there was some mo' blood caked up under his fingernails. We whooped his ass bad... tried to get him to talk."

"And happened?" I pushed further.

"Shit, the nigga sticking to his script. Sayin' he don't know shit. But he did say Cutta was out of prison."

I clicked my tongue against my teeth and let out a dry chuckle. So that nigga had been able to do it. He was back on the streets and that meant he was no longer untouchable for me. Now I definitely knew he was behind what happened to my moms.

"Okay, cut his head and his hands off and then place them on his mama's front porch. Neatly," I clarified, while pensively stroking my chin hair.

"Man, you buggin'?!"

"No, I'm dead ass. Or you wanna take his place?"

"I'm on it now."

"And make sure his mama see it 'fore you leave."

I hung up the phone and turned around, seeing LeTavia standing there. I had forgotten all about her that quickly.

"So, you're goin' to go kill some more people? Terrorize the city… place me and your daughter in harm's way?" Her voice had a sharp vehement tone of accusation.

I help up my chin and spoke forcefully, with deadly intent. I was so caught up in my murderous thoughts that I couldn't even appreciate the way a tiny glimmer of sunlight was dancing inside of her beautiful eyes through the window nearby.

"DeShaun, you're doing too damn much! When is this going to stop?! When will it end?! When you're dead and gone… or locked up in some white man's penitentiary for the rest of your life, what will we do then?!"

"Lower your fuckin' voice!" I gritted through my teeth with a stiff chin and grabbed her arm tight. "My mama was fuckin' killed! Slaughtered like an animal! Do you think I'm just gon' let that shit go? What kinda nigga you think I am, Tavi?!"

Shaking her head at me, she pulled away with her fist balled tight at her sides.

"Why can't you see that this is just makin' shit worse for all of us?!"

I looked her right into her eyes and said what was probably the truest words I'd ever spoken.

"I'm not stoppin' until I kill any and everybody who I even think may have had somethin' to do with this. Save your words because I'm not stopping until everyone who ever crossed me is gone. And I'm shooting first—I'm not waitin' for explanations or shit. I want everybody to know that this is what happens when you fuck with mine."

That's when my daughter walked back in. I tried to relax the tension in my face when I turned to her. Her eyes were wide and filled with tears.

"Daddy, are you going someplace? Are you leaving me?"

I swallowed a dry lump in my throat and lied with a straight face. Again.

"Naw, baby girl. I'm never leaving you again. I just need to go handle some business and then I'll be right back."

I heard LeTavia suck her teeth with disdain. Her body did some type of jerky motion when she shifted from one hip to the other and folded her arms over her chest.

We glowered at each other silently, giving credence to the assumption that mental telepathy was real. I knew damn well she could read my thoughts. I just wished I could have read hers better. I wished that I could be there for whatever it was she needed from me… the way that she was always here for me. But I would be able to do that as soon as I handled Rayshaun first.

I kissed both LeTavia and Imani on their cheeks, and headed out the door strapped with two bangers. The chopper was still in the whip. I was prepared to murder everything that moved.

Murder would be the case they gave me if I got caught.

Gunplay

The morning commute was dreadful in New York traffic, but it also served his purpose and gave me time to plot my next strategy. I drove past Rayshaun mom's house and nearly stopped. The devilish side of me told me to go inside and dump the entire small building unit with bullets until every single thing in it was completely annihilated. But she had been a mother to me when I was younger and I didn't want to move too quickly without proof. Maybe I needed to hear Rayshaun's side first.

Maybe…

After seeing that Rayshaun wasn't around, my next stop was his baby mama, Poochie. We all went to the same high school but Poochie and I had known each other since the third grade. Actually, Poochie met Rayshaun through me. I had been diggin' her but she kept me in the friend zone, said I was too street for her. She tried to hook me up with her friends and that was how I met Quisha. She ended up gettin' caught up with Rayshaun and they have been together since. Poochie piously stays by his side as the loyal girlfriend and mother of their two sons, regardless of the fact that she has caught him cheating on her multiple times and he goes to prison on the regular.

After checking around, I finally got an address for her and it wasn't too far away. They stayed in the drug-riddled part of town in

South Bronx. I parked my car right in front of their crib, a brownstone building that had seen better days. Next to it was a trash-littered vacant lot. From somewhere in the distance, a dog barked ferociously as I got out my car. I saw Rayshaun's black Chevy parked out front. It looked like it hadn't been driven in a while; one of the tires was flat.

Just as I walked up the stairs, a blue and white police cruiser passed by. I knocked on the door, waiting. I could hear a cacophony of voices coming from inside along with music. Soon the door opened and there stood Poochie, dressed in a housecoat with some type of wrap on her head that looked like a black plastic bag. Instantly, a large smile spread across her cheeks as she called me by my government name.

"DeShaun! What you doin' up this early in the morning, knockin' on my do'?" she said in a singsong voice radiating with love.

For some reason, she was wearing fake eyelashes that looked heavy on her pretty hazel eyes. Her almond-colored skin was aglow and I just happened to look down and saw the baby bump. She looked to be about four months pregnant. It took everything in my power to reciprocate her smile. After all, I was there to kill my old friend, her baby daddy.

"I'm good. I just stopped through to holla at my nigga, Rayshaun." It was hard to keep a straight face.

"Humph!" she sassed and twisted her face at me before rolling her eyes up at the ceiling. "*Somebody* need to holla at his ass! He ain't been out a hot second and his parole officer talking about violating his ass already for not going to work."

Out of nowhere, her oldest son, Kyle, appeared, squealing with delight.

"Uncle Gunplay!"

"Hey, boy!"

I ruffled his curly hair and made him laugh, wondering how he still remembered me. It had been so long.

"Guess what?" he asked with a guileful smile.

"What?"

"I'm playing basketball now."

"That's what's up." I reached into my pocket and handed him a twenty-dollar bill. His smile brightened.

"Thanks! When you gon' come with my dad and watch me play?" he asked, full of jubilance. My chest got tight and I shifted anxiously.

Never.

"I'on know…" Narrowing my eyes, I finessed my beard reflectively and then glanced over at Poochie. "I'll have to see."

"Mama, when we got another game?"

"Next week. Now get your butt upstairs and get ready for school so you don't miss the bus! Stop badgering folks!"

"He not folks, that's Uncle Gunplay!" She playfully pushed Kyle upside the head, shooing him up the stairs to his room.

The second Kyle disappeared, Rayshaun walked in. He was dressed in a wife-beater, blue jeans, and sneakers. His body was sculptured like an athlete, toned up with muscles, fortified from doing several years in prison and a juvie camp.

"What's good, nigga?" he greeted me, amped up. "Damn, I been tryin' to see you for a minute, fam!"

"Word?"

"Hell yeah! E ain't told you?!"

I mired, quietly observing him, getting the genuine feeling that I could be wrong about him. He seemed too cheerful. Too fearless.

That was until I looked down at his pants and saw what looked like tiny splatters of dried blood right at the hem. My heart dropped to my feet. I fought the urge to pull out on his ass and just start blasting. The only thing stopping me was my respect for Poochie.

With my teeth clenched, I bumped his fist and then prepared to lay my trap.

"What you been up to lately?"

"Shit! Dem white folks been on my ass! I got a part-time job painting but I didn't go to work a few days ago, and my parole officer tried to jam my ass up on some fuck shit. Made me spend three days in county."

I raised my brows.

"Real shit?"

"Yeah, I gotta get my G.E.D or somethin' because them day labor jobs ain't cutting it. Shit ain't been the same since—well, you know." He averted his gaze and shrugged his shoulders.

I nodded my head.

Since I got out of prison and he had to stop workin' with Cutta.

"They keep pickin' my ass up for silly shit. I think they just like fuckin' with me. I pissed dirty the other week and my fuckin' P.O. locked me up for a whole fuckin' month!"

"She might think you prefer it there as much as you stay locked up!" Poochie clowned him.

"Fuck outta here!" he chided with a laugh and slapped her on her ass hard. "Go fix a nigga an egg or somethin'. Shit, I'm hungry as fuck!"

"Nigga, fuck you!"

"I did and now you pregnant."

They continued to joke back and forth but I wasn't there. I didn't see any of it. My mind was instantly jammed with images of my mama's dead body, bloodied and lifeless as I held her while sitting on her kitchen floor. My veins pumped adrenaline, my heart began to race and my trigger-finger twitched. My mind began to chant lethal instructions, urging me to do what I'd come here to do.

"Come go for a ride with a nigga," I said casually, not wanting to let on to him that anything was wrong.

"What's going on?" The smile dropped from his face and his eyes narrowed on me. He was trying to read my demeanor.

"Nothing, I just want to holla at you about something, son. You can come right back."

Lies.

We drove into Queens and took 678 on the Van Wyck expressway as silence stewed all around us.

"Damn, we going a long way out," Rayshaun commented and

reached into my ashtray, removing a partially smoked blunt. Young Jeezy was bumping through the speakers as smoke began to rise. Finally, I broke my silence.

"So, where you been the last few days, yo?"

Rayshaun sighed and shook his head, letting the smoke flow out slowly through his nostrils.

"A nigga been on his dick. I been doin' bad, man."

"Somebody told me you asked about my mama... Asked where she stayed at. Why you ain't ask me that shit?"

"Man, stop it! I *tried* to call your ass about four times and you wasn't picking up. I had my shorties with me. It's been a minute since we let the kids kick it and I wanted them to meet Imani. I know she was fucked up after Quisha disappeared and I am her godfather after all. I thought it would be good for them to play together."

I shook my head curtly as I continued to drive on.

"I ain't get no calls from you, fam."

"Well, I—I did call you," he started to stammer, fidgeting with the blunt that was still burning in his fingers. "I even left a message! Check your voicemail, nigga. I swear I called. It kept goin' to voicemail... it was a couple days back before I got locked up for them couple days. I even saw your lady and asked her how to get up with you!"

Keeping silent, I thought back to how LeTavia had broken my phone and I couldn't see who was calling. Maybe he did call? I tried to make sense of it in my mind but my rage had pushed me too far. All I knew was that my mama was gone, my family had been touched, and all arrows pointed to Rayshaun as having something to do with it.

"But I been callin' you too, nigga," I told him, thinking about how I'd been blowing his phone up for days. "You ain't answered once."

"Man, my shit got turned off! I told you I was down bad. I'm using one of them Obama phones right now… them free government phones. I popped up at the club and gave the number to E and told him to give it to you when he saw you!"

He had an excuse for everything.

I saw a makeshift shack on a desolated dirt road right next to an abandoned junkyard. That day, the city was heavy with thick billowing fog, causing a gray ominous hue to hover nearly blocking out the sky, like an eclipse of the sun.

A perfect day for a murder.

Turning, I drove right under an old tree and placed the car in park.

"So, tell me something… when they locked you up the last time, was you fuckin' with Cutta? Must've been hard to survive in there being my nigga when, from what I heard, he runnin' shit in there."

Rayshaun sat all the way up in his seat and looked at me with a startled expression.

"Man, what's this all about—"

"Nigga, just answer the fuckin' question!" I said, pulling out my pistol.

"Nigga, you buggin'!"

"Answer the fucking question!" I looked around and saw I was close to 142nd. There was an abandoned graveyard over there. It would be his final resting place.

"Yeah… yeah… I ran into him. He was up there in Riker's with me before he got transferred. I saw him a couple of times in the chow hall and in the gym."

"What y'all talk about?"

"What all da one hunnid questions for, B?"

Click!

I cocked the gun and aimed it at him.

"Are you fuckin' serious right now, nigga? It's me… Ray. We almost blood, nigga!" he began to tremble as he looked at me, so tense that veins were popping out from his neck. The blunt continued to smolder between his fingers. I noticed his hand shaking.

"Just answer the fuckin' question!"

"Yeah, I saw him in there but BK niggas ain't really fuckin' with them Harlem clowns like that! So, we ain't talk 'bout shit!"

"How you get that blood on your paints?"

"B—blood? What blood, B?" he asked, throwing up both his hands in despair. He followed my eyes to his pants and flinched.

"M—m—man, I swear that ain't blood, that's paint yo! I told you I be paintin' and shit, tryin' to stack my chips."

My phone chimed right before it started ringing through my Bluetooth speakers. I peeked at the caller ID on the dash and saw it was Trigga. After glancing at my watch, I knew exactly what he was calling about. But Rayshaun had saw who was calling too and before

I could stop him, he pressed the green button on the center dash to answer his call.

"TRIGGA!"

"Nigga, I just wanna say I'm sorry. I heard what happened to your ol' girl," Trigga said, not realizing it was Rayshaun who had answered his call.

"Trigga, help me, man! This nigga got me in the car finna murk me on some fuck shit I don't know nothin' about. Help me, man, help!"

"Shut the fuck up, nigga!" Raising my fist in the air, I brought it down and cracked Rayshaun right at the top of his head. He dropped back in his seat, blood flowed down his forehead like a waterfall as his eyes fluttered irregularly.

"Who is that? I know it ain't Rayshaun, our homie. Not the nigga we grew up with!"

"Yeah, that's him," I answered dryly. "He finna be dead soon. I'm doin' this for my mama."

"Man, that nigga would never cross you like that! We grew up together. Trust me, Gunplay. You need to think this shit through. Stop bein' so fuckin' emotional, nigga, and get control of yourself!"

Of all my homies, Trigga understood me the most. I hated that shit. We were different in so many ways but in many others, we were alike. The same demons in me that urged me to kill were in him. The same way I didn't give a fuck about pullin' the trigger on a muthafucka, the same way it got my dick hard just watchin' the life leave a nigga's eyes... it was the same for him too. He could just control it better. He could squash the urge so that he could rationalize the situation. I couldn't. And I wouldn't.

"Take a deep breath, nigga. You need to settle your mind so you can think this shit through? You got a blunt on you? Matter of fact—where the fuck you at?! Let me meet you. If you so sure this nigga did somethin' to your moms, I need to handle this shit with you too."

He was baiting me. Stalling for time.

"SHUT THE FUCK UP!" I roared so loud that my head throbbed like I'd burst a blood vessel. "Stop fuckin' with my head, nigga!"

The boisterous sound of my voice brought Rayshaun back to full consciousness and he sat up straight in his seat, looking around confused as he mopped up the blood on his face with the sleeve of his shirt. He frowned down at it and I saw his face go pale as he began to remember the situation he'd found himself in.

"It's lights out, nigga," I taunted him and he flinched, turning to me with wide eyes as if he were seeing me for the first time.

"Don't do it, man!" Trigga continued his plea through the speakers. "You making a big mistake and if you hurt him, Gunplay, I ain't never gon' forgive your ass for that shit! Listen to me, just—"

I cut the phone off abruptly and turned around in my seat to face Rayshaun, to get a good look in his eyes. I was in search of any trace of treason. Deceit. Betrayal.

My phone rang again. It was Trigga. I ignored the call and then turned the ringer off.

"DeShaun, listen… yo' mama is like a mother to me. I'd never hurt her! She fed me; let me stay at her house when my mama was fucked up on dope. Man, please don't do this to me! Don't kill me, please!"

Without batting an eye to address his request, I moved on.

"E-Class told me you called him. He said you asked him about some hit Cutta had on me. You inquired 'bout the money on my head."

"Man, I don't know nothin' 'bout that! I swear on my sons' lives. You gotta believe me! I would never betray our trust! Last time I talked to E-Class, I asked him to give you my new number so I could holla at you 'bout some work. He told me you ain't wanna talk to me because you was still pissed 'bout that fake ass muthafucka I brought you to do business with so I should give you some space! I swear I ain't know that nigga was wearing a wire! I fucked some bitch named Chakeeta—"

"Chakeeta?" I cut in, my ears perked up. "Chakeeta or Shaquita?"

Rayshaun's voice wavered terribly as he responded. "M—man, I don't even really know. She had a badass body like a stripper. I—I had saw E-Class talking to her a few times, thought she worked there. She's who I got the info to him from. She said that she was messin' with some Haitian dude who used to cop his dope from him. I knew you was lookin' for a connect... I was tryin' to help you! Only thing I wanted was to get shit like how it was—when you and me ran the streets together! Don't' kill me, man, I'd never turn on you!"

Rayshaun broke down and began to cry but I didn't respond. My mind was on Shaquita. Her name was coming up too much for it to be a coincidence. She was connected to all this shit... she was probably playing us all. She tried to set me up with a case through using Rayshaun and ended up getting at Cutta, she used me to go at the

Haitian for some cash and now she had tricked E-Class into working with her. She was probably trying to get in good enough with him to tap the safe and steal the rest of the cash. She knew she couldn't get nowhere with me since I had cussed her ass out for asking me to be her sponsor. So, E-Class was her next plan. I looked at the blood on his pants again and shifted the gun in my hand to the other.

"That may be true. E-Class has no reason to lie on you though… and you been locked up with Cutta."

Then suddenly something else occurred to me. And it was what made all the difference.

"Imani told me she saw you… she said that she recognized one of the men who killed my moms. She said it was one my friends. But she only seen you and E-Class before. Nobody else been trusted around my seed like that, fam."

"I'on know, nigga." Tears began to trickle down his face as he started to come to terms with his fate. "I'on know why E-Class would say that, man. And I don't know who Imani saw but it wasn't me."

I felt a pang of sympathy for him and almost put away my gun. But then I looked down at the blood on his pants leg and an image flashed before my eyes. My mama, on the floor dying. My eyes filled with tears and I gritted my teeth together right before everything before me went red.

God help me.

Blocka!

I shot Rayshaun right in the face, the bullet entered right below his right cheek. The sound resonated like a cannon in the small confines of the car as it exited out the back of his head, shattering the window. Then the most eerie thing happened. His legs began to twitch as his body went into convulsions.

I freaked the fuck out! When I gave a nigga one to the dome, it was meant to be the quick ending to a lethal situation. But Rayshaun was *still* alive, moving in jerky motions, making a gurgling sound with his terror-filled eyes focused in on me.

"Fuck!"

I froze, watching him in utter amazement. And then there was a loud, clanging sound followed by the noise a car made when it backfired. I looked up and saw some type of security guard truck coming my way, slowly staggering up the steep hill. Rayshaun continued to kick and thrash while squealing in pain, making a horrific noise, so high-pitched that only dogs should hear. The screen on my phone illuminated. Trigga had sent a text.

Don't kill him. You got a rat but it's not him. Trust me.

Just as the truck neared, I drove away with Rayshaun kicking and gurgling to my side. The acid scent of his blood was heavy in my nostrils and quickly spread through the inside of the car, bringing with it the sour reminder of the same scent that had overpowered the inside of my mama's house.

I got back on highway 678 with Rayshaun on the passenger side, breathing and wheezing still although he wasn't moving as much. I had to do what needed to be done but the sight of him struggling hurt me to the core. I just needed to find a place to put another bullet in his brain so that I could end his misery.

About ten minutes down the road, I decided to check my voicemail after seeing that LeTavia called me. The sound of her voice through the Bluetooth speakers wasn't nearly as comforting as being with her in person, but I felt the calming effect she had on me set in, making it easier for me to drive on.

The blunt that Rayshaun had lit was still sitting on the middle console, burning. I reached over and grabbed it just as LeTavia's message ended. But I grabbed the wrong end and it burned the shit out of me.

"SHIT!"

Like a big ass kid, I stuck my fingers in my mouth to cool the singe and took a deep breath. But then another voice came through the speakers and my blood went cold.

"Aye, nigga! This Ray... I'on know if you got this number. This my new number, I told E-Class to give it to you but he on some fuck shit. Won't even give me a damn job at the club, you believe that shit?! Anyways, I got this paintin' gig but the shit ain't payin' me nothin'. I got a jit on the way and you know Poochie uppity. It's a lil' girl so she tryna buy her all kinds of shit! You already know she givin' me hell 'bout not bringin' no money in." He chuckled and then sighed deeply. *"I know I fucked up bringin' you that fake ass Colombian nigga... but we blood, fam! I would never intentionally do you wrong. Just hit me up when you get this... I just wanna work with my niggas again and get this money like we used to do. You feel me? One love, bruh."*

Unmoving, I listened to the message, stricken into place by my shock and disbelief. He had called me.

He was innocent.

I closed my fists tight, squeezing the blunt within, not even caring about the sharp, blistering jolt of pain that came when the fire touched my skin. Then I glanced over at Rayshaun who lay quietly with his head pushed between the small space between his seat and the window. Blood gushed from the hole in his cheek, covering his clothes and the inside of my car.

More innocent blood shed because of me.

"FUCK!"

CHAPTER TEN

Le'Tavia

Two Weeks Later

"This nigga must've forgot who da fuck I am," I mumbled as I marched straight into the building of some nice, posh high-rise apartments that I'd seen Gunplay's brand new dark blue Maserati parked outside of. As if driving around in a flashy ass Maserati wasn't enough, he even had double pistols on the plate and in the center of each tire so I could pick up on it anywhere.

He had me fucked up to the fullest. Matter of fact, there probably was not a man on this side of Heaven who ever had a woman more fucked up than Gunplay had me at the moment, but I was about to put things in order real fast.

DeShaun Banks, *my* man, was somewhere in this building, with some basic ass bitch, when he was supposed to be running the streets like the street king he was and coming back home at night to be with the chick who always had his back: ME! But instead of running the

243

streets, he was running up my blood pressure and running his ass all the way across town to chill with some random hoe that I was about to get together real quick.

After being there for him, taking care of Imani, and catering to his every need every single day since his mother was murdered, I started to get suspicious about him cheating again. He was doing a lot of late night texting but when I checked his phone, his texts showed nothing around that time, letting me know he was erasing messages. So, I did what I did the last time and pulled them records up. He'd been texting that Shaquita bitch again, tellin' her about how he was gon' be her 'sponsor'—in other words, a trick, payin' her ass for pussy.

What the fuck?! Can you believe that shit?

The messages had ended with her sending him a text with an address, which explained why after checking his messages, he peeled out of the house, around six in the morning, like he was on fire. As soon as he left, I pulled his messages and saw the address then prayed that he wasn't cheating on me. But as soon as I drove in the parking lot and saw his car in front of the building, I knew it wasn't true.

"Girl, I can't believe he would fuck around after you helped him through everything with his mama... made the arrangements and everything! That bitch he with ain't do shit to help nobody!"

Clicking my tongue, I shook my head somberly. Gunplay was used to women being so happy to be with him that they would sit happily in the position of 'main' bitch just so they could say they had them a fine ass gangsta in their bed at night. But that wasn't me. I didn't want to be the main, I wanted to be only and he would never be able to change that.

"DeShaun might be thinkin' he a thug 'cause he run the streets and shit but he really is just a big fuckin' baby. With me spending time with Imani to make sure she's alright, he probably feelin' neglected enough to run right up into this bitch. He's such a fuckin' liar and I hate that shit! It's the same as it was with…"

I didn't even want to say Quisha's name. Obviously, she was never the real problem. It was Gunplay. He had played her like he was playing me, telling us both one thing and then doing another. Now he had grabbed Shaquita and put her in Quisha's place. How could he claim to love me and then be somewhere laying up with this ole dusty strippin' bitch?!

"I'm sorry you gotta go and do this shit alone. I could definitely go for whoopin' some ass right now," Sonya said through my cellphone as I slipped right past the front desk and trotted quickly to the elevator.

"Ain't no need because I'm not gonna show out. I'ma just let him know he's caught and go on 'bout my business."

Sonya laughed. "Hell no, you aren't, Tavi. You *always* show out."

With a sarcastic twirl of my eyes, I stepped onto the elevator, ending the call with Sonya before it dropped. Pursing my lips, I slid off the new designer shades and stepped off the elevator, looking for the room number I'd seen on the text. In the matter of only a couple weeks, my whole way of life had changed. With niggas threatening his family, Gunplay moved the three of us into a brand new house. No… *mansion* would be the better word to describe it. It was beautiful, better than I could have dreamed, with a security system that surpassed whatever

thinking about it.

"What you mean, nigga?" Gunplay snapped, staring right into my face like I was the one in the wrong. "You already makin' a fuckin' scene!"

He stepped out the door and pulled it behind him, then casted a glance down the hall just as the Black woman turned the corner. With my arms folded in front of my chest, I glared at him, ready to go off.

"Tavi," he whispered and then glanced behind him through a crack in the door. "I need you to just trust me right now and leave—"

"WHAT?!"

He flinched, then reached out and snatched my arm into his hand, holding me firmly although it wasn't painful.

"Trust me. I need you to go back downstairs, get in the car, and *go home!*"

I cocked my head to the side and looked at him squarely like he had lost his mind.

"Hell naw, nigga! Move the fuck out the way."

I ducked under his arm and ran right up into the apartment. The Shaquita bitch that he was with was standing right behind him and had the audacity to be glaring back at me like she was gonna do something. Homegirl had heart, that's for sure, because she didn't look scared at all, standing with her hands on her hips, wearing nothing but some lace boy shorts and a bra while shooting a look at me like I was less than the scum at the bottom of a drain. Right as I walked up to her, she opened up her mouth and rolled her eyes as she began to talk.

"I don't wanna fuckin' talk to you! What you *need* to do is get da fuck outta my shi—"

Before she could even finish that sentence, I'd already hauled off and popped her one good time right in the nose. She crumbled in an instance, dropping her face into her hand as she wailed loudly, blood seeping steadily through her fingers. Did she really think I came in here to chat and talk shit?

"Bitch, ain't nobody come here to speak to your stupid ass!" I yelled right before diving on top of her, attacking her with punch after punch to the face and stomach. She was so shocked by the sudden assault that it took her a few seconds to get it together and start coming back with punches of her own. But by that time, I'd already one-upped her ass.

"Tavi! Stop wit'cho crazy ass!" Gunplay yelled, just as I felt him come behind me and grab me around my middle. Using my elbow, I came down on his arm, slamming it against him hard to make him release me.

"Stop this shit, Tavi! Damn! You remember what happened last time you beat a bitch's ass, don't ya?!"

He continued struggling with me, squeezing me harder to get me off his lil' bitch but I had her hair wrapped around my fist and the more he squeezed me, the harder I pulled. She began screaming and tossing punches every way she could but none of them were able to connect. Gunplay already knew what the deal was when I found out he was cheating on me. The least he could've done was get a bitch that could hold her own because this one couldn't fight for shit.

"Tavi, I ain't playin' wit' ya ass! LET GO!" he yelled but I only pulled tighter. The stress of everything happening in my life was getting to me, finally making me angry enough to snap after holding it all in. I felt a few strands of the chick's hair rip from her scalp and she screamed a bloodcurdling wail that was like music to my ears. But then Gunplay twisted around and locked my ass in a headlock, making me release her immediately only to turn on him, trying with all my might to get him off me.

"CALM DA FUCK DOWN!" he roared as he tightened his grip on the headlock. I immediately came to my senses when I saw that he had the upper hand and there wasn't anything I could do to match his strength.

"A'ight!" I yelled, trying to push Gunplay from off of me but he only clamped down tighter.

"Naw, drop ya fuckin' fists and I'll let go," he ordered me, his voice low and just barely audible over the moaning and crying from his side bitch.

Man, I just hope I broke that bitch's jaw, I thought as I listened to her sobs.

"Drop them," he said, once again and finally I listened, tucking my arms to my side.

He released me and I struggled to get myself together, fixing my hair and clothes as I breathed heavily, my anger renewing and increasing the more I looked at him. Standing in front of me with his arms crossed in front of his chest, Gunplay seemed just as put together as he had when he left the house. From the looks of it, I'd caught him before he'd been able to actually fuck the hoe but it didn't take away from the fact that it was what he'd planned to do in the first place.

"Here we are, once a-fuckin-gain, DeShaun!" I snapped on him and he only looked back at me, his eyes narrowed into slits as he glared at me angrily. Can you believe this shit? He was the one cheating but called himself being mad at me!

"Yeah, here we are a-fuckin-gain wit' ya ass showin' da fuck out over some bullshit!" he shot back, his lips pulled back in a sneer.

"Bullshit?! You think this is bullshit? You think I should be straight with the fact that you keep fuckin' cheatin' on me?!"

I paused, waiting for him to answer my question but when he didn't, it just pissed me off even more. My anger built up in me so steadily that soon I was huffing and heaving out my next breaths, my chest rising and falling at an increasing speed. Clicking his tongue, Gunplay shook his head from side-to-side and then turned around, walking away from me and towards Shaquita.

"She *hit* me!" the ugly ass girl was crying. "You let her hit me and—"

"I know, baby. I know."

My mouth dropped wide open when I heard Gunplay refer to that bitch as 'baby'. But imagine how much wider it dropped as I watched him carefully help her off the floor, using some paper towels he'd grabbed on the way, to clean her up. He tended to her every whine, ignoring me completely... like I was the side bitch instead of her.

My heart was broken.

I opened up my mouth and exhaled out a staggered breath. As the air left my lungs, so did my spirit. I felt shattered. My head began to feel heavy and I became dizzy, feeling like I had traveled into another universe. Instead of the girlfriend, the *main* chick, I was the accidental side bitch. This couldn't be happening to me! But when I opened my eyes, I saw Gunplay standing in front of me, his arms cradling his new woman who was standing at his side. With a smirk on her face, she glowered at me as she straightened up her clothes.

"Listen, bae, since she already knows what's up, I'ma take you back to my crib. Tavi, follow us there."

He gave me a look that chilled me to the bone. A glare so strong and twisted that it instantly ignited fear in me. He was nothing like the Gunplay I'd known. My Gunplay wouldn't do this to me.

I don't know why I did it… maybe I was afraid or maybe I was just dumb. Either way, I found myself following right behind Gunplay, not even paying attention to the road. Tears were streaming down my eyes as I drove without regard to anything around me. This couldn't be life. Not my life. I'd been through more hell than anyone should have in my time on Earth and most of it had come about because of my association with Gunplay. Still, I stood by him only for him to do me like this.

I was going to go back and pack my things so I could leave. While he tended to his new woman, I was getting the hell out. I didn't even have much to pack, I still had all my things that I'd left in my old apartment. Maybe it was a blessing. From the day I met him, I'd had a nagging voice in the back of mind telling me that he was dangerous, that I wasn't cut out for this life with him, that it would never be normal no matter how much I loved him and wanted him.

"I'll be just fine," I told myself, wiping the tears from my cheeks. "I can take care of myself, I got money saved. I just gotta get back and…"

It was at that moment that I realized I had no idea where the hell we were. I was still following Gunplay but we were nowhere near the new house. I squinted at my surroundings as Gunplay tapped the brakes, slowing the both of us down to a slow creep. It appeared that we were on some part of town that held all of the manufacturing transplants for the city. The sky was gloomy and dark with only a sliver of light partially illuminating the sky; somewhere in-between evening and night. I looked around, noticing that the area was nearly vacant with the exception of a few stragglers who were wandering about muttering to themselves.

Gunplay turned down a road and I followed him around what felt like over two dozen bends until we pulled up to an open field that looked like a large construction site, cloaked in shadows. He pulled over and I pulled over right behind him, following his lead, and killing my headlights. With my lips parted, I watched with bowl-shaped eyes as Gunplay jumped out of his side of the car and walked right over to me. He stood in front of my window and scowled right into my face, waiting before knocking hard on the glass.

"Get out!"

I heeded his command with alarming speed.

As soon as I stumbled out to my feet, legs wobbling and knees weak, he snatched my arm and jerked me forward, pulling me to the passenger side of his car. My heart was ripping through my chest as I looked around, wondering what he was about to do. Was he going to kill me? Is this how he wanted it to end? He always said there was no breaking up when it came to us… it was 'til death do us part. Obviously, he'd meant every word.

He hastily grabbed the handle of his passenger door and roughly pulled it open. I nearly screamed aloud when I saw Shaquita in the passenger seat with a bullet hole through her forehead. The sheer white dress she'd pulled on before we left was nearly covered in her rubicund blood, still spilling profusely from her injury, splashing a few droplets onto Gunplay's black leather seats.

"*This…*" Gunplay pointed with his bloody hand back to Shaquita's unmoving and lifeless body. "…is why I wanted you to leave."

He glared at me hard and I nearly crumbled from the myriad of emotions that were coursing through my body. The most prevalent one being fear with my need for self-preservation coming in at a close second. I did not want to have anything to do with another murder. I needed to get the hell out of here.

"What did you—why did you…"

"That's why I fuckin' told you to leave! This bitch is responsible for a lot of shit that may have led to my mama gettin' killed. I been tryin' to find her ass for weeks! I finally got her fuckin' number and had to sweet talk this bitch for days just to get her to tell me where the fuck I could meet her ass at. Spent all this fuckin' time tryin' to convince her that I didn't know she was part of that bullshit! All this was a set-up so I could find her and get answers on what she knows about who killed my moms. After that, I was gonna take her away so I could cancel her ass and get on to the next shit. But then here you fuckin' go!"

My eyes ping-ponged between Gunplay and Shaquita. I was freezing cold with my arms crossed in front of me, hands clutching my elbows, but it wasn't because of the temperature outside. I was a nervous wreck and about to have a complete mental breakdown.

"But I—I didn't know. I thought—"

"It doesn't matter what you thought," Gunplay cut in. Then he shook his head and beckoned for me to step forward.

"C'mon. Bring ya ass!"

I frowned lightly, flickering my eyes to him. I was confused by his words and ran them repeatedly over and over in my mind, trying to make sense of them with the part of my brain that hadn't turned to mush.

"Huh?"

"I said *'bring your ass'*!" He bent down next to Shaquita and pulled her out the car, dragging her by one arm. She fell to the ground with a loud *thud*, a sickening sound that I will never forget.

"Help me get her into that building. In there, we are going to chop her up, wrap the pieces up in saran wrap, toss it in a garbage bag, and bury it in that patch of dirt over there." He nudged his chin somewhere behind me.

I teetered, almost fell completely over.

"Help you do what?" He gave me a pointed look. "I—I can't do this. I—I don't want to... I'm scared!"

"See, if you had listened to a nigga, you'd be home sippin' tea or some shit."

I started to cry but Gunplay's facial expression stayed stony and cold. There wasn't a single shred of sympathy in sight.

"This better be the *last* time you don't fuckin' trust me, Tavi. It better be the *last* time you think I don't love you. Yeah, I hurt you before, shawty, but I ain't gon' do that shit no more. You got my word on that. You been the one who has always been there for me. I'll never forget that. Now that's some g-shit for your ass."

I nodded through my tears, squeezing my eyes shut before I wiped them away. He was right. I was trippin' hard. In fact, I was driving myself crazy thinking he was doing shit he wasn't. I had a good nigga in love with my ass and I was about to ruin it. He made a mistake right when he got out of prison but he was trying to get things right. I couldn't punish him forever.

"Okay." I nodded, gasping out a small sob.

"Good." He returned my nod with one of his own and then turned to look down at Shaquita's body. "Now let's go."

I didn't move a thing but my bottom lip, which dropped wide open in disbelief, an obvious indication of my internal thoughts. He still wanted me to help? Wasn't this little lesson over now that I understood his point?

But with Gunplay, there was no zero understanding of anything outside of what he commanded. Coming over to me, he waved his hand in front of my face, making me wince. And then there was a grimace when I glanced down at Shaquita's body. It was like déjà vu. Here I was in another Quisha-type situation once again, disposing of another dead body.

"Hurry up before somebody fuckin' see us!" Gunplay's warning scared me and I nearly jumped out of my skin. "Next time, I suggest you trust me."

I will, I thought as I leaned down and grabbed one of Shaquita's arms.

It felt cold and stiff in my hands. I began to feel nauseated and my stomach flopped. Swallowing down the sour-tasting bile at the back of my throat, I reached down and grabbed the other. Gunplay's eyes pierced through mine as we began to move quickly, cloaked by the night, towards the place where we'd butcher her into pieces. He was holding most of her weight but she was still heavy as a thousand bricks. Damn, I wish I'd stayed home. I wish I had trusted him.

I vowed this would be the last time I didn't.

We were approaching our destination, an old forgotten about shack of a place that, to the untrained eye, looked like an abandoned shelter for rats, roaches, and whatever other disgusting, creepy, crawling creature may have decided to take residence there. But one thing I'd learned from dealing with Gunplay was that nothing was ever exactly as it seemed.

"Drop her," he told me and I eagerly did just as he asked. A few of her fingers grazed my open toes and it startled me, jumping backwards with what was probably supernatural speed, being that I was still wearing my stiletto heels. Gunplay glanced at me, his stone face breaking as a smirk crossed his face.

"Oh, I thought you was big and bad, now you wanna act all scary and shit. Ain't nothin' to fear 'bout the dead."

I pursed my lips and didn't say a word as I watched him reach down and tap something under a slab of cement near the door. A keypad revealed itself and he entered a code, then there was a clicking noise and the heavy steel door was open.

Hours later, we were ready to leave and I felt like shit. I hadn't done a single thing once we got Shaquita's body in the building, as I'm sure Gunplay knew I wouldn't. While he handled and disposed of her body, I took constant trips back and forth to the small bathroom located inside to throw up until I was left with absolutely nothing in my stomach. Even still, the nausea remained and I dry-heaved into the empty toilet bowl.

"In a few minutes, we can go."

After showering and changing up his clothes, Gunplay walked over to me looking and smelling good, perfectly put together and eerily calm for someone who had just murdered, butchered, and buried someone. He was pure goon, unmoved by the stench of death or any aspects of it. He carried on like it was just a normal day. I guess to him, it was.

He glanced at his watch and I lifted a tired brow, almost too fatigued and worn out to speak.

"Why can't we go now?" I whined but he didn't reply.

About ten minutes later, he was texting someone on his phone when I heard movement at the door and I started to panic. My adrenaline shot through the roof and I jumped to my feet, my heart slamming in my chest, and my eyes darting around for a place to hide. Then I focused on Gunplay who was sitting totally calm, eyes on me with his lip curled up and a crazy expression on his face.

"Tavi, sit yo' crazy ass down, nigga! You gotta learn how to calm the fuck down if you gonna be rollin' with me. Damn... you the type to fuck around and get a nigga locked up. Just chill!"

Still trembling, I fell back into the small chair that I'd been sitting in and turned my attention to the steel door that was now being pulled open. Who was it? What was about to happen?

God, I swear I can't see somebody else get killed today. I won't be able to fuckin' take it!

LaTavia

The door opened and in walked three men I'd never seen before. I cowered in the corner as I watched them step in, each of them carrying two big, heavy duffle bags in their hands. All of them had that same thug appeal that instantly attracted me to Gunplay. It was like they didn't have to say a single word or do a single thing to show you they were deadly, bold and fearless. They strode in the building with all the confidence of kings and all the swag of the street niggas they were. No introduction was needed.

Then one of them stepped forward, laughing a little as he surveyed the area, his nose high in the air. I frowned at him, my interest instantly piqued. He looked curiously like Gunplay, with long loose hair pulled in a ponytail that flowed down his back. He was covered with tattoos everywhere but his beautiful, smooth-brown face and sported a mouth full of gold teeth, just like Gunplay. His style was impeccable, flashy and, I had to admit it, sexy. He upper body was covered in jewelry that adorned his ears, neck, and both wrists… Damn, he had to be wearing at least a couple hundred grand in gold.

I pulled my eyes away from him quickly, not wanting my crazy ass nigga to catch me ogling another man. But damn, he was fine. And if Gunplay had never become a necessity in my life, there was no doubt in my mind that *this nigga* could get it!

"Damn, fam. It's stank as fuck in this bitch!" the man exclaimed right as he walked in. Then stopped in his tracks and narrowed his eyes at Gunplay before turning slightly and glancing at me. I almost blushed from the intensity in his face as he ran something around in his mind.

"Ah shit… you done chopped somebody up in this bitch, huh?" he asked with a smirk on his face. "Cuz, you know big bruh gon' mollywhop you on yo' muthafuckin' ass for that shit! This our *stash* spot and where we conduct bidness… no bodies in this bitch, nigga!"

Gunplay chuckled heartily as the guy dropped the duffle bags on a large metal table in the center of the room, the same one that had just been covered in blood before he'd cleared it of Shaquita's body and its remains.

"You know I don't give a fuck what Kane tell me to do!" Gunplay laughed. The other one laughed too as they bumped their fists.

"Aye, you know I don't either."

Then another one stepped forward and his ass was sexy too. He had skin a couple shades lighter than the other one, light eyes with his curly hair cut low on his head. Draped around his neck was a pair of Beats headphones, blasting some trap song. He dropped his bags on the table and greeted Gunplay by slapping his hand and giving him a half-hug.

"Y'all know Kane be makin' them rules and shit to look out for us. It ain't a bad thing," he added right before the last popped in, snatching Gunplay's arms before doing some fancy handshake, bumping their fists three quick times in row like they were best friends reunited.

"NIGGA! What's good?!" the last one greeted him.

And I know you think I'm lyin' but his ass was sexy too! He had a bright ass yellow complexion and was dressed like a hood model, perfectly put together in a way that I could barely explain. He was a true pretty boy, his edge up was crafted to perfection, his shoes matched his shirt, socks matched both colors in his jeans, fitted cap matched every damn thing… Who the hell were these niggas and why was I just seeing them for the first time?!

"Aye y'all, I need y'all to meet somebody," Gunplay started, turning his attention to me. The eyes of the other three men followed and I felt a little self-conscious about my appearance. I sat up straight, forgetting all about how miserable I had been feeling only moments before.

"This my lady, Tavi. Tavi, these my cousins… blood cousins," he boasted with a smile. "I don't get to chill with these niggas too often because they think they too good since they got college degrees and shit but—"

"Get da fuck outta here wit' all dat bullshit, fam," the one with the golds joked. "Naw, he don't chill wit' us because he stay gettin' mad at me for pullin' all the bad bitches!"

My eyes widened and I looked at Gunplay who jabbed the guy in the shoulder. They both laughed.

"My bad," the guy added. "I guess since you his lady and all, we might hear from his ass more often."

"This—" Gunplay jabbed his thumb at the one with the golds. "—Is my lil' cousin who we call Outlaw." Then he pointed first to the one with the headphones and then the pretty boy. "This is Cree and this right here is Young Yellow but we call him Yolo."

Cree and Yolo came up and politely greeted me with a handshake. Outlaw, however, stood back with his chin balanced on his fist while he shamelessly looked me up and down while licking his lips. Feeling awkward under his stare, I froze and shot my eyes over to Gunplay who had a confused look on his face, also waiting to see what was up with his cousin.

"Aye, she fine as hell, Gunplay! Who knew you could pull somethin' like this!" Outlaw said finally. He walked over and held his hand out for mine. I placed it in his, shaking it gently but then he pulled it to his lips and gave me a light kiss. I blushed.

"Nigga, get da fuck off my bi—woman!" Gunplay snapped, pushing Outlaw away but he only laughed, keeping his eyes on me.

"Listen... you got a sister that look like you or somethin'? A twin?"

I mired, glanced over at Gunplay, Cree, and Yolo who stood silently watching and then nodded my head.

"Yes... I mean, she's not my twin though. Sh—she's younger than me."

"Jailbait young?" he questioned with his eyes wide. "Like almost eighteen?"

I nodded. "She's about to be a senior."

"Oh." He paused for a minute and then looked away for a second before his eyes came back to mine, a light flickering within them.

"Well, as long as you don't snitch on my ass, I'm good. Tell her I said what's up—"

"Nigga! Stop settin' appointments up for your dick and let's get down to business!" Cree jumped in, slapping Outlaw on the back.

They all laughed and turned towards the duffle bags on the table but I was still in a state of shock. I couldn't erase the boggled expression from my face. I'd only spent a few hours doing this street shit with Gunplay and it was much too long. His ass was crazy and so was everyone else who ran with him. Then suddenly, Yolo turned to me, obviously the most sensitive one of them all—the only one to try and provide me some comfort as I sat in my seat, stricken, awkward, and praying to be anywhere but there.

"Don't worry nothin' 'bout that crazy nigga. Luke ain't got 'em all but, being with Gunplay, you should know how that is, right?" I nodded my head slowly, assuming that Luke was Outlaw's real name.

"And, most importantly, I ain't 'bout to let Outlaw's ass fuck around with my future sis-in-law," Gunplay shot over his shoulder as they pulled out a few things from inside the bags. Guns… every kind imaginable, the duffle bags were packed full of them and everything you needed to go along with it. There was a war about to be waged in the Brooklyn and Gunplay now had everything he needed.

"Lil' sis might like bein' turned out!" Outlaw joked and I pushed my lips tightly together, fighting the urge to cuss his ass out for even suggesting something like that about Nori. "If she ain't been already."

That was it. I had to say something.

"My sister is *not* a hoe!"

He turned to me, smiling bright, in a way that made my stomach flutter a small bit. Now, I wasn't crazy… he was sexy so my body reacted to that but I would *never* in my life try to do anything with him. Gunplay was a handful enough for me.

"She ain't no hoe, huh? Well, maybe I can make her wifey."

"Nigga, stop yo' lyin'! You ain't never gon' settle down," Gunplay joked as they closed up the duffle bags. "Every time I see you out somewhere, you wit' a new bitch."

Outlaw cocked his head to the side and thoughtfully ran two fingers along the small piece of hair right under his bottom lip.

"Aye, I might one day," he said in a low voice. But in the next second, he frowned up his face and started to laugh. "Naw, I'm lyin' like a muthafucka. Fuck bitches, get money. That's the muthafuckin' motto, right, fam?"

With a devilish smirk, he looked at Gunplay who only smiled before placing his eyes on me, staring at me dreamily.

"I'on know nothin' 'bout that life no' more, cuz."

He licked his lips and I squeezed my thighs tightly together. Damn, even after the crazy ass day we'd had, he was stirring up all of my most erotic emotions.

All four men grabbed the duffle bags and placed them in the trunk of Gunplay's car before helping him clean up all the traces of Shaquita's blood that remained outside. They poured some kind of liquid on the ground to kill even the traces of it that we couldn't see. After that, they piled up in their ride and each of us jumped in ours. It was time to go and I couldn't have been more relieved. As soon as I was in the car, I called Gunplay.

"How come I never met them before?" I asked him after I was able to breathe a little bit easier. We were now a good distance away from the warehouse.

"I don't really fuck with none of my family members like that," he explained. "But I fuck with them niggas the long way, even though we don't meet up too much. I got a lot of peoples but my mama was like the black sheep and it was my doing. I did so much shit in my past that most of our relatives ain't want shit to do with either one of us. I got brothers and sisters you don't even know. Them three, and their brothers Kane, Tank, and Tone, the only ones I fuck with."

"If y'all both runnin' the streets and shit, why y'all don't do it together?"

"Because they don't do the shit I do. The drug game is my area. Them niggas ain't into movin' no work… they take shit. Guns, cars, money, gold bricks… anything they can scheme up a way to grab, they go and get that shit. Our businesses cross whenever I need to cop some artillery and that's it. They smart as hell, every single one of them went to college and got degrees so they can't be stopped."

Interesting, I thought. I was intrigued.

"What can I say? Boss niggas just run in my fam." He could hear him through the phone smiling boastfully, his ego on max. I rolled my eyes and sighed.

"Whatever, nigga. I just can't wait to get home so I can get some fuckin' sleep. I'm done strollin' the streets with you."

CHAPTER ELEVEN

Gunplay

As mad as I was at LeTavia for the shit she'd pulled following me to Shaquita's house, I had to admit that watching her ass was funny as hell. She was nuttin' up completely. In fact, she had me feeling like I needed to get her home quick because I wasn't certain that she wouldn't lose her damn mind. But I needed to teach her a lesson, it was a hard one to learn but she needed it.

When it came to street niggas like me, it was important for a woman to stay in her fuckin' place. It was important for her to trust me. Doing the opposite could get her killed or worse. She had to understand that. And, from looking at the terrified look on her face when I made her help me with Shaquita, it seemed to me that she finally got it.

"I just want to take a shower and lay the hell down. I don't want to bothered or touched, I need to get all that crazy shit out of my mind's eye," she said right as we got to the house. We'd been out all night and now it was nearly nine the next morning. She jumped out the car and stomped right up the steps, walking through the front door before I even had a chance to get out.

Following behind her, I walked inside as well. But relaxing and lying down may have been on LeTavia's list of things to do but it was not on my mind. My spirit was unsettled and my mind wasn't at ease. It would be that way until I figured out which bold ass muthafucka had the guts to lay his hands on my family. I had a lot to figure out after getting Shaquita's dying statement and I needed to make sense of it all.

According to her, everything on her end had been about money. She was a hoodrat through and through, always looking for a way to make a buck without regards to what she had to do or what consequences came out of it. According to her, she was offered a couple grand just for connecting the Colombian up with Rayshaun and then even more after connecting him with Cutta once I refused to work with him. She swore over and over that she didn't know anything about who murdered my moms, but whether she was telling the truth or not about that, I'd never know. Even if she had no parts of it, she had almost gotten me locked up for life over a couple grand and I couldn't trust her to not set me up in the future just to line her pockets up. She was a dangerous woman and she had to go.

However, now I was back at square one.

"Aye, what you doin', babygirl?"

With a smile on my face, I sat down right next to my daughter as she flipped through the television stations, trying to find something to watch. I nodded my head in greeting to Sonya who was lying on the couch adjacent to Imani, flipping through the pages of a magazine.

"Nothing," she said with a shrug. She didn't even look in my direction but I could see her sad eyes from where I stood. Leaning over, I gave her a kiss on the forehead and then stood up to walk to the room to take a shower. I had cleaned up at the warehouse but another one wouldn't hurt.

"After I get out, we are going to take a ride... have a little fun. You down for that?"

Smiling, she turned to me and nodded her head excitedly, her pretty little eyes lit up like Christmas lights.

"Where are we going to go?"

"Wherever you want to. You say the word and I'll make it happen," I told her as I walked down the hall.

"Okay, well, I'm going to get on out of here now that y'all are back," Sonya said with a sigh. "This nigga been blowing up my fuckin' phone since last night."

"Word?" I replied without a shred of real interest but not wanting to be rude. "Well, just make sure that nigga treatin' you right."

I grabbed my phone and started sending out a text to Gunna to let him know that I was going to hang out with Imani and get with them later on that night. In the background, I heard Sonya chattering on, mistaking my presence for my attention.

"He is... I just have to allow myself to relax enough to let a new man into my life. This is the first time I'm thinking of being serious with someone without having him meet my dad..."

Her voice trailed off and I looked up, right into her eyes. Guilt built up in my chest, making it uncomfortably tight. I was the reason her father was gone.

"Listen… I can't change the past. If I could I would but I want you to know that I appreciate you for never blamin' for that shit that happened with your pops. Real shit, we both know that I share the blame—" She shook her head dismissively but I continued. "I do, and I'm man enough to accept that shit. But because of that, I'll always be here for you. Even if me and Tavi break up for some stupid ass reason, you can always depend on me and I put that on God. It's my word and my word is bond. So, bring that nigga around next time I see you and I'll check his ass thoroughly to make sure he ain't with no fuckery. Good?"

She smiled genuinely, her entire face lighting up. "Thank you. You don't know how much I appreciate that. I really do."

Before I could say anything further, Imani cut in.

"See?! There it is, Daddy—that man has the teardrops, too. Except they are on his face!"

"What teardrops?" I asked, frowning as I walked over to where Imani was and looked at the TV screen.

It looked like she had come across some show on HBO showing some prison yard and some fake ass gangsta lookin' niggas walking back and forth grilling each other like they wanted to start some shit. The one she was referring to was light-skinned with a trail of teardrops along the side of his face. Just as I focused on the screen, the light-skinned one pulled out a shank to jab another guy with and Imani gasped, placing her hands to her face. Tears filled up in her beautiful eyes.

"Maybe we should change this…" Sonya said, grabbing the

remote from her and flipping the channel.

"It's the same as the man who hurt Grandma," Imani cried out, tears immediately streaking down her tiny cheeks. "He has them on his face though but it's the same…"

I frowned, narrowed my eyes and walked in closer to Imani. Something she said had thrown me for a loop.

"What do you mean he had them on his face though? The man who killed---I mean, the man who hurt Grandma didn't have them on his face?"

Wiping the tears from her eyes, she shook her head softly.

"No… they were on his arm."

His arm? I thought, completely perplexed. Who the hell puts teardrops on their damn arm? Imani must've been mistaking. But it didn't matter because either way, it didn't get me any closer to figuring out who it was. Reaching out, I grabbed her up into my arms and held her tightly in a hug, rubbing her back until her crying began to subside.

"Calm down, Imani. Let me take a quick shower and then we're out of here. We'll do something fun, okay? Just calm down…"

She nodded her head and I placed her carefully down back on the couch. Grabbing the remote, I turned to the Disney channel, peeled off a few big face bills for Sonya to thank her for looking over Imani while LeTavia and I were away and then walked down the hall.

I needed to be running up and down the streets, wreaking the utmost havoc, but I couldn't stand seeing my daughter sad. My only role in life was to protect her and keep her happy but I was fucking up with that in the highest sense. I was all she had now… I had to figure out how to be a full-time dad and a part-time goon. That shit was going to take some adjustment.

"Damn, shawty, what yo' name is?" I teased LeTavia as I came in the bedroom and closed the door behind me, seeing her standing naked in the middle of the room.

"Don't even try that cute shit with me, DeShaun! I'm looking for a hair-tie to get my hair up and then I'm getting in the shower to wash the last twenty-four hours off of me. I still can't believe that you actually made me be involved in that crazy ass shit after…"

She continued ranting even after she'd walked inside of the master bathroom and closed the door behind her. I chuckled and collected my clothes and other items I needed so that I could shower in the other bathroom down the hall.

After cleaning up and getting dressed, I decided to check the messages on my phone. There were a few text messages from a few people on my team, giving me updates on some things I had them working on but nothing I wanted to hear. I saw I had a voicemail message and listened to it, the entire time feeling stressed as hell. Still, I didn't want LeTavia or Imani to see me like that so I kept shit strong for them.

"Aye, Imani… you ready?"

When I came into the living room, Sonya was still there. Imani was sitting between her legs on the floor as Sonya braided up her hair in a fly ass design. Something that Quisha used to do. In fact, I hadn't seen Imani's long hair braided up in that way since Quisha had done it last.

"Aww, Daddy, I really want Aunty Ya-Ya to finish my hair. She does it just like Mommy used to do it, except she doesn't have any beads."

I looked at my watch and then back at Imani. "Maybe she can finish it later. We have to get going now… I gotta make a quick stop and then maybe we can check out a movie or something."

Imani rolled her eyes and gave me a smirk. "Daddy, you don't like seeing the movies I like to see. And I really want to get my hair finished… and with the beads in them. Can you just wait for a little while?"

I stood silently, torn between my duties as a father who needed to spend time with my daughter and my duties as a father who needed to protect my daughter. I couldn't sit still and wait because I didn't have time to waste. Spending two hours at the movies was something I was willing to do to make Imani smile but I'd be lying if I said it didn't push shit back. Sonya must've seen the conflicting thoughts in my mind through my eyes.

"How about you do whatever it is that you need to do while I finish up Imani's hair? We can go to the store to get some beads and then I'll meet you somewhere so you can pick her up and have your time together."

"I thought you were going to go meet up with your nigga," I replied but she shook her head.

"I'm not going to rush over there just because he wants me to. He doesn't own me and I don't have anything else to do."

I thought on that for a few minutes and then nodded my head.

"Sounds good."

LeTavia slipped behind me and sauntered towards the kitchen, leaving in her wake, the sweet scent of Jasmine. I grabbed her by her arm and pulled her back towards me, pressing her soft body against mine.

"I'll be back," I told her and then laid a kiss on her soft lips. I felt my manhood rising up, ready to convince me that I needed to stay but I simply stepped back, creating some distance between us before things got out of control.

"Okay," she replied, her eyes searching mine for an answer. I stared back at her with a blank face, not saying anything but I knew she picked up on the words I didn't say anyways.

"Just be careful. I'll be here when you get back."

I nodded my head, walked over to kiss Imani on her forehead, and then I was out.

Less than thirty minutes later, I was pulling up to one of the last places that I wanted to be. But I had no choice.

"You been in there yet?" I asked Trigga as soon as I walked up to him. He pressed his lips together firmly and shook his head 'no'. There was fire in his eyes, and although he didn't say anything, I could feel his fury.

"The doctor just walked out of there... told me it was touch and go at this point."

"Fuck," I cursed, feeling a pain in my chest. "This shit got me feeling fucked up for real... I just can't believe I did this shit."

Trigga sighed but didn't say another word as he took the lead and walked inside of the hospital room that stood before us. I followed quietly behind, feeling a sense of dread come over me. For the first time in a long time, I felt like I had no control over my own life. Other muthafuckas were around me calling all the shots, leaving me only reacting to the bullshit.

"You have thirty minutes," an attractive and petite brown-skinned nurse said just as my feet passed over the threshold into the room.

I nodded my head at her. "We won't be that long."

It was dark inside, the blinds were closed and the only light came from the small television on the upper part of the wall. It was playing but there was no sound. The entire room was quiet except for the light beeping of the machines all around the bedside, everything working together to keep him alive. The bullet I'd shot into him had went in through his cheek and pushed straight out right behind his ear, miraculously avoiding any major areas that would have ended his life.

He was lucky.

"Damn, Ray..." Trigga said as he walked over and looked at him.

Rayshaun was in a coma, but to us, he already looked dead. His skin seemed slightly discolored and dry but there was a peaceful look on his face. His hands were clasped on top of his midsection as if he'd been positioned to be pushed from the bed and right into the casket.

"I swear I didn't know..." I paused and shook my head somberly. This wasn't how this was supposed to be. I was fucking up bad— murking niggas who had always been there for me.

"E-Class come up here to see him?" Trigga asked with one brow lifted. There was a serious look in his eyes but I had the impression that he was asking me for a reason beyond just making small talk.

"I'on know. E been out of town on business. He left before the shit went down with my moms. I haven't even talked to him to tell him what happened or to know if he's back."

Trigga clenched his jaw and looked down at Rayshaun and then back to me. He licked his lips and sighed, making me focus all of my attention on him. There was something he needed to tell me and from the looks of it, it wasn't good.

"Look, nigga, I'ma be real wit' you right now. I ain't feelin' like—"

"What the *hell* are you doing here?!"

Frowning, I turned around to stare at the source of the voice and was shocked when I saw Poochie, standing with both of her sons holding her hands, her protruding belly looking even larger than when I'd seen her a few weeks before.

"Poochie, what you mean? I'm—"

"I know this happened to him because of *you!*" she declared, releasing her oldest son's hand so that she could jab her pointer finger at me accusingly. Her beautiful face was curled up into a malicious sneer as she walked slowly but steadily towards me, the entire time I got the impression that she was like a volcano getting precariously close to the moment when she would blow.

"I know you did this. I don't know why but I know you did and you're not going to fuckin' tell me anything different! How could you?! All he's ever done is be a friend to you! A friend who needed you but you abandoned him when he was at his lowest moments! He never had one bad thing to say to you even after he reached out over and over again and you refused to answer his calls!"

I placed my hands up, my eyes darting from her face down to the boys that I'd regarded as my nephews, who were staring at me with accusations and hate in their eyes. What had she told them about me?

"Poochie, listen... all I knew was—"

"I don't give a fuck about what you have to say!"

And with that, she lunged forward, using her long nails like talons and scratched me right across my face. Trigga jumped in between us and grabbed her around her waist, pulling her away as she screamed, kicked, and punched, trying with all her might to reach me.

"I FUCKIN' HATE YOU! I KNOW YOU DID THIS! I KNOW IT WAS YOU!"

I ran my hands through my locs and looked from her to the boys who were glaring at me. Young boys that Rayshaun had raised to be future goons. Future goons who would think of me as the man who tried to kill their father. Or the one who killed him, if Rayshaun didn't make it.

"Gunplay, you gotta go, nigga," Trigga told me as he continued to hold Poochie tight, struggling to keep her from coming at me. She calmed down and started to sob, loud, tormenting wails that chilled me to the bone.

"A'ight, I'm out."

I began walking to the door just as a couple nurses rushed in, eager to see what all the commotion was for. Slipping by them, I was just about out the door when I felt a small foot kick me right in the calf muscle.

"I should kill you, nigga."

Kyle spoke to me with all the seriousness of a gangsta. Even in his youth, I picked up on the truthfulness of the statement in his eyes, eyes he'd inherited from his father, and the way that his upper lip turned up in disgust as he glared at me.

"You should," was all I said as I exited the room.

It wasn't until I stepped onto the elevator at the end of the hall that I turned around, pressed the number for the lobby, and realized that Kyle's sinister eyes were still glowering right at me.

Le Tavia

Oh no.

Mouth open, all I could do was stare down at my phone, unmoving, as tears streamed down my face.

After everything that I'd been through, the worse was still to come. Once Sonya and Imani left, I laid down in the bed and tried to relax. But I had too much on my mind and I couldn't. I felt paranoid after dealing with death so much in the past few days and it was freaking me out to be in this big ass house all alone. So I turned on every single light, checked all the locks on the doors, made sure the alarm system was turned on, and holed myself up in the room. I wanted to tell myself to relax and get a grip but I still couldn't shake the feeling that something was wrong.

Then, less than an hour after, right when I started to get comfortable and breathe a little easier, the worst possible thing happened next. I received a text from a number I didn't recognize and when I opened the message, I was greeted with a video. The same video that Quisha had played for me five years ago, of when Cutta raped me. About five minutes after receiving the video, a call came through from the same number. Having no choice otherwise, I answered it right away.

"Hello?"

"LeTavia, right?" the icy voice said on the other side. From his

279

tone, I could almost see the cruel smile that was on his face. It was Cutta and just the sound of his voice made every hair on my arm rise.

"How are you calling me? Wh—what do you want?" I asked, trying to steady my wavering tone as I licked my dry lips with an even drier tongue. My hand was shaking so badly as I held the phone to my ear that it nearly fell.

"Don't act like that, LeTavia. You should consider me an old friend," he continued with a coarse, dry laugh that didn't sound the least bit pleasant. When I didn't reply back, he continued on.

"I'm callin' to give you a heads up on some shit. I'm back on the streets and I'm gonna destroy Gunplay, that's fact. But before I do that, I'm gon' send him this lil' video of you and I to brighten up his day before the real shit starts to kick in. Now we both know that nigga gon' fuck yo' ass up when he see it… just sayin', if I was him, I'd kill ya ass for this shit. I mean, you in here lookin' like you havin' a good ass time with a nigga, which I'm sure you was…"

He laughed again and I felt my blood go cold in my veins.

"But before I send this to him, I'm gonna give you a choice. Ever since I been locked up, I been thinkin' about you. Maybe 'cause I ain't have shit but this video to keep me company or maybe it was somethin' else."

I didn't even want to think about what the something else may have been. And I definitely didn't appreciate the suggestive laughter that followed. He was really enjoying my misery.

"Gunplay gonna try to kill ya ass when he sees this. Your fuckin' life as you know it is over. But if you choose to be with me, I'll take care of you forever. All you gotta do is tell me a few things to prove ya loyalty and I got'cho back. From what I heard, that nigga been fuckin' around on you since ya'll been together. He done proved he ain't worth shit. Probably been knocking your ass out like he used to do Quisha too, huh? See, I'd never put my hands on you..."

My thoughts merged in my mind and I felt a tear fall down my cheek but I couldn't find the strength to wipe it away. It was true... everything he was saying was true. Gunplay had treated me like shit some of the time we'd been together. The cheating, the lying... he'd done it all. But those days were behind us. He'd never put his hands on me in the past even though he'd come close. But if he saw this video, would it push him over the edge? I knew better than anyone about the demons that Gunplay had within him and how they controlled him through his fury, squashing out any evidence of rational thought. When they took over, there was no love, there was no sympathy and there was no mercy. There was only the desire to create pain.

I'd waited too long to tell him about what went on with me and Cutta... I'd spent too much time waiting for the perfect moment only to realize that there was never going to be a perfect moment to tell him this bullshit. But at this point, he'd never believe me if I said what really happened and I feared what he would do to retaliate. Even so, there was no way that I'd ever betray Gunplay for Cutta. Even if it meant my life.

"So, what you choosin'? I can have a Bentley with your name on it parked outside in the next thirty minutes for you if you choose to roll with a nigga. All you gotta do is say the word," Cutta's voice oozed through the other line, dropping to the sexy tone he'd used when we first met. But this time it didn't have the same effect at all, just the sound of it made me nauseated.

"No," I told him, my voice cracking.

"What?"

"No!" I repeated, this time with more bass in my voice. "I will not betray Gunplay for you."

There was a brief pause on the other line before Cutta began to laugh. It was a boisterous, deep laugh as if I'd told the funniest joke he'd ever heard.

"And do you think he'll be that loyal to you once he sees this video? Do you think that he'll give a shit about you then? Or what about when he finds out about your lil' trip to the clinic?"

My breath caught up in my lungs and I instantly felt dizzy. How in the world did Cutta know about that?

"Oh you didn't think I knew about that, huh?" he asked, mimicking my thoughts. "You don't think I had eyes on you after I was locked up? Well, I got eyes every fuckin' where, you better believe that shit."

Then his voice dropped to an even lower decibel, dark and deep enough to send a shiver up my spine.

"I heard he's lookin' for the niggas responsible for killin' his moms. From what I heard, it was an inside job since only a few had her new address... from the video I'm lookin' at, I'm thinkin' he might figure that inside person is you."

I gasped, my mouth dropped open, and my tongue felt dry and limp in my mouth.

"What?! I would *never* do anything to hurt his mother and he knows that!" Tears stung my eyes.

"Yeah, I'm sure right now that nigga don't know what the fuck to think. You know he just killed his homeboy 'bout this shit, right? That nigga, Rayshaun. And he grew up with that nigga! I'm willin' to bet he don't give a shit about you."

My entire body was trembling with fear and devastation. I kept trying to tell myself not to let Cutta's words get to me but the only thing I could really focus on was what Gunplay had said to me the day after his mother had died when he and Imani returned from the police station.

I'm not stoppin' until I kill any and everybody who I even think may have had somethin' to do with this... And I'm shooting first—I'm not waitin' for explanations or shit. I want everybody to know that this is what happens when you fuck with mine.

Did this apply to me? Would he give me a chance to explain? The sound of Cutta's voice pulled me from my mental deliberation.

"So, I'ma give you one last chance before I send this video over to him. You gon' roll with me or you gon' wait for Gunplay to put a bullet up your ass?"

I chewed on my fingernails, tasted the metallic paint chips in my mouth, my tongue even drier than before.

"No," I said once more, this time tears were streaming down my cheeks. I was conflicted. My mind was telling me to save myself but there was no way I could do what Cutta was asking. He couldn't be trusted. I had to take my chances with Gunplay.

"I won't betray Gunplay for you. Ever," I told him, solid in my decision. Sniffing, I wiped away my tears and waited for him to respond.

"Okay," he said after a long pause. "Look at the clock… in five minutes, I'll be sending your lil' boyfriend this video. Five minutes."

And with that, he hung up the phone. Still, I couldn't move. I sat frozen in place with the phone to my ear as I stared at the clock.

Five minutes and Gunplay will know, I thought to myself. *Five minutes.*

The digits on the clock changed and I felt my throat tighten. Should I stay and try to explain or should I leave? What kind of man did I give my heart to? Would he really kill me once he found out? Just how crazy was he?

The digits flashed once again as I continued to battle with myself on what I should do. The one thing I had in my favor was Gunplay's love for me. But the opposite of love was hate. When you loved someone so strongly, the intensity of those emotions never changed, they only shifted over time. So just as strongly as you loved someone, if things changed in a negative direction, you'd hate them just as much. I'd seen Gunplay's fury up close and I'd heard stories of what he'd done to those he didn't like… but what would he do to someone he'd begun to hate? What would he do to me?

The clock changed once more. I had two minutes. Two minutes between now and the time Cutta promised he would send the video to Gunplay. Looking at my phone, I wondered once more what I should do. If I called Cutta and he did what he promised, that meant I'd be safe. Otherwise, I had nowhere to go that Gunplay wouldn't find me. I'd be on my own.

My phone chimed and with a shaky hand, I grabbed it to check the message.

Last chance.

It was Cutta giving me one last shot at deciding to team with him and betray Gunplay. My fingers hovered over the keypad for a few seconds before I typed up a reply.

I'll do it.

Of course, I didn't mean it but I needed to stall him. I needed more time to decide what I could do and how I could fix this. I needed to speak to Gunplay before Cutta got to him first.

Sucking in a deep breath, I hesitated before I hit the 'send' button. Closing my eyes, I took another deep breath and then hit 'send'. A few seconds later, a message came in.

Good choice. I'll see you tonight.

CHAPTER TWELVE

Gunplay

I had just grabbed Imani up from Sonya's spot when my phone rang. The day had been productive for the most part but the rest of the night was going to be even better. Gunna called me to tell me that he'd gotten the names of the niggas who had grabbed me and tried to kill me that night at E-Class's club. Turns out they were affiliated with Cutta. As soon as I took Imani home, my next stop was to meet up with him so we could run up on them niggas. It was late as hell and I knew Imani was sleep. Part of me really wanted to just tell Sonya's I'd pick Imani's ass up in the morning so I could get an early start on squeezing the information out of Cutta's men. My mind was already ruminating with the many ways I would torture all the information I needed out of them.

Nothing got a nigga's tongue wagging like a little bit of suffering before meeting their tragic end. I toyed with niggas before I sent them on though. Before taking their last breath, I loved to see that little ray of hope in their eyes they got once they were done snitching on everybody they knew. They always thought after they told it all, I would shed some mercy on their asses and let them free. NOT!

"Wassup, E?"

"I got some good news! It's about the plug and—"

"Aye nigga, hold up!" I cut in, interrupting him. See, E-Class wasn't no real street nigga but I was. I had two phones, a personal one and my trap phone, and his ass was on the wrong one.

"Aye, I'm right 'round the corner from your crib, nigga. I need you to tell me this shit in person."

"Bet, I'm about to get dressed to make a few stops but I'll be here when you get here."

I pulled up to E-Class's spot less than ten minutes later. E-Class stepped out at the same time I jumped out the whip, closing the front door behind him. He rubbed at the short hairs on his chin and then took a long look around us before bringing his eyes to mine. I stared back at him, noting his appearance was far different from what I was used to. E-Class has always been the pretty boy of the crew. And after buying the club, he had even taken it up a notch, wearing nothing but custom-made suits, dress shirts, and tailored slacks whenever I saw him. Now, he was casually dressed in some shorts and a white tee.

"Damn... Nigga, it look like you still on vacation," I joked, bumping fists with him after I ran up the stairs to his front door. I'd left Imani in the car so instead of walking inside; I sat down on the top of the stairs.

E-Class seemed perplexed for a moment, bunching his brows together in confusion but then his face relaxed into a grin.

"Oh yeah, I just got back."

Ready to get back to the point of my visit, I crossed my arms in front of my chest.

"So, what's goin' on with the plug? He still meetin' up with us tonight?"

I still had a bunch of product left over but business was booming and I needed more. Plus, the plug had fronted me some dope on the strength that he knew I was the type of nigga who could double it in no time and make us both rich. Or richer, I should say. The meeting tonight was to pay him back for what he fronted and to buy even more… all cash. I ain't need him to front me no more because I had enough cash to buy my own. I wasn't the type of nigga who liked to take favors.

"Yeah that's still on!" E-Class exclaimed, rubbing his hands together hungrily. "And he said he got some new shit, some pills, they taking over in Cali that niggas here ain't even got yet."

"Word?" I rubbed on the hairs on my chin, thinking about how shit was working out even better than I'd planned. "That's what's up, fam."

"Fuck! I was so happy to tell you that shit that I forgot to say… I'm sorry to hear 'bout what happened to moms," E-Class said, exhaling a heavy breath. He looked at me with a sad expression in his eyes and reached out to pat my shoulder. I looked from my shoulder, where his hand lay, up to him, noticing that there was something plastic hanging just from below his sleeve.

Clearing my throat, I pushed my emotions away and replied

quickly, eager to change the subject.

"Thanks, man. What's that on your sleeve?"

E-Class smirked and shrugged. "Ain't shit really. I added on to a tat that I got a while back. It's the grim reaper standing in the rain. Each drop of rain that surrounds him means something. I'on know if you seen it. But yeah, I'm fucked up 'bout not bein' able to see ya moms be buried, man. I wish I could've told her goodbye."

I shifted from foot-to-foot, suddenly eager to get out of there. The only way I could deal with the shit on my plate was to not think of my mama's murder. I pushed it away from my mind and tried to heal my grief by holding onto my anger. Only once I found out who was responsible, could I grieve over the fact that I'd lost her.

"Aye, I got my shorty in the car so I gotta go. I'll holla at you after I drop her off at the crib... I need to catch you up on shit that's been goin' down since you been gone."

With a deep frown on my face, I turned around without waiting for him to reply back. I needed to hurry up and get to Gunna and Nuke so we could run up on the niggas who had jumped me. They had to know something and whatever it was, I was going to find out.

"Imani in the car? Damn, I haven't seen her ass in forever. She gotta be big now," E-Class said from behind me. I simply nodded my head and kept walking while I responded.

"Yeah, she tall as hell now. Almost as tall as..."

My words died off when I looked up and my eyes honed into the backseat of my car right on Imani. Her beautiful little face was pressed against the window, her eyes stretched wide in horror along with her mouth. Tears were running down her face as she looked, not at me, but behind me. She was terrified.

Without finishing my sentence, I took off and grabbed the car door, pulling her straight out of it and into my arms. She began to cry even louder, howling in my ear and I felt myself about to panic. What the hell had gotten into her?

"Imani! What the hell—Imani?!" I tried to hold her tight but she continued to scream, kicking, and lashing out as if I was hurting her.

"Damn, she good?" E-Class started off the stairs, walking closer to where I stood but Imani became even more hysterical.

"I got her," I said, my eyes still on her as I rocked her in my arms. "Calm down, baby girl. Daddy is here... I won't let anyone hurt you ever again. Not ever again."

She began to quiet down and stopped kicking and thrashing, although she was still crying, sobbing profusely as she dug her face into my chest.

"She was there that day," I said, glancing to E-Class to give him a look, sending him a hint of what I was talking about. "She was hiding in the house with my moms and the shit still gives her nightmares. I gotta get her home."

Glancing at E-Class, I continued to rock her in my arms. He had a wide-eyed look on his expression as he stared at Imani who was still weeping quietly as I held her against my chest.

"Word? That's cray, bruh. You might have to send her to a therapist or some shit."

I ignored him and sat her down gently in the back seat and strapped her into the seatbelt. I glanced at E-Class and gave him a nod before jumping into the driver's seat to leave. I needed to get Imani home. She'd been having nightmares every now and then, which I figured was normal after seeing her grandmother murdered but this was the first time she'd flipped out like that. Maybe my nigga was right. Maybe I did need to get her some help.

Imani fell asleep in the back and I was thankful for it because it gave me some time to run through my thoughts and make plans. My cell phone rang when I was about ten minutes out from the house and, seeing it was LeTavia, I picked up immediately.

"What's good, bae?"

"Um, hey, baby," her sweet voice came through the speakers and spoke peace into my soul. My mind was instantly at ease.

"I'm goin' to go visit my grandma for a little bit to make sure she's doin' okay. I'm goin' to ask Ya-Ya if she can keep Imani tonight. Is that okay?"

"Damn, bae, I just picked her up. I was on my way to bring her to you."

"I'm sorry, I didn't know… but I really have to—"

I shook my head and cut her off. "Naw, shawty, you good. I'll turn around and drop her back off at Ya-Ya's. Her crib is on the way to where I gotta go anyways. Call her and then let me know if shit changes before I get there."

She agreed and I told her I loved her before hanging up the phone and making a U-turn. I glanced at Imani through the rearview mirror and saw that she was still sleeping peacefully.

"Fuck!" I cursed, frustrated that my daughter was having issues due to some shit I was involved in. What made me feel even worse was the fact that she was dealing with this shit and I couldn't even spend time with her because I was so busy in the streets trying to right my wrongs.

My role as a father, a goon, and a boyfriend were beginning to conflict but I knew there was no way I would fail at either one. I just had to get business taken care of, end Cutta and everybody else who wasn't on my team, and then everything else would be straight. I was sure of it.

Now I know I couldn't have been more wrong.

LeTavia

Oh My God!

It was hours later and I had no idea what I was going to do but I had to do something. The warning from Gunplay's mother kept circling around in my mind. There was no way in hell I could tell him about what happened between Cutta and I. He'd given me a preview of his reaction and I definitely didn't need anything else to go off to ensure me that the advice she'd given me was the truest shit anyone had ever told me. To protect Gunplay, and to protect myself, I had to come up with a plan.

With my purse in hand, I grabbed the keys to my car and ran out the door, on my way to Sonya's. If anyone knew how to help me come up with a plan, it was my best friend. Not just that, I had no one else to turn to. For the first time since Gunplay had returned to my life, I felt alone. As soon as I opened the front door, I ran out, knocking right into a tall, thin man with an athletic body. My first thought was that it was Cutta. He'd found out where I lived and had come to make sure that I made good on my promise. I nearly jumped five feet in the air from sheer surprise and fear, squawked out a scream, and scratched with panic at the door, trying my hardest to get back inside to safety.

And that's when I realized it wasn't Cutta. It was Gunplay's friend, E-Class. Letting out a deep breath, I relaxed, placing my hand to my chest to still my racing heart.

"You scared me!" I panted out, chuckling a little from embarrassment as I shook my head. "I'm so sorry."

He laughed and bent down to pick up my purse that I'd dropped on the ground right before trying to claw my way through the front door.

"You're good, pretty lady." He held my purse out to me and I grabbed it. "Your evil other half up here?"

A sharp pain went through my chest when he mentioned Gunplay. The guilt that I'd managed to keep at a minimum had returned to me with a vengeance and I was sure that it showed all in my face. Mustering up a fake smile, I looked at E-Class and shook my head.

"No... did you try calling him? He left early this morning."

E-Class chuckled and shook his head. "That would have been the smart thing to do, right? Naw, I didn't call him. But... you good? Looks like somethin' bothering you. You know Gunplay is like my brother, which makes you fam. If you need anything, I got you."

Pursing my lips, I thought about what he said and wondered if there was any way I could get any advice from him. Being that he'd been friends with Gunplay for so long, I was sure that he knew the same thing his mother did: that in order to protect him, there were some things it was better for him not to know. Then again, I couldn't take the chance. And, most importantly, I didn't know his ass like that to be telling him my business.

"No... I'm just havin' one of those days. You know what I mean?" I laughed, trying to play it off. "Just a woman thing."

He squinted his eyes at me, taking a step closer and not at all sharing my laugh. His face was serious as he stared at me like he could see right through me.

"You sure? I mean, I know that Cutta is out and that had to be hard on you. I heard that something happened between y'all… has he contacted you?"

My eyes stretched wide and I felt my heart begin to slam in my chest once again. How did he know about my situation with Cutta? Was it that talked about? How many other people knew?

Sensing the panic on my face, E-Class placed his hand on my shoulder and gave me a gentle look.

"Listen, Gunplay comes to me a lot because I know shit. I work at the club and people talk. I heard some shit 'bout you and Cutta before he got locked up. I ain't said shit to Gunplay because we both know how crazy that nigga is. I know that certain stuff that nigga can't deal with. And you havin' sex with another nigga is one of them."

I winced.

"I *didn't* have sex with him. He raped me."

The tears came to my eyes before I even knew it. I bit my trembling lip and tried to urge myself to get it together. But it was hard. I was trying to be strong for everyone around me but I wasn't that kind of woman. I wasn't strong enough to overcome what he'd done to me or to get over the fact that I had to abort my first child. I had managed to forget it for a little while, using Gunplay as my motivation and my perfect distraction, but now the reality of it all was in my face again. I was scarred by my past and I was desperate to figure out a way to stop it from haunting me for the rest of my life.

"I didn't know that shit, Tavi," E-Class said, pulling me into a hug. "I swear I ain't know or I would've got at that nigga my damn self."

I cried hard as he held me. I needed to let it all out. I'd spent so much time holding it in and keeping it all to myself. And then, I opened my mouth and it all started to come out. I told him about the rape, how I was drugged, how Quisha had recorded it and sent it to me, I skipped the part about her coming to my apartment and her accidental death but I did tell him about Cutta contacting me to set up Gunplay.

"Damn," he said once I was done. He pulled back from me and lowered his head, running his finger over his top lip, pensively. Then he looked up at me with a light in his eyes that ignited hope in mine.

"I got an idea. We can set that nigga up together." He nodded his head slowly, as if still thinking over the details in his mind. I felt jittery and began to fidget as I waited for his response. When he didn't answer right away, I pressed.

"How?" I asked.

"Let's go inside and I'll tell you."

E-Class's plan was simple. I'd meet up with Cutta that night in Harlem with a duffle bag of Gunplay's money. Gunplay had a small stash that he left in the house and I had access to it in case of emergencies. I'd never used it because there was no need to. It was his money and I had my own little cash saved from the financial aid I was getting from my online classes. But Gunplay counted his money every morning before leaving the house so I'd gotten a visual of how many stacks were inside and it was *a lot*.

E-Class told me to meet with Cutta to give him the money to gain his trust but he advised me to lay it on extra thick. Now this was the hard part and just thinking about it made me feel nauseated but I knew I had to do it because it made sense. So the plan was for me to do everything to convince Cutta that I wanted to be with him and that I'd actually enjoyed the rape as much as his twisted mind already had him thinking I did. Then, once I was able to distract him enough to get him alone, E-Class would shoot him dead and my problems would be over. The trick was that I had to convince Cutta to complete the transaction in an open location and to promise that we would be alone.

I had a hell of a performance to put on and my ass was not ready for any of it. E-Class had told me that Cutta would definitely have me checked for weapons so he advised me not to bring anything on me. I told him I wouldn't but it was a damn lie. I was a lot of things but a fool I was not. Gunplay had given me a gun to protect myself with and even though I couldn't figure out how to hide that on me without getting caught, he'd also bought me a blade and it was just what I needed to do the job.

Gunplay

After making a few stops while Imani was sleep in the car, I was back in the whip, Imani was at Sonya's and I was on my way to meet up with Gunna to put all this drama to rest at last. But then my phone rang once more. It was E-Class calling again. This time it wasn't with good news.

"Aye, E. I know I said I'd call you back but Gunna and I need to handle some shit so I gotta fill you in later."

"Naw, I ain't callin' 'bout that, bruh. Listen, I got some crazy ass news."

Just from his tone, I knew something wasn't right and I only hoped that it wasn't nothing dealing with either of the two women I'd give my life for.

"What is it?"

"It's 'bout Tavi."

Instantly, I felt my throat get tight and I pulled off onto the side of the road. If anything happened to LeTavia, it would be the end of me. I'd have to pull myself together to take care of my daughter but truth is, I didn't even know how I would manage to do that without my queen by my side.

"Man, remember when you told me not to say shit 'bout her and another nigga unless I know the shit is true?"

I frowned. "Yeah."

"Well… Nigga, she foul," he continued, blowing out a breath. "She fucked Cutta. I thought she had fucked with one of his men but it was *him*. She got pregnant from that nigga and everything but aborted it when he got locked up. I guess she figured she might as well work it out with you then. But word is, she's meeting up with his ass *right now!* She over in Harlem giving him yo' muthafuckin' money, nigga! I knew it was a reason I ain't like that bitch!"

This shit couldn't be true. LeTavia, the woman I loved more than even myself, would never do this to me.

"Naw, I'on believe that shit, bruh. Check yo' fuckin' sources."

"Nigga, look at yo' phone. I just sent you the records from when she got the abortion. I got the hook up at the clinic. One of my strippers is a clerk over there and…"

He was talking but I wasn't hearing shit because I was already searching for the photo he said he'd sent me. I looked at it but the main thing my eye focused on was the date. It was the same day I was questioned by the police. The day I showed up and LeTavia was looking like shit, cramping, and telling me that her period was on when I asked about that big ass pamper she was wearing on her ass.

Blowing out a sharp breath, I ran my hand over my face and looked down at the image, reading over the notes quickly. Before I could get to the end, I tossed the phone to the side, feeling my breathing get heavier.

"You there?" E-Class said. I'd forgotten he was on the phone until his voice came through my car speakers.

"Where are they meetin' at?" I snarled. My chest was aching. I put my hands up to my ears and pressed down hard as I squeezed my eyes shut. I was about to literally lose my fuckin' mind but I needed to keep my anger at bay for a moment longer.

"Harlem. I got the address from a nigga who talks too damn much. I'll send it to you. But listen... I need the combo to the safe because the plug comin' by in a couple hours and—"

"Nigga, send me the fuckin' address! I don't wanna hear shit 'bout no fuckin' safe!"

E-Class was about to make me nut the fuck up. My fuckin' world was crumbling into shit and he was talking to me about a fuckin' plug.

"I know, man. That's why I'm tryin' to handle this for you, B. I know you gotta check on shit with yo' lady, so I got this. Just send me the combo."

I squeezed my eyes shut and gritted out my response through my teeth. "I'll reply back to you with it after you send me the address."

"A'ight, I'll do that now. Don't forget now, nigga. If this nigga show up and we ain't got this money, you gon' have bigger problems."

I didn't see how the fuck he figured that. What could be bigger than this shit I was dealing with right now?

"Bet," was all I said before hanging up the call so I could get my mind right. It couldn't be true. There was no way LeTavia could do this shit to me.

But she *did*.

All of the blood in my body rushed to my head, filling my vision with red. My breath started coming out in heavy grunts and I felt my anger rising up in me in a way that I'd never felt it before. It was powerful and all consuming, destructive to the highest degree. I squeezed my eyes shut, clenched my teeth, and ran my hands over my face, pressing down hard on my eyes to try to extinguish the image of LeTavia in bed with another nigga… the nigga who was most likely behind my mama, and almost my daughter, being murdered. All this time I was searching for answers on what had happened and who was involved, not even knowing that the woman I loved might be right in the center of it. My rage was incomparable, magnificent, and uncontainable.

I couldn't control it and I couldn't stop it.

Ripping my door open, I got out of the car and pulled my pistols out from behind my back, squeezing them so hard in my hands that my fingers began to ache. I clenched my teeth hard as I dropped down to my knees, trying with my last bit of mental strength to control my wrath. But my efforts were futile. My heart was bleeding but it was nothing in comparison to the fury that I felt. Then there was an uttering in my mind and it continued on, over and over, cycling like a chant while growing more and more powerful each time.

Somebody is gonna die.

I felt it. I knew it. And it was going to be LeTavia.

Even though I knew without an inkling of doubt that I was gonna kill her, there was a small part of me that was urging me to calm down and think rationally. There was a small part of me telling me that I didn't want to kill the only woman I loved and that there had to be another explanation for this level of betrayal. A small part of me continued to say that LeTavia would never do this to me. She *couldn't ever* do this to me.

But the only voice that I could understand right then was yelling out 'fuck all that bullshit.'

"FUUUUCK!" I roared to the top of my lungs. "FUCKIN' BITCH!"

Raising my hands, I started firing off shots into the air as I cursed LeTavia's very existence. Tears stung my eyes but it wasn't because I was sad. If anything, they were tears of happiness. My mind had accepted that I would be burying the one person I'd loved most and I couldn't fuckin' wait to do it. The more I thought about it... the more I listened to the voices chanting for the end of her life within the small confines of my mind, the more I craved ending her life.

"I'MA FUCKIN' KILL YOU, BITCH!" I yelled, clutching the guns in my hands.

On the road beside me, cars were speeding by at top speed after hearing the sound of shots fired. I knew that in a matter of time, the police would be coming because I was certain someone had called them but I didn't give a shit. Nothing else mattered.

Fuck. Everything. Else.

Lifting my head up, I narrowed my eyes at the road ahead of me and clenched my jaw tightly together as the murderous thoughts continued to run through my mind. There was no longer any question about whether or not I would kill LeTavia because I definitely was. The only thing left to consider was whether I was going to kill that bitch fast or would I kill her slow. Either way, she would be taking her last breath tonight. My phone chimed and I saw that E-Class had sent me the address. I replied back with the code to the safe, not even worried about meeting with the plug or anybody else right now.

The sound of sirens erupted in the distance and I jumped in the car and took off. I wasn't worried about being picked up by the police because after what I was about to do, they'd definitely be after my ass. But I wanted to handle this first.

"FUCK!" I yelled, punching the steering wheel as I drove through the streets at top speed.

The city passed by me in a whir of lights. I was going so fast, I couldn't make out a single thing around me but it didn't matter because my rage was leading the way.

"You thought you pulled the wool over a nigga's eyes, huh, bitch?" I said as if talking to her. "Probably still fuckin' with that nigga now. I'ma light yo' ass up and his ass up right after. You can suck his dick for eternity while y'all rot in hell."

I was almost to Harlem when I stopped and pulled my car on the side of the road. I needed to plan out what I was going to do. Reaching into my pocket, I pulled out a blunt and lit it. While puffing on it, I pulled out my pistols and dropped a couple rounds inside to replace what I'd just used.

"I'ma name this one 'bullet up ya ass,'" I said with a sinister chuckle, scrutinizing each bullet as I dropped it in. "And this one is 'bullet in ya neck.' And this one... this one is 'bullet between ya eyes,' you punk ass bitch."

Niggas said I was crazy. When I was little, they tried to convince my mama that I needed medication. Tried to tell her that I was schizophrenic... a sociopath, incapable of normal relationships. It was bullshit. I wasn't crazy. Muthafuckas drove me crazy. There was a difference.

I took another puff on the blunt and then something suddenly occurred to me. They say you do your best thinkin' when you're high as fuck and whoever 'they' is, they ain't never told a fuckin' lie.

"Naw, I ain't lettin' this bitch get off this easy," I said with a snarl on my face. "Naw, I'ma kill her, nigga, quick, but I'ma make that bitch suffer slow before I end her ass. That's what I'ma do."

Turning around in the road, I headed to a hardware store that was on the corner, not even a quarter mile away and swerved into the parking lot. With the burning blunt still firmly placed in between my lips, I jumped out the whip and walked inside with my eyes scanning the interior of the store as I searched intently for the things I needed.

"Sir, can I help you?" a gentle voice said from beside me.

Turning towards it, I shook my head at the older white woman who had walked up on me. I saw her flinch when she looked into my face, freezing when she peered into my eyes. And then her gaze narrowed in on the blunt between my lips. Her own lips pulled into a thin line before her eyes came back up to my face.

"W—we don't allow smoking in the store," she informed me as I grabbed a roll of duct tape.

Matter of fact, I may need two more, I thought to myself, ignoring her, as I grabbed a couple more rolls.

"I said—"

"I ain't gon' be in here long," I muttered, walking away from her. "Shit… I'ma need a buggy."

Walking to the front of the store, I grabbed a buggy and dumped the duct tape inside. Then I went to the back and snatched up some rope, a large roll of dark blue tarp, heavy-duty black gloves, a hatchet, and a chain saw. With my buggy full off everything I needed, I stomped to the front of the store, puffing on the blunt as I checked the buggy over and over again to make sure I had everything I needed. Satisfied that there was nothing else left to grab, I continued to the front.

There was a young white boy at the register; he looked as if he might have been in his teens. As soon as his eyes fell on the blunt between my lips, a smirk rose up on his. Snorting out a low laugh, I pulled the blunt from my lips and held it out to him.

"You wanna take a hit?" I asked with a smirk and he nodded his head. Then, there was the sound of someone clearing her throat behind me and his smile dropped as he shook his head. Shrugging, I began to place all of my materials on the counter.

"Geez!" he exclaimed as his eyes ran over everything I was buying. "Looks like you're assembling a kill kit for a serial killer!" He laughed and I shot him a crooked smile.

"You think you need some Pine-Sol to clean up the blood?" he joked as he motioned with his finger towards a few bottles of Pine-Sol on the counter to the right of me.

Narrowing my eyes in on it, I thought for a second and then grabbed two bottles along with a few cleaning rags that were next to them.

"Good lookin' out," I muttered as I placed them on the counter with my other purchases.

The boy's cheeks flushed red. He shot me a wide-eyed look and then began to hurriedly ring up my items without saying another word. Chuckling lightly, I put out the blunt with my hand and stuck the rest of it in my pocket. I pulled out a knot of cash, peeled off a hundred dollar bill and dropped it on the counter just as he finished bagging everything up.

"Keep the change," I told him as I grabbed the bags and began to walk out of the store.

LeTavia

Show time.

I thought as I saw Cutta's dark blue and white car creeping up the street. My game face was on but my stomach was a bunch of fluttering nerves. I felt sick and the closer he got the more that I could taste the throw-up building up in the back of my throat. I was hit with the sudden urge to pee but I simply pressed my thighs together and forced out a smile, pretending to be happy to see him as his car came to a stop ahead of me.

Darting my eyes about as I clutched the duffle bag in my hands, I tried to pick up on anything that seemed out of place. Or anyone. I didn't see E-Class but I sent him the address hours before and he'd assured me the last time I'd texted him that he would be here before I was. I hadn't wanted anyone to see me driving in over here so I'd driven in, parked my car, and took the train in. It was a dangerous thing taking a train to Harlem while holding a duffle bag full of money but it couldn't even compare to the shit I was about to do.

I felt the crazy feeling like I was being watched but I probably was, either by E-Class or one of Cutta's men. I was in the middle of his city… right in Harlem where he'd once reigned. While Cutta was locked up, Gunplay ran drugs all through Harlem but he didn't come here often for the simple fact that Cutta still had too much power. And here I was, standing in the middle of Harlem in the dead of night, meeting up with the one man who he would have killed me for meeting with.

Fuck.

Cutta's car came to a halt and I threw on my most convincing smile, hoping he couldn't see through it to the hate which lay beneath. Taking a few steps forward, I licked my lips as I gazed at him from inside of his ride. He looked exactly the same as he had the last time I'd seen him, making my mind flood with images of everything that had happened that night. The prickly sensation of fear and panic rode up my spine but I shook it off with a toss of my hair, trying to rid myself of my anxiety.

Shutting off his car, Cutta stood outside the car and waited for me, his dark skin illuminated by the moonlight, creating a sinister glow that chilled me to the bone. With a sickening smile on his face, he looked me up and down.

"Come to me," he urged and I cringed beneath my clothes before willing myself to obey.

Once I walked over to him, he wrapped me up in his arms in what might have appeared to be a loving embrace but I knew it was anything but. As he wrapped his hands around my waist and then ran them down to my ass, I knew he was checking for a gun. He was no amateur but neither was I.

Pulling me close, he continued to grope my ass as I tried to keep myself from pushing him away. I used the duffle bag in front of me to create a barrier between us but it was to no avail, his hands were having his way with every part of my body.

"Just makin' sure you ain't trick a nigga," he said with a smile but I picked up on the serious undertone beneath it. "Wouldn't wanna have to bust a cap in yo' ass for fuckin' with me. I'd rather bust a nut, na'mean?"

His joke sickened me to the core but I laughed hard, delivering my best attempt at a flirtatious giggle to mask the fact that everything about him was utterly disgusting to me. Wanting to get this whole ordeal over quickly, I lifted the duffle bag and handed it to him. He took it quickly, unzipping it without saying a word. My heart nearly stopped when I saw that instead of simply looking inside, he actually grabbed a few bands and inspected them carefully. Then he began to flip through them and my knees nearly started to knock. It was getting harder and harder for me to keep my cool.

Cutta's eyes went from the bands to me and then he gave me a nod before placing them back in the bag.

"So... you know, I'on just want you to help me get rid of this nigga. I also want you to be my main bitch. You down wit' dat?" he asked. His eyes pierced through me and I felt uneasy, feeling as though he could see my thoughts as they ran through my head. Could he tell how much I hated him? Could he tell that I wanted him dead?

"I wanna be whatever you want me to be," I cooed as I twisted up one of my long locks of hair around my finger and gave him my best 'fuck me now' face. "I'd settle for any position you wanna put me in but 'main bitch' sounds appealing to me."

"That right?" he inquired with one brow raised and a smirk on his face.

Nodding my head, I strolled up close to him and used my index finger to begin making a design on his chest. Cutta's smile deepened and I knew he was loving that I had my hands on him but, in my mind, I was making a diagram of exactly where I wanted to place my blade that I'd camouflaged beneath a belt.

"Aye, boss," a voice came from behind, startling me. I jumped and turned around, seeing a group of armed men walking in a fast pace towards us.

I shot my eyes up to Cutta's face, trying to keep my cool but my heart was speeding and I could barely breathe. My bottom lip was trembling and my legs were beginning to go numb.

"You told me that it would just be us," I hissed into his ear.

He'd tricked me. I told him that I'd wanted a one-on-one meeting but, of course, he wasn't about playing things my way. He had back up ready. I watched as each of the men stationed around us, surveying everything around us with their weapons out. This was really about to fuck up my plan. Cutta told the men to go back in the building with a wave of his hand and then turned back to me.

"Don't worry about them niggas. I got word on the way here that we might have some company joining us so I called for some back up," he uttered under his breath just as they walked away.

I froze, no longer able to continue with the plan. My fear had become too great and I was afraid I'd been found out. Had someone seen E-Class coming here to help me? Did they know I was part of the set up?

"We're surrounded by a group of niggas who are ready to take a fuckin' bullet to save either one of us. See how it is when you roll with a boss nigga?" Cutta asked me and I forced out a smile as he wrapped his hand around my waist once more. "I would never let you wander the streets on yo' own because I know you're precious and need protection. That's the difference between me and that fuck nigga you roll with. Feel me? Now let's go inside, baby."

He grabbed my hand to tug me towards the building and I snatched away in a seductive manner, eyeing him as if I had an attitude. I had to stall for time.

"You mean the fuck nigga I *used* to roll with. But yeah, I feel you," I told him, eyeing his throbbing Adam's apple. My smile deepened as I imagined pushing the blade right through it.

"Them lips look good as fuck," he said, licking his own and I giggled hard to hide my disgust at how close he was to me. "What about giving a nigga a little kiss?"

My stomach churned like rolling waves and I swallowed down the bile stinging the back of my throat. This couldn't happen. I couldn't do this.

Oh God, I thought to myself as I saw him lick his lips once more.

I needed to distance myself from him so E-Class could get a good shot but Cutta wasn't letting up on me one bit.

"Of course you can." I hoped he couldn't detect the bitterness in my tone.

Leaning down, I closed my eyes tightly and pushed my lips right on top of his as I tried to force down the urge to throw up in his mouth. He flicked his tongue through the barrier our lips created and once it hit my teeth, I knew I couldn't take it anymore. I had to end this now. Cutta still had his keys in his hand and I couldn't drag out this moment any longer. My only hope was that E-Class was watching and could distract the men in a shoot-out so that I could jump in Cutta's car and escape to safety.

Just as I was about to reach for the blade, I heard the sound of a car door slamming closed and I nearly jumped out my skin. I felt Cutta's hand move from my waist to his side and the both of us turned our heads towards the noise at the exact same time. Once I saw who it was, all of the blood drained from my face.

"Gunplay!"

But it was no use. Murder was in his eyes and I knew at this moment, he was not about to give me the same grace he'd lent me the day he'd told me to leave out of our house. When he raised his pistol in the air, I was shocked but not at all surprised. Gunplay had his mind set on ending my life.

THE PAST
MEETS THE PRESENT

Gunplay

An ominous full moon was high in the dark sky, creating a ghastly shadow on the side of Gunplay's face as he crept through the hood; his eyes focused ahead of him, alert and attentive as his fingers wrapped tightly around the pistol in his lap. There was a deadly silence in the night as he pressed lightly on the brakes of his all-black Chevy Camaro, bringing the car to a slow halt. He peered into the distance ahead of him into a hue of murky gray fog that almost seemed dreamlike as he looked, straining his eyes.

There, only about three blocks from where he sat on the corner near one of the many Harlem projects was the object of his search: LeTavia. He furrowed his brow as he absentmindedly ran a single finger along the line of his goatee as if heavy into concentration. He watched her intensely, wondering what reason she could have for being on this side of town so late into the night.

Appearing nervous, LeTavia shifted from foot-to-foot, her eyes occasionally glancing around at her surroundings as she held on tightly to a duffle bag so big that she had to handle it with both of her hands. Gunplay eyed it with suspicion as he wondered what was inside. Although he had an idea of what it could be, there was no way in the world that LeTavia could be that stupid, so he dismissed the thought quickly and continued to watch.

Suddenly, a car turned onto the block behind where Gunplay sat parked on the side of the road. Looking into his rearview mirror, he saw a dark blue and white Bentley pulling up behind him and he gritted his teeth in anger.

"Fuckin' Cutta," he said under his breath as he watched the car drive by him.

He looked through his tinted windows into the car and saw that he was correct in his assumption. There was Cutta, sitting behind the steering wheel, leaning back in the seat and driving with one hand as if he hadn't a single care in the world.

When Gunplay saw the car cruise up to where LeTavia stood and begin to come to a stop, he grabbed tightly onto the gun in his lap and grabbed the handle of his door, ready to get out and start firing in Cutta's direction before he had a chance to hurt her.

But something made him stop suddenly before launching his assault.

His eyes traveled to LeTavia's direction and he saw that, not only did she not seem afraid about being approached by Gunplay's number one enemy, she appeared to have expected his presence. Under Gunplay's confused glare, she smiled with ebullience and took several steps towards his car.

"What the fuck?!" Gunplay muttered when he saw Cutta shut off his car and get out as LeTavia walked over to where he stood.

Seething with anger, Gunplay narrowed his eyes into tiny slits, barely able to contain his wrath as he watched Cutta stroll over to where LeTavia stood waiting for him, and slid his arm around her waist, grabbing onto a handful of her plump, round ass. LeTavia responded *with what appeared to be a flirtatious giggle before handing him the duffle bag. Pushing gently away from LeTavia, Cutta opened the duffle bag and pulled out about three bands of money and flipped through them. Satisfied with what he saw, he closed the bag and gave LeTavia a curt nod before whispering a few words in her ear.*

Gunplay gritted his teeth and tried to calm himself down as a burning inferno of rage barged its way into his mind. LeTavia was his lady and Cutta was his enemy, the only nigga on God's green Earth that he could truly say he hated with a passion. There was no reason for LeTavia to ever have any contact with Cutta. Period. But here she was, meeting up with him in the middle of the night and allowing him to squeeze on her ass. To add insult to injury, the past month or so, Gunplay's personal cash stash had been coming up short, but he'd had too much going on to ask LeTavia about it. Now he was beginning to understand why.

"Fuckin' bitch!" he raged as ice cold blood raced through his veins.

Running his hand over his face, Gunplay took several deep breaths, fighting the ebb and flow of mounting anger, and began pulling his long locs up into a rubber band, the way he always did when he was planning on getting his hands dirty. In his mind, LeTavia had committed a cardinal sin and he was about to bring final judgment upon her in the most vicious of ways.

It's death before dishonor, fuck ass bitch!!

Just as he grabbed at the door handle to jump out of his whip, his phone began to chime. He looked at the name displayed on the screen and then back at LeTavia and Cutta. They were still standing, talking quietly to each other as Cutta lay with his back against the side of his vehicle. LeTavia was standing in front of him, twirling a lock of her hair between her fingers, and making goo-goo eyes, while listening intently to what he was saying and responding occasionally with a nod of her head.

"Enjoy the chat. Those will be your last words, bitch," Gunplay muttered as he answered the phone. "Aye, Trigga, let me call you back. Tavi—" He struggled to keep his composure. "I'm fuckin' watchin' this bitch over here smilin' in this nigga's face! I'm about to kill everything moving in this bitch!"

"What?!" Trigga shouted through the phone. "Gunplay...nigga, calm the fuck down! You and Tavi always fightin' and shit. That's what y'all do. I keep tellin' you that your fuckin' temper is gonna get you in some shit one day if you don't—"

"Trigga, it ain't like that this time. I'm in Harlem watchin' Tavi cheesin' and shit at Cutta while he's grabbing her ass. She been fuckin' around with that fuck nigga!" Gunplay said with his jaw clenched so tightly his teeth made a grinding sound as he got more and more furious while he spied from a distance. LeTavia had strolled up close, coquettish to Cutta and was making figure eights on his chest with her fingernail.

"I'ma kill this punk bitch, I swear on err'thang I love, and I'ma spatter that fuck nigga's brains right there next to hers. Closed caskets," Gunplay grumbled. Just then, he watched two men walk out of the building behind where LeTavia stood. They said something to Cutta, and then walked back inside. Gunplay eyed the building they'd come out of with curiosity.

"Whoa..." Trigga started. "Tavi and Cutta?" Trigga paused before speaking again. "Naw, nigga, I ain't believin' that shit. You gotta calm *down. Don't get cased up on some bullshit. Think that shit out before you move. Where the hell you at exactly?"*

Gunplay ran his hand over his face again and exhaled heavily, frustrated, not trying to hear nothing Trigga was spitting.

"Nigga, I told you, Harlem. Right up in this nigga's zone where we did that hit together a while back." Gunplay's voice was laced with deadly intent as he spoke, with his finger on the banger so tightly he could feel his palm getting sweaty, his trigger finger itching and his pulse racing. He looked over at the building again.

"It looks like I might be right in front of one of his trap houses or some shit. I saw a couple of his niggas walk inside and a few junkies moving around."

"A'ight. Then you know what the fuck that means. Don't do no stupid shit, my nigga. You by yourself and you don't know what the fuck he got goin' on inside..." Trigga paused and Gunplay heard shuffling on the other line as if he was moving quickly.

Shaking his head, he tried to let Trigga's words sink through to his brain because he knew he was right. There was no way in hell that LeTavia would betray him in this way. She'd been the love of his life for years and the hate between him and Cutta ran deep. It didn't matter if they were together or not, LeTavia knew that if she fucked with Cutta in any capacity, it meant her life. There was no way the woman he loved could do this shit to him. There had to be an explanation.

Finally, Gunplay expelled a deep sigh of frustration that ended with a throaty grunt of his discontent. He banged his fist on the dashboard.

"You're right, man. I'ma wait this shit out and see what happens.

319

Tavi would never do this to me. There has to be some shit going on..." he said, stopping when a movement from ahead of him grabbed his attention.

"Exactly, nigga. That's your bitch...she done looked out for you through everything. Ain't no fuckin' way she fuckin' around with—"

"THAT FUCKIN' BITCH!" Gunplay roared all of a sudden, instantly stopping Trigga from speaking.

LeTavia began to move away when he wrapped his arms around her waist and pulled her closer to him. She obliged and fell on top of him, lacing her arms around his neck and then lifted her head up, placing a tender kiss right on his lips.

"Gunplay, don't—"

"Nigga, fuck that shit," he responded in a calm tone, completely void of emotion. In the blink of an eye, LeTavia instantly became dead to him. There was no explanation she could come up with that could save her.

"That bitch finna die tonight."

Muting Trigga's pleas, Gunplay ended the call and threw the phone in the passenger seat next to him before jumping out of the car. With his face pulled into a menacing frown and his finger pressed gently against the trigger of his Glock 9, he slammed the door hard, garnering the attention of both LeTavia and Cutta at the same time. Both of them turned towards him with two very different expressions on their faces; while Cutta had a gloating grin on his, LeTavia wore a stunned and guilt-ridden expression on her face. She knew as soon as she laid eyes on Gunplay that it was all over. Her life would come to an end on the other side of his gun.

Before she could react, Gunplay raised his banger, painfully aware of the fact that he was about to murder the only woman he'd ever been willing to die for. LeTavia was the only woman he'd given his heart to… the only one who had what it took to be by his side. But she was now also the only one who'd brought so much pain into his life by betraying him in the worst kind of way. And for that she had to die.

Out of the corner of his eyes, Gunplay saw Cutta move but he was too focused on killing LeTavia to care about what he was doing. His heart was bleeding and the only way he could see to end the pain that LeTavia had created in his heart was to stop the beating of hers.

Death before dishonor, bitch, he thought to himself one more time.

"May you go straight to hell," he gritted as he aimed directly at the space between LeTavia's stricken, stretched-wide open eyes.

Clenching his jaw, he took a sharp breath. And then he pulled the trigger.

POW!

CHAPTER THIRTEEN

LeTavia

*P*OW! *POW!*

Heart racing, I dove to the ground as soon as I saw Gunplay raise his weapon but he hadn't wasted a single second. Before I could completely fall to the ground, I heard the sound of the gunshots echoing in my ears and a sharp pain erupted right in my shoulder blade. I hit the floor hard, nearly knocking the wind from my lungs, as I grabbed at my shoulder. A wet substance came from the wound and leaked onto my fingers. Blood.

Wincing in pain, I tore my head up from the ground so that I could look back at Gunplay. He was standing up, his rage-filled eyes still glued on me. They were smoldering with murderous intent and focused on completing the only mission he could concentrate on the moment, and that was taking my life.

"Please, DeShaun…" I pleaded as I watched him walking towards me with his gun out in front of him. But my words did nothing. They were falling on deaf ears.

323

Before I could say a thing, Gunplay turned towards Cutta and took aim prepared to fire another shot. Again, he didn't hesitate.

POW! POW! POW!

The gun Cutta was holding flew from his hand and fell a few feet from where I lay on the pavement, watching the deadly duel in sheer terror. Cutta's body dropped to the ground like the sack of shit he was. I didn't even have a second to feel relieved by the death of the man who had made the last bit of my life a living hell because a vicious gun battle ensued between Gunplay and the other men on Cutta's team.

They were trying to kill him and I couldn't let that happen. My love for him was so much stronger than my will to survive. A little voice at the back of my mind was saying I was crazy to spend what could be my last moments defending the life of a man who had tried to take mine. But my heart knew that he hadn't meant it. He didn't know the truth. He didn't understand how much I loved him.

Grinding my teeth together and narrowing my eyes, I lunged for Cutta's gun and flipped around, taking aim at Cutta's men who were closest to me as I pulled the trigger hard in rapid sequence, determined to end them all. I took aim at a man only feet from me who was firing off shots from a long barreled weapon in his hands. But something about him made me pause before shooting. He wasn't aiming at me or Gunplay but at Cutta's men. He was helping.

"Oh GOD!" I cried out, wincing from the pain in my side.

I dropped the gun and grabbed at my side. When I pulled my fingers away, they were covered in blood. I felt sick to my stomach and my body was weak. I needed to get to a hospital quick. I was in so much distress that I hadn't even realized that the shooting had stopped until I felt the presence of a figure looming over me. I looked up and was alarmed when I found myself looking right into the iciest gray eyes I'd ever seen in my life. In his hand was his weapon. I saw a subtle movement and then heard a sound.

Click!

He'd dropped one bullet in the chamber. He was going to shoot me.

"Oh my God... please don't shoot!" I said, throwing my hands up in the air. "I'm not with them!"

"Tell me you didn't have nothin' to do with this shit, Tavi," the voice said and I looked back up at him, frowning that he'd used my name. How did he know me? He looked oddly familiar but I couldn't yet remember why.

"Tell me you didn't set Gunplay up for this shit."

Dumbstruck, I moved my lips to speak but nothing came out right away. And then I heard his voice and it made me freeze in place.

"Don't ask that bitch shit, Trigga! I ain't kill her ass because I got other plans. Get da fuck up!"

Before I could say a word, or even turn into his direction, Gunplay reached down and grabbed me by my hair, pulling me straight off the ground. I screamed out a high pitched wail as I held onto my throbbing side, the pain coming from it and now my scalp almost made me go blind.

"I didn't—this was a set up on Cutta! E-Class, please tell him!

E-Class!" I didn't know where the hell E-Class was but I prayed to God that he was somewhere hovering around to bear witness to my innocence.

"E-Class?" Gunplay scowled, still gripping me so hard by my hair that my head was back and my neck was stretched at an odd angle that only intensified my pain.

"He—he's here! We came up with this plan earlier today after Cutta contacted me! We were supposed to kill him, I swear! I swear, please!"

I didn't have anything else to lose so I started talking, fast, a mile a minute, hoping that somewhere in my story Gunplay would see that I was telling the truth. Two people in love shared a connection so deep and intense that science couldn't even explain it. But what I had for Gunplay was beyond that. Our relationship started with the ultimate sacrifice, the kind of sacrifice that came about when you were willing to give yourself to save the life of another. From the first time I saw him, that day he'd walked into my job, bleeding and broken, the day I covered for him when I barely knew him, lied to the cops even after being threatened... from that day on, I'd been willing to sacrifice myself for him and today the shit was still the same.

He knew it and so did I.

He relaxed his grip on my hair and then finally let go, backing away from me with wide eyes as he looked from my face, covered in tears, down to his hands, one of which was still holding the gun he'd shot me with.

"Fuck..." he whispered. He let his hand go limp and it slipped from his fingers, crashing to the ground with a loud clang that made me jump. I was still tense and paranoid about every little thing.

"You said E-Class told you to meet up with this nigga?" Trigga asked, his eyes tight as he spoke.

Nodding my head, I squinted at him, recognizing his name as someone Gunplay had spoken about many times before. I'd only seen him in passing and didn't recognize him at first.

"He showed up at our house earlier when Gunplay was gone and told me what to do. He said he would be here to kill Cutta and—"

"Somethin' ain't right," Gunplay said shaking his head as he cut me off. "E-Class the same nigga who told me you would be here. He called me 'bout an hour ago, sent me the address and all… said you and Cutta was workin' behind my back." He glanced at me, his eyes tight with suspicion as if he was thinking twice about what I was saying. I shook my head vigorously. Trigga gave me a look with one brow lifted and then walked over to Cutta's body, grabbing something from off of him. Staring at Gunplay, I continued talking.

"I have the text in my phone from him. I sent him the address and he said he would be here before I got here, waiting. It was only supposed to be me and Cutta here but then his men came out, saying that they received word someone would be joining us. I thought they meant E-Class but they had to be talking about you."

"She's tellin' the truth," Trigga said, holding up a phone. "This is Cutta's phone. The number he last texted isn't saved in it but someone told him you were on the way and the same someone told Cutta to meet him at the stash spot once everything was said and done. Wherever the fuck that is."

Gunplay's eyes widened a little and then I watched as he looked at the bodies all around us. It was a miracle no one had called the police just yet. Or maybe someone had and they were just taking their sweet time to come, as they usually did on this gang-ridden side of town. They made sure to wait until everyone had killed each other before they arrived on the scene, toting their big guns and pretending to actually care about protecting the people and upholding the laws.

"OUCH!" I cried out, grimacing as I pressed my hand against my side.

"Let me check you out," Trigga said and I nodded my head, biting my lip hard as I pulled my hands away for him to examine my wound.

"She hurt?" Gunplay asked, not coming close to me. I could tell from the look on his face and the way he seemed to stop breathing that he was fearful that he'd actually caused me harm but his guard was up. He was still trying to work everything out in his mind.

"Yeah, it's just a flesh wound. Keep pressure on it."

I nodded my head and that's when Gunplay said something that made me suck in a breath.

"E-Class set us all up. We weren't supposed to make it out of here alive."

I looked up at him and frowned, wondering what he meant but his eyes weren't on me. Neither was Trigga's. Both of them were looking at the scene, analyzing in ways that only true street niggas could.

"He set Tavi up to come here, knowin' I would kill her ass. He must've leaked it to Cutta that I was on my way. I was supposed to kill her and them niggas were gonna kill me. He's been working with Cutta all along. But he didn't count on you bein' here to help my ass out, Trigga."

The air around us got so thick that I felt like I would choke on it. I felt dazed and my head was heavy.

I told Gunplay and Trigga about everything that had occurred with him earlier and they both exchanged murderously glances. There was no need for them to explain what they were thinking. I could read it clearly as if it had been written in the sky.

"We gotta find that nigga, fam. You know where he at?" Trigga asked and Gunplay looked off in the distance, his eyes clear and glassy. Then they went dark and I knew there was trouble brewing beneath.

"Naw, not really. But I got an idea." He looked at me, the love that I was used to seeing in his eyes returning, as he held out a hand. I grabbed it and immediately fell into him, tears coming to my eyes as I felt his body pressed against mine. Something I hadn't thought I'd feel ever again.

"I'm sorry, baby. I swear I can't believe I almost hurt you. Fuck!" His voice cracked with emotion as he said the words low, just barely above a whisper and it almost made me cry even harder.

"We gotta move," Trigga said, checking his weapon.

Gunplay nodded his head and then looked at me, "You able to make it?"

I nodded my head and put my game face on. He was close to ending the nightmare we'd been living in and I didn't want to hold him back a second longer. Gunplay helped me into his car and Trigga got into his, telling us that he'd follow behind us. Once we were on the road, Gunplay drove at top speed, so fast that it made me dizzy so I laid back in the seat and closed my eyes. He called someone up on his phone and I listened as I held my side, pressing the t-shirt he'd given me against my wound.

"Aye, Yolo, I need a favor, cuz. I need you to check on my lady. She got shot."

"Damn! She a'ight?" Yolo asked and Gunplay answered him quickly, telling him it was just a flesh wound. "How the hell she got shot?"

He paused and I felt his eyes on me but I kept my head turned towards the window and my eyes closed.

"I'll explain later," was all he said. "Meet me at E-Class's club in Brooklyn. She'll be in the car waiting on you."

"On the way now."

They hung up the phone and the next thing I felt was Gunplay grabbing my hand. He placed it to his lips and kissed it softly, keeping my fingers to his lips even after the kiss had ended.

"I'll never hurt you again. I put that on God. Not ever again."

I believed him.

Gunplay

"He said the man on his shoulder was coming to get her. He said he was going to add a tear to honor her death... what does that mean, Daddy?"

"It's the grim reaper standing in the rain. Each drop of rain that surrounds him means something..."

How the fuck could I have missed that shit? Imani had been telling me everything I needed to know all along but I had missed every damn clue she'd given me.

The terror-stricken look on Imani's face when she saw E-Class had been cycling through my mind the entire time I gunned my whip down the streets of my city. She had been too broken, too devastated to physically tell me the words but her body language had said it all: she was looking at her grandmother's killer, the same man who would have killed her had he known she was there. And I had been too off my game to see it.

Everything was adding up, finally it all was making sense. E-Class had been at the bottom of everything, carefully planning my demise and all the while smiling in my face, pretending to be on my side.

"You ready?" Trigga said and I nodded my head.

"Been ready, nigga." I walked ahead of him with my gun at my side.

It was late and E-Class's club was closed but I knew where he was and I knew he would be there alone. He was over at the house where we'd stashed the cash and he wasn't meeting up with no fuckin' plug. Probably never was. His ass thought I was dead and I was more than certain that he was in the safe, running through all his new hard earned cash. Money he earned through betrayal, blood money that was supposed to be his reward that he would share with Cutta.

My mind was quiet the entire time as we walked into the club, a club that I had been in so many times before. But this time, I wasn't here to have a good time, toss money, and blow smoke in the air while watching the best entertainment this side of the city. I was here to settle a score. I was here to take a life. The life of one of my brothers. Someone I considered my blood, my nigga, somebody I had broke bread with and possibly would have died for, if need be. I was here to murder him, my own so call friend. The dope-game was ruthless like that and honor among thugs is a myth often flaunted but betrayed.

They say the love of money is the root of all evil and they were right. In my short time on this Earth, I'd witnessed many who I put my trust in turn their backs on me for the almighty dollar. Each one of them had met the same fate that E-Class also would.

But like I always said, it was death before dishonor, nigga!

We were already waiting for E-Class when he came up the stairs from the basement, both of his hands clutching large duffle bags that I already knew were full of cash. I saw the surprise in his eyes when he gawked at me like I was a fuckin' ghost. One of his legs wobbled and one of the duffle bags slipped out his hand and landed on the floor with a thump as his mouth moved but no words came out. Of course, he was shocked to see me. I was supposed to be dead, right? He'd made sure of that.

I didn't move a muscle. I was sitting on the top of a table, right in front of him with my AK-47 right in my lap. Trigga was by my side with that big boy, an AR-15. Wasn't nothing he aimed that shit at going to escape out this bitch alive. But Trigga was just back up… E-Class's life was mine.

"G—Gunplay! What you doin' here, bruh?" He made a snorting sound that was supposed to be a laugh but it was anything but that. Instead it came out as a dry, nervous chuckle. The kind when a nigga was attempting to come to terms with the fact that his life was about to be over.

"I'm probably the last muthafuckin' nigga you wanted to see, huh, bruh?" I said with my mouth twisted like I wanted to spit venom.

"No, no, no." E-Class flailed his arms taking a step backwards and bumped into a table.

"You one of the last muthafuckas I would have ever thought would have crossed me and you damn near pulled it off," I hissed. My eyes were bloodshot red and I felt my jaw begin to twitch uncontrollably.

"It ain't what it seems, man. I got all your money here. I was just getting ready to move it to a safer place. I swear on my mama life!" E-Class said with tears in his voice, his entire body was noticeably trembling all over.

"You're a liar. You set this whole fuckin' thing up with your smart ass," I spat with my jaw clenched tight as I fought to control my anger.

The entire time I was heavy into my thoughts and things were starting to become crystal clear. What E-Class had attempted would have been nothing short of brilliant, except for one major fuck up. He had underestimated his opponents.

"It's just a big misunderstanding! We can resolve this shit. In fact, it's not even about the money. Take the money, all of it. I got more at the other club and you can have that too, man."

Trigga couldn't help but chuckle at his groveling antics.

"Man, shoot that fuck nigga and let's go."

I didn't even pay Trigga any mind, it was as if I was in trance.

"You set this whole thing up from the very beginning to the end. You even tried to get me to kill Tavi," I spoke, never letting my eyes leave E-Class's face. Trigga mused and took a step closer with the AK-15 level at his chest.

"Man, that was Cutta. I didn't wanna have nothin' to do with that!" his pleas fell on deaf ears.

"Stop fuckin' lying!" Trigga yelled spraying spital, lowering the assault weapon in his rage. I continued to speak, giving the eulogy for before E-Class met his end.

"You killed my mama and set up Rayshaun… My mama bled to death right in my arms, I felt her take her last fuckin' breath as I held her in my arms."

KA-BOOM!

Trigga pulled the trigger and the lower portion of E-Class's leg blew off just above the knee cap causing him to topple on the floor in a heap. His severed leg landed on the other side of the room, next to a case of beer. E-Class howled like some type of wild beast, antagonized by his tremendous pain, as blood spurted out of his fresh stub, spewing like an open fire hydrant.

"Man, you fuckin' shot me! You fuckin' shot me and blew my fuckin' leg off!" E-Class wailed in agony as Trigga stood stoic over him, impassive and cold.

"You even tricked me into shooting my dude, my own fuckin' best friend, a nigga that been in the trenches with us. He ain't never did nothin' to nobody and that shit hurt, bruh. Hurt me to my fuckin' core! I gotta look at his kids and Poochie in the fuckin' eyes, knowin' what I did!" I paused and swallowed the dry lump in my throat.

Trigga stood rigid and wiped his face with a weary hand. Shit was real.

"My leg! I'ma fuckin' bleed to death! I gotta get to the hospital, pleeeaaase, man—"

"Nigga, you holla one more time 'bout that punk ass leg, I'ma shoot you in the other one, fuck nigga!" Trigga raged before rushing up and placing the barrel of the assault weapon against E-Class's other leg. He let out a wail and then started to squirm away, slithering in the large pool of his own blood. Trigga pushed the barrel further in his leg, his threatening expression making E-Class clamp his mouth shut.

Silence.

"He had this shit planned from day one," Trigga said distant, like his mind was heavy in thought. "I fuckin' knew it. I was goin' to tell you at the hospital before Poochie came in. I knew somethin' wasn't right with this nigga. I knew he was foul."

"No it wasn't, I mean, it ain't… man, I'ma bleed to death." E-Class began to cry like a baby and babble incoherently.

"Tell me everything and I'll get you help. Then you gotta leave this city and never fuckin' come back."

Grimacing from his pain, E-Class looked up at me as best as he could being that his entire body was trembling. He was probably about to go into shock. He needed to hurry.

"Speak!" I pushed him and he flinched, then opened his mouth and got to talking. "When you started workin' with Cutta?"

"I—I mean, I ain't never stop workin' with him. Before you came home, he was payin' me and shit to use my club. He paid me to give him info and shit… I he—helped him keep his money clean and legit, same as I do for you. I—I ain't know y'all was gon' start beefin' once you got home!"

I couldn't believe this shit.

"You set me up to kill Tavi because you knew she was meeting with Cutta. You gassed her up to do it then you went and played me to the left, knowing I was going to show up."

"Naw, man! That ain't it. I swear, you wrong! Please, lemme go!"

I continued with my hand cuffed under my chin as if heavy in thought.

"So, while I was in jail, you was doing business with Cutta. You were workin' with him, laundering money through your club. When I came home you tried the same get rich stunt with me, only I wouldn't give you half and you got greedy. Had larceny in your heart for a nigga."

"Man, I was tryna help you!" E-Class yelled. His pain was becoming his torment and the acid stench of blood began to permeate.

"Yeah, you right. Help me into my grave so you could relieve me of my chips, fuck nigga."

Trigga nodded his head approvingly and then spoke. "You tried to play us all at both ends. That's a dangerous game, especially when you did all this shit over some fuckin' money. Blood fuckin' money."

"Man, I swear'ta God, I ain't have nothin'—"

Wham!

I came down so hard with the butt of the AK-47 on E-Class's face that one of his eyeballs seemed to nearly spring forward out of his head.

"Goddamnit, man!" Trigga cursed with a scowl on his face as E-Class fell on his back and began to pant like he was having trouble breathing.

Death would come soon but I was trying to exacerbate it.

"Nigga, this for my mama and all the fuck shit you did. Open your fuckin' mouth!!" I yelled so loud my voice echoed as I stood over him with my weapon aimed at his face. There was a puddle of blood enveloping him like a virulent red plague, spreading.

"Come... on... man...puh-leeeassse..." With E-Class's meager strength waning, due to his injuries, he could hardly talk.

"Nigga, I said OPEN YO' FUCKIN' MOUTH!"

Violently, I shoved the barrel of my gun in E-Class's mouth and partially down his throat as far as I could get it, causing several teeth matted in blood to dislodge. It was like a scene from a horror movie.

"This for my mama… This for all the fucked up shit you did, you BITCH ASS NIGGA!"

KA-BOOM!

I pulled the trigger and E-Class's head exploded like a watermelon, knocking a huge hole in the floor, the size of football. I was covered in blood but I barely noticed. I felt something break loose inside of me and I fell to my knees, dropping my head. I was exhausted and emotionally drained but most of all, I was finally able to really grieve the death of my mother's murder. Heaving over, I dropped down, placing the palms of my hands on the floor to support my weight and finally let go of my emotions.

In the chaos of all the madness, murder and bloodshed, I bereaved the loss of my mother, and the tragedy of it all. Trigga came up behind me and stood close, not saying anything but making sure his presence was felt. After a while, I felt his hand on my shoulder and he helped me up, never saying a word or looking me in my face. Some things were personal, especially when a thug mourns.

"Nigga, you rich for life now. Take the money move away with your shawty and get out the dope game," Trigga admonished.

"Yeah, I'll think 'bout it." I wiped my hand at my face. There was no use; it and my hand were covered with blotches of blood.

As we both picked up the heavy duffle bags loaded with money, Trigga added, "My nigga, you gotta get some kinda medication too. The way you killed that nigga, you don't think that shit was a little over kill?"

"Fuck outta here! Medicate these nuts, nigga," I chided with a hint of a smile.

Trigga shoved me as we both walked towards the exit, "Oh, you got jokes now."

EPILOGUE

"*D*amn, girl! You big as hell. You remember me?"

Rayshaun smiled down at Imani who immediately wrapped her arms around his legs, pulling him into a tight embrace. He reached down and grabbed her up in his arms and she immediately wrapped her tiny arms around his neck.

"Yes, I remember you, Uncle Shaun!" she told him, giggling like it was the funniest thing she'd ever heard.

"I taught my baby never to forget a face," Gunplay said, walking behind Rayshaun. "Put that big ole girl down, Ray. Your ass just got clearance to stop walking with a cane. You tryin' to get sent back to the rehab center?"

"Hell naw, I'm not." Rayshaun placed Imani carefully back down to the ground and she took off, joining Rayshaun's sons in play in another room.

"Welcome home, Rayshaun," LeTavia said before walking over to Gunplay and kissing him softly on the lips. He pulled her closer, deepening the kiss and then smacked her hard on the ass, squeezing tight before letting her loose. LeTavia popped him on the forearm and rolled her eyes.

Standing up straight, Rayshaun focused his good eye and took a good look around. He was blind in his other eye from where he had suffered the horrific gunshot wound. Gunplay had personally spent several hundred thousand dollars for his friend's reconstructive surgery. He'd also blessed him with enough money that, if he spent it wisely, he wouldn't have to work another day in his life, Rayshaun was happy and lucky to be alive.

He marvel at the site around him. Vaulted ceilings covered his head and custom tile floors, flown in from some foreign country he couldn't even pronounce, were beneath his feet but that was minimal in comparison to the splendor that lay throughout the new home he'd stepped foot in. There were rooms on top of rooms, each one decorated with the most luxurious furniture money could buy. It was evident that no expense had been spared.

"Damn, Gunplay… I'on even know what to say," Rayshaun began and then paused when he felt himself getting choked up. His eyes glistened with tears and Gunplay, seeing them, already knew what it was his friend wanted to say.

"Don't even say it, bruh. This right here is the least I could do. From now on, I'ma make sure you good. You my right hand. This house ain't shit compared to what you got comin' to you, nigga. I know this don't make shit right but—"

Rayshaun lifted his hand up, stopping Gunplay from bringing up the past. In his mind, Gunplay had done no wrong because, had he been in the same position, he knew he'd have done the same thing. Like Gunplay, Rayshaun also played by goon rules and was aware of what that really meant. At this moment, he couldn't say that he wasn't happy about how things had turned out in the end. He was alive, he'd never have to worry about how he was going to provide for his family, and his relationship with Poochie was even stronger after she'd almost lost him.

And, as if summoned by his mind, Poochie appeared from down one of the hallways, holding in her arms the most precious baby girl, a perfect mixture of her parents with light brown eyes, caramel skin, and curly brown locs of wild hair. Rayshaun smiled brightly, showing every single one of his teeth, as he reached out to grab his baby girl into his arms.

"Fatherhood looks good on ya, bruh!" Gunplay chuckled as he watched Rayshaun with his newborn daughter. "Ole baby makin' ass, nigga."

Grinning so hard that his dimples showed prominently in both of his cheeks, Trigga walked up to Gunplay and tapped him on shoulder, playfully.

"Aye, nigga, that's gon' be you next! So talk no shit, bruh." He grabbed Gunplay in a mannish greeting that consisted of Trigga holding him in a headlock. Gunplay resisted, pushing Trigga away as he joined in on his laughter.

"We'll see."

Once he'd escaped from Trigga's grasp, his eyes locked in with LeTavia and in that vast moment in time, he heard her voice in his thoughts as if she were whispering the words to him herself. She needed his love right then. She needed to feel it, be assured that things between them would be okay. Softening his stare, he tried to feed her his emotions through his eyes and then licked his lips before mouthing the words.

I love you.

She blushed and looked away, bashfully. Once her gaze returned to his face, he continued.

And I always will. No matter what.

Her heart swelled in her chest and a warm feeling invaded her body. It was Gunplay's love falling over her. She felt even more in that moment than ever before.

The night that Cutta died, LeTavia had finally confessed the whole truth to Gunplay, telling him, with tears filling her eyes, that she would never be able to have children.

"Before I tell you this," she'd said to Gunplay before revealing one of her most devastating secrets. "Tell me… will you always love me? N—no matter what? Will you?"

Tense and on edge after the events of the past few days, Gunplay's level of patience was at an all-time low, just a smidgen below the double negatives. His mental fortitude didn't have the juice to deal with the extra dialogue. He needed her to get straight to it.

"Tavi… I can't play no fuckin' mind games with you right now. What is it?!"

Dropping her face into her hands, LeTavia let out a long sob and then sucked in a breath, bit down hard to still her quivering lip and then spoke her words with all the strength she could muster. She told him about the abortion, the pain, the fear, and the loneliness. And then she told him about her last visit to the doctor and the news she'd been given. There was no cancer and while she was grateful for that, she wasn't out of the dark completely.

She would never be able to have children again.

By the time she finished her story, she had collapsed into tears. Gunplay ran to her side and grabbed her, held her tight in his arms to console her. She cried until her throat was sore, her eyes and lips were swollen pink and her cheeks were crusted by the stains of her dried tears. And he held her, rocked her, soothed her with his voice all the while saying the same thing over and over and over. His breath blew against her cheeks and she closed her eyes, finding herself at ease as she let her mind meditate on the words he said.

"I love you... I always will. No matter what."

And now, here they were months out from that day and though LeTavia's prognosis was still the same, Gunplay was constantly bringing in the best doctors his money could afford to study her case until one of them found a breakthrough. Until then, she was a wonderful mother to Imani and an excellent godmother to Rayshaun's daughter, NisaRay, a combination of her parent's first names.

Gunplay was settling into his role as a father, boyfriend, and kingpin so, truth be told, he was in no hurry to expand their family anyway. It had taken him no time at all to spread his empire further than he'd even thought it could go, stretching out of New York and into other areas of the country. Out of respect for Trigga, he stayed out of the territories ran by Queen, the fearless leader of the Queen's Cartel and Trigga's friend. If he were honest, he would admit that it wasn't just out of respect for Trigga. Queen was *that* bitch and Gunplay didn't want no parts of waging war against her. If ever there was a woman who could be as crazy and cold as he, it was Queen.

Queen thought like a man when it came to running her empire and there was none like her. Gunplay had major respect for a woman like her who could reign in New York, as well as in many cities throughout the U.S., without ever taking a loss. But he wanted to grow even bigger than she had. He had his sights on being international and he knew that he wasn't far away from getting there if he only stayed focused.

LeTavia continued to go to school and even started a jewelry business on the side that she ran in her spare time. She took care of her grandmother and, with Gunplay's help, moved her out of the Brooklyn projects and into a nice home in her same neighborhood. Every day she grew closer and closer with Imani, falling easily into the role of a mother and caring for her as if she'd come from her own body. Unknown to anyone but herself, she still dealt with the guilt of killing Quisha and there was never a day that went by without her praying to God for forgiveness for it.

The End?

And as faith would have it, some time later and well into successfully fitting his roles as a father and kingpin, Gunplay had purchased a 7-karat diamond ring—but hadn't time to pop the question yet—when he got an urgent phone call from Trigga. Gunplay answered his cell phone on the first ring.

"Man, you're not going to believe what's going on! The fuckin' bitch set me up, I'm on a search and destroy mission." Trigga spoke as if he was winded; it sounded like he was walking through the woods. Gunplay could hear the crunching of the crisp leaves from under his feet and he tromped on hurriedly as if jogging.

"Oh, man! What now? Fuck!" Frustrated, Gunplay groaned and ran his hands through his locs as he drove his new customized 750 BMW, doing nearly hundred miles an hour on the highway.

"Here we go again. You always got some shit going on!" Gunplay grumbled and banged his fist on the steering wheel. This wasn't the time to be getting caught up with Trigga. Not when LeTavia was going through yet another round of treatment with a new group of fertility doctors to see what they could do. She was taking it like a champ but he had promised her she wouldn't have to deal with any of it alone.

Then here came Trigga.

"Nigga, I know you ain't talkin'! Besides wait until you what's going on. This shit just might affect you, too."

"Da fuck? Naw, nigga, tell me right now!"

"Can't do that, bruh. I don't trust my phone. It might be bugged," Trigga replied with ease and Gunplay sent off a full round of curse words, spouting enough words for a full three sentences before Trigga was able to pick up on anything he could really understand.

"Fuck! Dammit! Lemme find out you got some secret squirrel shit going on, nigga!"

"Just come!" Trigga shot back, his voice tight and low. From the sound that Gunplay could pick up on in the background, his jog had slowed to about a snail's pace as if he was creeping up on someone.

"I sent you the address already. Just meet me there now."

The urgency in Trigga's tone let him know that he meant business. So Gunplay let off a sigh and then skidded to a stop in the middle of the street and did an illegal U-turn so he could head back into the city instead of to Jersey, where he'd planned to pick up some money his traps had earned before meeting with LeTavia. The money had to wait but he wouldn't miss his appointment with LeTavia. Whatever Trigga needed, it had to be done and over with quickly.

"A'ight. I'm on my way and I'ma bring that muthafuckin' chopper and AR-15 with the hundred round drums on that bitch. We sprayin' everything movin' so I can get in and get out that bitch," Gunplay said and swerved, nearly hitting another car as he headed into town.

It was just another day in the hood.

Do you want to hear more about GUNPLAY?
Let us know in your review!

We can't wait to read your thoughts, but,
please, NO SPOILERS!

THANKS FROM PORSCHA!

I really hope you all love Gunplay & LeTavia's story and appreciate what we did with the development of these characters!

Gunplay is a character in the Keisha & Trigga series, and though he is like Trigga in a few ways, there are MANY ways that he is drastically different. He is obviously, the more savage of the two and has many demons he's dealing with. He's a bit emotional (and definitely very unstable) but he's capable of loving and being loved.

Thanks to the readers who support our team! We love you and appreciate you! Please connect with us and definitely leave a review. We read them and take your input seriously. It's a great help to us, as authors, to know what you think and what you want from us.

Thank you to my #DOPEAUTHORS who make up ROYALTY PUBLISHING HOUSE! Y'all are amazing! I appreciate you ALL!

Thanks goes to my son, Al, and to Leo! Neither one of you will ever know how much I appreciate and love you two! Leo, you inspire, mentor and motivate me. And, for that, I will always be grateful!

Keisha & Trigga Reloaded 2 (Part 6 to the Keisha & Trigga series) IS COMING SOON! But in the meantime, as you wait, check out the books written by our authors. They are some of the most talented authors who have ever done it!

I hope you enjoyed this novel. Until we meet again… #StayRoyal

Porscha Sterling

THANKS FROM LEO

First, I would like to thank God for, once again, allowing me to do what I have been blessed to do and that is writing and creating with my mind and capturing the vivid imagination of millions. I would also like to thank you, the readers, without you none of this could be possible. I would also like to thank my family.

Right now, some of the most important people in my life are the team of writers on my roster. I call them Family. Shout out to the entire staff and writers at Sullivan Productions LLC Films and Literary.

I thank my very beautiful and talented co-writer Porscha Sterling. As always, this has been a labor of love.

Thanks for the reviews, they motivate me to write. I read them all and if you tell me to hurry, I do my best. One thing is for sure, my next project will be the last and you won't have to wait long.

So until next time, peace and blessings.

You can follow me on Facebook or Instagram.

Want to read more books from these authors for FREE?! Get ready to Get LiT!

LiT is an eReading application where you are able to download hundreds of books, many of them free! You'll also be able to read more books from the authors you love FIRST before they are available anywhere else!

Text GETLIT to 22828 to join our mailing list and stay up-to-date on new releases going to the app!

Join our mailing list to get a notification when
Leo Sullivan Presents has another release!

Text **LEOSULLIVAN** to **22828** to join!

To submit a manuscript for our review,
email us at leosullivanpresents@gmail.com

BCPL
Baltimore County
Public Library

CPSIA information can be obtained
at www.ICGtesting.com
Printed in the USA
LVOW03s2121250717
42602LV00017B/725/P

9 781548 950552